# Praise for Looking Through the Water

*This is a must read. The author takes you through a myriad of emotions that most adults have not felt since their childhood. Looking Through the Water captures life through the eyes of a child who views the world with wonderment, innocence, amazement, and imagination all the while yearning for parental acceptance and love. What a fantastic book!*

—Lyndel Herrmann Compau, book club reader,
Brooklyn, Michigan

*Wonderful, wonderful book! Bravo, bravo! Besides the storyline I so enjoyed "feeling" all the feelings described. I have felt like the characters over different situations in my own life, so I enjoyed the book for that reason too!*

—Cynthia Alt, book club reader,
Grand Rapids, Michigan

*As you read this book, you will see all that Cassie sees, from the flower gardens to the peeling paint on the porch to the splash pool, not to mention all the rainbows that she finds.*

—Dara Morgan, book club reader,
Ypsilanti, Michigan

*If you need to renew your faith and hope, this story is sure to unlock your heart. I admire this author's use of imaginative language in an amazing story through the eyes of a child. This surprising story of innocence and bravery keeps you turning the pages. I recommend this book to every reader, young and old. A heartwarming story, Looking Through the Water gives you all you need.*

—Karen E. Ricci, book club reader,
Winter Garden, Florida

*Ginae Lee Scott tells a bittersweet story of inextinguishable hope and undeserved grace. She has an uncanny knack for cutting through the heart to touch and heal buried wounds. I found myself on a rollercoaster ride of emotions as I walked beside the courageous seven-year-old Cassie and experienced life from her perspective. Somehow, despite the gritty reality of her existence, she was always able to see beauty, and her childlike optimism brought transforming light to everyone she encountered. Like a cool rain on a hot day, this inspirational story left me with the refreshing reminder that I do not walk this journey alone. The Light was and is always there.*

—Lori Nederveld, book club reader,
Byron Center, Michigan

# LOOKING
# THROUGH
## THE
# WATER

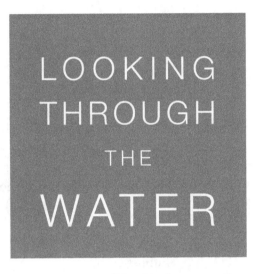

LOOKING
THROUGH
THE
WATER

A Novel

GINAE LEE SCOTT

ISBN: 978-0-9837208-6-7

Published by:
Turn the Page Publishing

www.GinaeLeeScott.com

*This book is dedicated to*
*Dan, my uncle and good friend, and*
*Lori, my friend who totally gets it.*

*Looking through the water*
*To the other side*
*The glorious light comes through*
*So bright, so white*
*It changes my world*
*What I see...*
*The beauty is there...*
*It was always there...*
*As I lie down in the water*
*Looking through, I reach for the light*
*It calls me... it beckons me...*
*The colors reach out to me*
*Distorted but true*
*As I reach the surface I am new*
*Tears of water pool up in my eyes*
*I do not blink them away...*
*I see him through the water*
*He is on the other side*
*Looking through the water*
*I see him reach for me...*
*As the light twinkles on the water*
*It reaches out to my soul*
*Rainbows of color cover the world*
*Looking through the water*
*I see to the other side*
*I want to step through*
*To where the rainbows are*
*It is so transparent*
*So clear, so pure, so true*
*I see the light... I am a child of the light*
*My refuge was there all along*
*Always with me, covering me*
*I am refreshed so I may share the beauty of*
*Looking through the water...*

*—GLS*

# CHAPTER 1

Summer 1973 • Tipton, Missouri

The screen door slammed shut with a loud bang, sending vibrations through the wooden door. The old chipped white paint didn't have a chance. It flew off the screen door like fluttering snowflakes, floating down to the unswept front porch. Cassie Marvin was kicked out of the house again, and for the second time that day.

"What are you doing in here? Get outside and go do something." Her mother had gone to the front door. Opening it wide, she made room for Cassie to pass through. "Go find something to do I told you. I don't want you in here." Cassie got a cuff across the back of her head as she exited the house. With a flick of the wrist, the screen door was slammed shut. For a young girl of seven going on eight, she handled these emotional outbursts from her mother well. As she sat down on the worn-out front porch, the second step down, so her feet could touch the ground, she wondered what she'd done wrong … this time. She loved her mother and tried to please her, but again, she did something wrong; she just knew it. As she searched her mind, she could not come up with the answer though, no matter how hard she tried—and she did try.

*What did I do to upset Mom this time?* Cassie asked herself with a sigh, her small shoulders slumped forward with bewilderment. She was deep in concentration. The frown between her eyebrows was too big for her face. Mary Marvin, Cassie's mother, never gave any real explanations about these outbursts to Cassie. Mary would kick her out of the house just to get rid of her. She didn't want to be bothered. At least that's what Mary said to Cassie. Just talking to Cassie was a bother for Mary on most days. Even looking at Cassie annoyed Mary Marvin. There was no good reason. Mary never felt she had to have a reason. She did what she wanted and never explained herself to anyone.

Hot and high in the cloudless blue sky, the sun was beating down upon Cassie, making everything hot to the touch. Spring and summer air in the Midwest was too hot and humid to breathe, scorching her lungs. And if she moved much, she felt like a melting piece of butter on a hot platter. Cassie was thirsty, but she knew not to ask her mother for a drink of water or anything else for that matter. She'd made the mistake of knocking on the back door once when told to stay out. "What do you want?" Mary yelled.

"Could I have a drink and something to eat please? I'm hungry and thirsty." A few minutes later Mary yanked open the screen door and threw a plastic cup out at Cassie with a smashed sandwich inside. "Use this at the faucet outside and don't bother me again, Cassie, or else." Cassie's cup and food had tumbled to the ground. She wasn't choosy; she wiped off the dirt. She could still hear her mother slamming things around in the house. The house had a broken-down feel to it. There were times Cassie felt sorry for her house; it definitely took a beating. Cassie could picture her mother slamming and banging things a little too hard one day, and then the house would come down around her. It would just topple over from the stress of it.

The portable radio was on in the kitchen. Mary had it turned up loud, but it never drowned out the other sounds she made, yelling and slamming things down in an angry, stormy huff. Sitting on the porch, Cassie could mentally picture the scene of her mother in the house, phone in one hand and a cigarette in the other. Or if she was busy doing something with both of her hands, then her mother would dangle the cigarette from her lips and hold the phone against her cheek and shoulder. When the phone rang, the conversations were always the same. "Yeah he's out again. Don't he know I want to get out of here too?" Mary would say. Listening to the caller, she usually added, "I get so sick of his excuses. He doesn't do a thing around here." On and on Mary went. It was also usually the same for Cassie when the phone rang, "Get on out of here, Cassie. I am on the phone." Sometimes raising her leg, Mary kicked her in the bottom to get her moving. Cassie never moved fast enough for Mary. "Yeah, she don't need to be in here while I'm on the phone." Mary acted like she was mad with everything. Cassie could picture the little black rain cloud that followed her mother around.

Just like in *Winnie the Pooh*. Cassie thought as the image of the black rain cloud over her mother had come to her mind. Smiling now, Cassie remembered fondly that her grandmother had given her the book, which featured a story about a little black rain cloud. As Cassie had held the book her grandmother Elizabeth had given her, Elizabeth told her, "Cassie my favorite thing about Pooh is the honey pot! And you are my honey pot, Cassie. You remember that." Cassie remembered. She treasured it. It was a fancy hardcover book with a cover made of red material. Cassie took special care when she read from the book. It had pictures on some of the pages. Pictures helped tell the story, Cassie believed.

It made Cassie nervous when her mother was in her mood. She could be in her own little world drawing or playing when Mary would slam something down in an annoyed huff, and Cassie would jump in reaction to the vibration that would riffle through the house. She was so unprepared at those moments. Cassie picked up the habit of talking quieter when speaking to her mother. Cassie remembered a time when she was looking at a book. She was quietly involved with figuring out the words when Mary slammed a basket of clothes on the hardwood floor in her bedroom. Cassie had jumped and let out a small scream she was so startled. "If you weren't so engrossed in that book and helped me once in a while you wouldn't have jumped and screamed like a sissy," Mary said. Cassie remembered she didn't say a word. She hadn't known what to say. Mary went on, laughing. "I swear, Cassie, you get off in that la la land of yours. Where do you go, Cassie?" Not waiting for an explanation, Mary had left the room.

Making the mistake of daydreaming, Cassie was still on the front porch. "When I said get outside, that did not mean sit on the front porch, Cassie. Go do something!" Mary yelled through the screen.

Cassie jumped up from the step, "going now, sorry."

Cassie thought she would take a walk around the neighborhood. Maybe some of her friends could play. She knew it was best she left anyway. But before she ventured out, she would get a much-needed drink of water from the backyard hose. She knew she'd heard somewhere a dirty garden hose wasn't the healthiest place to get a drink of water. Maybe she heard it from her grandmother, but she was thirsty so she headed in the direction of the backyard hose anyway. *It can't be that dirty*, Cassie concluded.

The water was very cool against her lips as she bent over for a long drink, having let the water hose run for a while, getting all the steaming hot water out of it. Cassie watched the water flow down like a fountain to the ground. She loved looking through the water. It looked like some distorted glass to her, making the world change through its eyes. The shapes of things were different, but the wonderful colors still showed through.

*Well, I've had enough,* Cassie thought as she turned the water hose off. Her small hands were still plump from her baby fat and had dimples on top of each knuckle. Cassie twisted the knob tight, making sure the water would not drip.

Cassie did not venture far from home. Her little world consisted of an area of two blocks and sometimes, when feeling brave, downtown to the candy store, which was four blocks from her home. Two blocks north then two blocks west was the distance for Cassie to walk there. Downtown had a pharmacy, which was also a gift and candy store. Then there was a meat shop, a couple of diners and doctors offices, one of which was the local dentist. There were a few other buildings—Cassie didn't know what type of businesses they were—and a few churches. Though her parents never took her to church, she knew they were there. That was her big town. The candy store was Cassie's favorite, and then the meat shop because the butcher had an ice cream counter and homemade cookies and donuts in the morning. The donuts and cookies never lasted past the morning hours, if she wanted one of them, she had to get there very early.

Mr. and Mrs. Winters, who owned the meat shop, never let Cassie pay for anything after her first few visits. They loved it when she visited their store. On her first visit, she had looked so sweet standing at the counter, taking all her coins out of her pocket, and laying them up on the counter and asking Mrs. Winters to help her count them out. Cassie had ordered an ice cream cone and was trying to pay for it. Cassie's dad gave her his quarters once in a while, so Cassie saved them for her downtown trips. Mrs. Winters had checked the store for her parents while Cassie was floundering around trying to get the coins out of her pocket, but Cassie was on her own. A lot of children ventured into town but none as small as Cassie. On her first trip into town, she could not have been more then five or six years old. And being petite in size, Cassie looked younger.

Some time later, Mr. and Mrs. Winters put together who her parents might be. When Mary Marvin shopped at the meat market, most of the time she was alone, without Cassie, so it had taken Mr. and Mrs. Winters some detective work to figure it out. Ignoring the public ashtrays outside the businesses along the main street, Mary would fling her cigarette butt on the sidewalk. Then she would make a half attempt at smudging it out before entering the market. She was very gruff, not friendly, and always looking for a problem with her order or a problem with the way her meat was cut. Mr. and Mrs. Winters were always friendly to her, but both of them did not think much of the mother of Cassie. The Winters got to know Cassie really well when she stopped in their store; she was a friendly little girl. They gave her a cookie or an ice cream cone, always asking her to try it for free. Mr. and Mrs. Winters told Cassie they needed to know if the cookies tasted good or if the new flavor of ice cream tasted good.

"Why, Cassie, I can't taste everything here, so you are my little helper. I have a lot of customers who ask me if something tastes good, and if you tell me it does, then I know what to tell them."

Mrs. Winters, Bobbie to those who knew her, had told her husband, Fred, early on when Cassie visited the store, "Why, she must be only five or six years old, Fred! I just love Cassie. She is such a little angel. We can't ever take a cent from that child. She just blesses me with her visits, I tell you! There are days when the bell rings I look up and I just hope it is Cassie. I wonder why that is, Fred."

Mr. Winters just smiled at his wife and said, "Bobbie, you always wanted to adopt something; if it's not an animal, it's Cassie. You know, though, I feel deep down in my bones the child needs your kindness, you just be kind to her all you want."

"You know, I love you, Mr. Winters! You are a wonderful man!"

"I know, Mrs. Winters, but I am a wonderful man because I have a wonderful wife!"

Cassie walked down the side street that would bring her to Mrs. Vashon's backyard. Mrs. Vashon's house was different than anyone else's on the street. She had a huge yard compared to most of the neighbors. She owned two lots back to back instead of side to side. Her backyard was on one street, and her front yard was on the street a block over. Her lot went through the middle of the block, which could have given her an entrance from both streets, but she used only the street out front of the house. Mrs. Vashon had planted a beautiful garden on the extra lot, her backyard. The garden took up the whole yard.

Mrs. Vashon's garden was all flowers. Cassie had never seen such a beautiful garden before. All the flowers were in neat rows or gathered in bunches, forming circles. At this very flower garden, Cassie fell in love with tulips. They were her favorite flower now. Mrs. Vashon planted the tulips in perfect rows, all color coordinated. In the spring, there were rows of yellow, red, peach with pink, white, white with red tips, and almost every other color. She even had purple tulips or a dark blue that almost looked black. Cassie wasn't sure. They were Cassie's favorite color of tulips because they were so unusual.

Because Mrs. Vashon's backyard was where everyone else's front yard was on the street, Cassie could walk up to the rows of tulips from the sidewalk. Cassie thought no one could see her up at the house. She would sneak into the garden uninvited. Mrs. Vashon had always seemed really nice to Cassie in the past, but with each visit, Cassie always hoped she would not get shooed out.

Cassie would stand as close to the tulips as she could and look down at the star inside. Cassie would squint her eyes to get a good look. The inside of the tulip looked just like a star in a beautiful heaven to her. She felt like God put what looked like a star inside the tulip just for her. What a beautiful surprise the inside of a tulip was. Cassie thought God was a very special person to think of little things like that, remembering not only to make the outside of the tulip beautiful with all the different colors of the petals but to make the inside something wonderful also. At the end of spring, new flowers came up where the tulips had been. Cassie was sad the tulips were all done until next year; she already missed them.

What Cassie did not know was Mrs. Vashon looked forward to Cassie's visits to her garden. As Mrs. Vashon sipped her coffee at the kitchen sink, she would watch Cassie from the kitchen window. Mrs. Vashon's flowered print curtains in the window made it possible to watch Cassie but not be seen. There was something about Cassie that moved her heart. Mrs. Vashon never felt quite alone with little Cassie in her garden, and as she watched Cassie being so careful as to not step on any flower, she felt the love right there at her kitchen window—the love Cassie had for her flowers and her garden. All the work Mrs. Vashon put into her garden was worth it to her with Cassie appreciating it.

Mrs. Vashon had recently bought a yard statue—a garden angel—and was waiting for the perfect time to go out to the garden when Cassie was there. Putting the statue in the garden without sharing it first with Cassie would not have been as special, she wanted to wait for just the right moment when Cassie was visiting the garden. When Mrs. Vashon bought the statue, she had Cassie in mind. She hoped sharing it would be something very meaningful to Cassie and hoped she would accept it as a small token gift to her. Since Cassie was going from flower to flower, Mrs. Vashon thought this might be a good time to go out and talk to Cassie. Mrs. Vashon never wanted Cassie to think she was not welcome. She wanted to somehow express to Cassie she was always welcome in the garden, and if Cassie ever wanted to consider it her garden too, Mrs. Vashon would love to share the flower garden with her. Maybe this garden angel would help Mrs. Vashon accomplish just what she wanted to do.

Opening the back door, carrying the garden angel statue, Mrs. Vashon hurried out to the flower garden, hoping not to scare Cassie away. Cassie reminded Mrs. Vashon of a skittish little colt. She was so kind looking in the eyes but not sure of anything yet, and her legs were on the longer, skinny side. Cassie was very petite, but her legs were long for her body, maybe it was an indication she would be on the taller side when she was grown-up. It wasn't long ago when Cassie started venturing into the garden. Mrs. Vashon was hoping to become good friends with the sweet little girl. But their meetings in the past did not last long. Cassie was in such a hurry, and she always went on her way after quick small talk.

"Hello, Cassie. How are you today, honey?" Mrs. Vashon called out.

Looking up, Cassie smiled. "Oh, hello, Mrs. Vashon. I hope you don't mind that I am here," she said, raising her eyebrows in concern.

"Oh no, honey. I am so glad you're here, which is why I came out. I have something I bought for the flower garden, and I wanted you to help me pick out the best place for it."

"Me?" Cassie questioned, unsure. "What did you get?" Cassie wondered, not sure she had heard Mrs. Vashon right, but she was excited to see what was in Mrs. Vashon's arms, so she hurried forward.

"I found a garden angel statue while I was shopping in town and thought of you! Don't you think she's beautiful?" Showing Cassie the statue of the garden angel, Mrs. Vashon could not hide her excitement over the happiness that came across Cassie's face. Cassie's face lit up like the sun coming up over the horizon; the brightness shone through her eyes and her smile.

Reaching out to touch the angel statue, Cassie told Mrs. Vashon, "She's beautiful… and you want me to help you?" Amazed and already thinking, it only took Cassie a few moments to say, "You may want to put her somewhere she can see the whole garden. She'll watch over it, right?"

Touched by her answer, Mrs. Vashon said, "Yes, she will watch over it. See, I knew if you helped me, Cassie, you would know the best place to put her."

They both started looking around the garden to see the best place for the garden angel statue. Cassie did a little twirl to take in the whole garden. Squinting her eyes and pursing her lips, Cassie was thinking. Mrs. Vashon could tell by her face when she found the right spot. Her eyes opened wide with excitement.

Pointing across the yard from where they were standing, Cassie said, "Right there, Mrs. Vashon! If you put her there, she can see the whole garden, and when the sun comes up, it will shine on her and wake her up to let her know it's morning!" Cassie was so excited, she went running to the spot that she'd picked.

Mrs. Vashon, carrying the angel statue, followed Cassie across the yard. "Why, Cassie, this is absolutely the most perfect spot for her."

Cassie reached down and started flattening the grasses and made a flat spot for the garden angel to be placed. Turning back, she reached out to help Mrs. Vashon lower the statue to the ground. "This is very heavy, Mrs. Vashon!"

Standing back, they both looked at their work. Cassie proudly folded her arms and tilted her head, admiring the garden angel.

"Cassie, she looks wonderful there. She adds a nice touch to the garden, don't you think?"

"Oh, yes, she's beautiful!"

The angel statue was close to three feet tall and had flowers thrown at her feet. Her flowing dress seemed to be blowing in the wind. In her hands, she held garden tools so detailed Cassie could almost picture her bending down to move the dirt with one of the garden tools she held.

Mrs. Vashon, who wanted to make sure Cassie knew a little of what she felt, said, "You know, Cassie, you are welcome in this flower garden any time. I actually want you to visit as much as you would like to. I have this feeling you may like this flower garden as much as I do, and it would make me very happy if you visited regularly. Flowers need someone to appreciate them. I believe they bloom healthier and prettier if there is someone to watch over them."

"Oh, thank you, Mrs. Vashon! I could help again, you know. I could water the flowers and pull weeds if you'd like." Cassie beamed with the knowledge the flower garden could be a place she could come to and not worry about being shooed out.

"Cassie, you are welcome here every day for as long as you want to stay. You don't have to help me to be welcome here, but if you'd like to help, then I will leave a bucket out here for the weeds. Up here by the shed is the water hose, so you can water if you'd like. They will just need a light mist and some water to the roots. Then just remember to turn off the water." Mrs. Vashon was busy showing Cassie. "Most days I will be here, and if I see you, I will come out and we can do those things together. Would that be fine with you, Cassie?"

"Oh yes, I would like visiting with you, Mrs. Vashon. Thank you!"

"For your wonderful help today, I have some cookies for you. Just follow me to the back door, and I will give you the cookies in a napkin so you can take them with you." Mrs. Vashon turned to go back to the house with Cassie following her. "Is your real name Cassandra, Cassie?"

"Yes. My grandma told me my mom named me Cassandra after hearing the name on TV. But my whole family calls me Cassie for short."

Looking back at Cassie, Mrs. Vashon thought she was such a sweet child. Then she said, "Well, Cassie and Cassandra are both beautiful names. I like them both."

As the afternoon wore on, Cassie wandered around the neighborhood. Stopping to kick a rock here and there, she kept her hands deep in her pockets with a serious, thoughtful look on her face. She continued on her walk and stopped to play at the school playground. When Cassie was bored, she benefited from having the school so close to her house. Swinging on the swings, Cassie was going as high as her legs could pump her. The pretty flowered fabric of her shirt was flowing out behind her. Cassie loved to lean back, her hair blowing in the breeze, and pretend she was flying. If she closed her eyes to small slits, then she could only see the sky. Way up there she felt she could fly away. She would picture herself jumping from one fluffy cloud to the next. She wondered if she would bounce on the clouds or fall right through them. The afternoon never felt as long getting lost in daydreams. With the wind against her face and arms, Cassie did not feel the heat of the day. The damp curls against her neck were the only indication she was as hot as everyone else that afternoon in Tipton, Missouri.

She sat on the swings for a while thinking this was a good time to eat her cookies. Her stomach was letting out little growls. Pulling the cookies from her pocket, she unfolded the napkin Mrs. Vashon had given her. Her cookies were a little crushed but still delicious. Holding the napkin in her hands, Cassie picked at the broken pieces, enjoying every bite while twirling slightly on her swing. Digging her foot into the sand, Cassie looked around the playground. She was alone. None of her friends were at the playground. They were probably at home in a backyard splash pool… if they were lucky enough to have one.

Walking home, Cassie took her time. Cassie opened the screen door, hoping she'd been gone long enough. "Where have you been?" Mary asked.

"I, ah, been out playing."

"Didn't you hear me? I asked *where* have you been."

"Oh, I went to the school park."

"And…"

"I stopped by Mrs. Vashon's garden and looked at the flowers." Cassie felt afraid to add more.

"Mrs. Vashon, huh? You aren't bugging these neighbors, are you?"

"Oh, no!"

"You better not be going where you aren't wanted, Cassie. I don't know if I like you going into these people's yards to look at anything either," Mary said.

Cassie waited. Nothing more came from Mary. She was finished. Cassie felt hopeful about the garden; she wasn't told she couldn't go there.

# CHAPTER 2

Mary wouldn't allow any of Cassie's friends over in their yard when she wasn't home. Even when Mary was home, the children of the neighborhood were not made welcome. Cassie had been embarrassed more than one time by her mother's yelling.

"Cassie, get in here!" Mary yelled. "What are you doing writing all over the sidewalk?"

"Larissa brought some chalk over, and we were drawing." Holding her head down, Cassie knew she'd done wrong.

"Quit it now. I don't want that junk all over my sidewalks. She can go draw on her own sidewalks!"

Cassie knew Larissa had heard. When she went back outside, Larissa was already packing up the chalk. "It's okay. We can do this at my house later," Larissa whispered.

"Okay. Sorry." Cassie sat down on the porch watching her friend go home.

"See ya later."

"Later."

Her friends Larissa and Samuel lived next door. Larissa was Cassie's best friend. They were used to Cassie's situation, but the embarrassment was always there for Cassie. Both Samuel and Larissa enjoyed playing with Cassie. She had a wonderful imagination and kept them all busy with made-up games to play. Cassie loved the convenience of her two friends living next door; it made seeing them easier for her. Less for Cassie to figure out and less trouble.

Cassie got Larissa involved in her make-believe on a regular basis. "All right, Larissa, you stand there and run this way, and I will stand here and run the other way. Keep your arms up and flap them. We are butterflies."

Larissa extended her arms and followed the directions. Keeping an eye on Cassie, Larissa did everything she did.

"This is fun. What kind are you?" Larissa asked.

"Oh, I don't know, maybe a blue one."

"I'm green!"

"Are there green ones?" Cassie asked.

"You know, I don't know." Larissa laughed.

After circling around, both girls got dizzy. Laughing and almost colliding, they fell to the ground in a fit of giggles.

. . . . . . . . . . .

The neighbor Mrs. Lillian Chambers was home all day and had Cassie's parents' work numbers just in case. Cassie was told she could go to Mrs. Chambers in case of an emergency only, which really did not qualify as a babysitter. Cassie did not have a babysitter. Those who knew Cassie volunteered to help out, but Mary did not want charity. More to the point, she did not think Cassie needed someone to look after her. Mrs. Chambers was kind to Cassie. She invited Cassie over every year to pick rhubarb from her backyard. Mrs. Chambers would have liked to watch Cassie full time if Mary would have allowed it, but she was elderly and had an elderly husband in a wheelchair she had to take care of.

Once in a while Cassie would knock on the Chamberses' door just to say hello to Mr. Chambers, knowing he did not get out much. Carl Chambers would enjoy her visits so much. He would have Lillian look for her on his better days and see if she could wave Cassie over.

"Hello, Mrs. Chambers, is Mr. Chambers awake?" Cassie asked.

"Why he sure is, Cassie. Come on in."

"I want to tell him how good the rhubarb is."

"Go tell him yourself, honey. He is sitting there in the living room. Carl, Cassie is here," Mrs. Chambers called out.

"Hello, Mr. Chambers, how are you today?" Cassie asked.

"I am good now, Cassie. I am so glad you stopped by. Come on in, have a seat."

"I just wanted to tell you the rhubarb is getting real good. I've had a few pieces you know, and thanks for sharing." Cassie smiled.

"We could never eat all that, so you just keep helping yourself. Maybe Mrs. Chambers will make us a pie soon. Hmm?"

"Oh, I've never had it in a pie. But I sure love it raw. What's it like in a pie?"

"Well, it's got to be one of the best tasting pies I've ever had, Cassie!" Mr. Chambers exclaimed.

"Yum!" Cassie rubbed her stomach just thinking about it. Her stories were the highlight of his days. Cassie would tell him an update of everything that was happening on the outside of his home, from what bug she caught in a plastic cup to how tall his rhubarb was getting. At night, Cassie would sit on the front porch in her pajamas and peel off the stringy outside of a thick stick of rhubarb and then eat it. She loved the sourness of it.

To stay busy during the day, she also cleaned her house when her parents were away at work. For a young child, she knew what to do to keep her home somewhat clean. It was expected out of her by her mother, but even if the list from her mother was not rattled off most mornings, Cassie would have still picked up the house. It was just her way. She kept her room clean, and she organized everything. She had one junk drawer in her dresser, and it was her one "fun" drawer. When it got really messy, she would clean the drawer out by dumping everything out and start all over by straightening up all the items in it. It was still a junk drawer though. She liked having at least one. One drawer when she was in a hurry to clean-up the drawer would hold all her stuff. Then she would know where to look for her things when needing them again. If a toy or pencil wasn't where it should be, Cassie knew it would be in her junk drawer.

When she went to a friend's home in the neighborhood, she loved when they had chores to do because then she could help them. For whatever reason, Cassie loved to help her friends with their chores. A few mothers in the neighborhood finally gave up telling Cassie they were not her chores but their children's because they realized she liked helping and she was a joy to have around.

At the Stockards' next door, Larissa and Samuel were sweeping out the garage one morning when Cassie had asked to help.

"Cassie, this is not your chore to do, honey," Mrs. Stockard said.

"I know, but I got a broom and would like to help them if I could."

"Well, I don't know…"

"I don't mind really," Cassie said.

Mrs. Stockard gave in. The broom was bigger than Cassie. But her eyes were even bigger hoping she could help.

Smiling, she said, "Go ahead, and thank you for your help, Cassie."

. . . . . . . . . .

The neighbors had to wonder, did Cassie ask too many questions when her mother came home from work? Was she *too* excited to see her mother? Did she not do a chore right? What would make her mother send her outside like a dog all the time? The neighbors felt for Cassie. Because if they could not figure Mary out, how could a girl of seven figure out her mother enough to be treated better?

Cassie's dad, Paul Marvin, was a stranger to the neighbors for the most part. He seemed to be a hard worker, quiet. He was friendly enough, but once he parked his truck out front, he was gone into the house. He always had a quiet, kind word for his daughter, at least in public. The yelling always came from Cassie's mother. When the door slammed, about ninety percent of the time, Cassie was put out on the porch like a dog. She would sit there swinging her feet, trying not to look embarrassed or bored. When Paul was home and this kind of behavior took place, the neighbors had another set of questions to wonder about.

# CHAPTER 3

Sitting on the back porch having a cherry Popsicle, Cassie was thinking of the old movie she'd seen on TV. It was an old black-and-white movie about a young girl who was visited by an angel or a saint of God. Cassie did not know for sure. She did not understand the entire movie, having just watched from the middle of it. She wanted to talk to God, be a saint, or an angel for God, just like the girl in the movie.

Just like the grown-up she was, Cassie was a very serious girl when she talked to God. Hoping for an answer Cassie talked to God that very afternoon.

"God, I want to be a saint. Is there anything special I have to do to become one of your special people? Could I be an angel?"

Cassie, enjoying the last of her Popsicle, told God how she knew it was him up there in the thunder. "Are you bowling?" she asked him.

"I like how you made the apple tree branches. They are easy to climb for me and my friends, Larissa and Samuel," she continued as she looked in the backyard. "Oh, and I really like the feel of the grass when I am barefoot. It's soft and cool under my feet. The tulips are one of my favorite things though, you made them in so many colors, and how you put the middle decoration in there that sort of looks like a star is pretty good too. I wonder how you do those things. Oh, and thank you for

Mrs. Vashon. I helped her in her garden the other day, and we put one of your garden angels there to watch over it. She also gave me cookies, and they were very good."

Leaning back on her elbows on the back porch, Cassie looked around, wanting to make sure she wasn't forgetting anything now that she *knew* she had his attention. "Oh, and I love how you made water see-through because I love looking through the water. It makes things pretty. Thank you for Grandma, God. I miss her. Do you think she will be coming to visit me soon? Um, I think I am done for now, but if I think of anything else, I will let you know."

Looking up, Cassie finished up her conversation. "Oh, and when you get time, let me know what I can do to be a special person to you like in the movie I watched today. Thank you, God. This is Cassie. Cassie Marvin from Tipton, Missouri; it's me sitting right here on the back porch if you can see me."

Cassie continued to sit on the back porch, waiting for her parents to get home. She watched the flies circling the garbage cans in the back of the driveway. *They really want in those garbage cans,* Cassie thought. *They aren't as much fun to watch as ants,* Cassie decided. Ants worked hard, and they could lift a food crumb that was four times as big as them or bigger. Cassie loved their fancy houses. All the sand twirled up and twisted to make it a work of art to her. She tried not to ruin their homes on purpose while she walked through the yard. *Let them be,* Cassie thought. *They aren't hurting anybody.*

Cassie hummed to herself, wiggling her feet, which were covered in pink slip-on tennis shoes. Her legs were crossed at her ankles. She looked totally relaxed and was enjoying herself in her reclining position. Someone else would have said they were bored and complained all afternoon, but Cassie just sat there and hummed a tune, perfectly content with sitting on the back porch.

. . . . . . . . . .

Her mother, Mary, was in the kitchen putting dinner together having just recently gotten home from work. Mary worked at the local dry cleaners. She told Cassie she worked in the back where it was hot. "But at least I'm not up front having to deal with customers."

The smells of dinner were coming out the back door, making Cassie's stomach growl. All she had to eat during the day was a peanut butter and jelly sandwich and the Popsicle. Her belly was almost empty, which would explain the loud growling monster that was making a lot of noise in there at the moment.

"Cassie! Come set the table. You haven't done that, girl! Your dad will be here soon, and I'm starving!" Mary yelled from inside the kitchen, her voice loud and clear. Did her mother think she was down the street and not as close as the back porch?

Cassie scrambled to get in the back door. "Yes, Mom, here I come." Reaching the kitchen, Cassie continued, "I would have set the table, Mom, but I couldn't reach the plates. They were up there in the cupboard today." Cassie pointed to the cabinet that held the dishes and glasses. They were hardly ever put away in the cupboard. Usually they were in the dish drain so Cassie could reach them.

Mary just looked at her long and hard. "You could have climbed up on that chair, girl." Mary nodded her head toward the kitchen chairs. "Don't you have brains to figure something like that out?"

Cassie had thought of doing exactly what her mother just said but didn't think it was a good idea to climb on the kitchen chairs and then to the counter with no one there to help her.

Cassie knew better than to say anything, so she just said, "Yes, Momma," looking at the tiled floor. Cassie started to count the speckles in the tile. It helped her with her nerves.

"Well, next time then make sure it's done before I get home," Mary said as she handed Cassie the plates for the table.

The three plates weighed almost as much as Cassie. Cassie set the dinner dishes and silverware out in their places. She was hardly any taller than the table. She was a petite child, which made a lot of the chores her mother had her do more difficult. It was almost funny to watch Cassie vacuuming. The machine was taller than Cassie. Though she never complained, it was a ridiculous chore for her to do. Their vacuum was very huge in size and very heavy for a girl to push around furniture. What was more ridiculous was Mary would never have cleaned the house before. But with Cassie a little older now, Mary bossed her around like she was her personal maid.

Dinner was uneventful, ending with Cassie on a chair at the sink washing the dishes with her dad drying them.

"I cooked dinner, Paul; the least you can do is the dishes tonight. It's too hot for me to do anything else. Get Cassie to help you; she can wash them dishes!" Mary said, going out the back door for a cigarette.

Pulling over the kitchen chair to the sink, Cassie told her dad, "I can help you, Dad." Cassie didn't mind washing the dishes. She washed them better than her parents. They left grease on the edges of the pans, and Cassie had noticed the film of leftover grease on the glasses in the strainer. Cassie scrubbed until they were clean. Cassie did it right. If she washed a dish, then she washed it clean.

Paul Marvin just nodded his head at Cassie. The small pull to the side of his mouth may have been considered a smile. Cassie, for the most part, thought her dad was a kind man, though his eyes seemed sad to her. His face was prickled with his beard stubble, and he never had a close shave. His light-brown hair was always plastered down on his head from the worn-out ball cap he wore and from the heat. Cassie's dad was a big eater, but he was very skinny, Cassie thought. His arms working the dish towel on the wet dishes looked like long, bony twigs.

Cassie smiled to herself. *Yep, that's what Dad looks like—a twig man, a tall and thin twig man!*

Washing and drying the dishes silently, Cassie and her dad finished up what needed to be done.

"Cassie, let me get those pans, and you put the ketchup and other stuff away in the refrigerator," her dad said with a tired sigh. He looked as hot as everyone else. Cassie knew those factories were really hot during the day—at least she had overheard her parents talking about it all the time. They would argue whose job was hotter: Mary's at the dry cleaners or Paul's at the factory.

. . . . . . . . . .

Later on in the middle of the night the noise grew louder and louder. For a moment, Cassie did not know where she was or what she was hearing. Blinking a few times to wake herself up, she lay quietly and tried to listen to what was causing the noises. The voices were coming from the living room. *Are there people here?* Cassie wondered. *What time is it?* It was still dark, so it had to be the middle of the night. Her bedroom door was closed, she tiptoed to her door and opened it just a crack to she if she could see something or see someone. Too curious to be afraid, Cassie peeked down the hall. Her mother and father were yelling at each other. She quickly closed the door. Cassie silently thanked the door for being quiet as she did this. There was no squeak to give her away. Cassie found her way back to her bed and covered herself back up with the covers just in case one of her parents came in her room. They never did but just in case. She didn't want to get into trouble with her mother.

Cassie lay there listening until it was all over and the doors quit slamming. At one point, she thought she heard a car door. Had one of her parents left? She didn't want to get up and check. Her bed was safer. Her stomach hurt now. It felt tight and nervous; it jumped around in her body, and Cassie just wished it would stop. Curling up on her side made it feel better. Maybe it was safe to go to sleep. Cassie wondered if sleep would come as her eyes stared into the darkness. Part of the moon was out tonight, the soft light filtered into her room, giving her a glow in the darkness. As she lay there, her eyes adjusted to the darkness. Cassie was thankful for the light the moon made. It made it easier for her. Falling asleep a while later, Cassie dreamed of nothing she could remember the next morning, feeling only exhaustion when she woke from having so few hours of sleep.

· · · · · · · · · ·

Her mother and father worked the early day shift at their jobs. Her dad worked at a factory right out of town. Her mother worked in town. Her father made some kind of parts that went into tractors, Mary had told Cassie. "A nasty job, just a nasty job; you better hope you don't have to work a job like that one day, girl. Mine's no better. I work over that hot machine all day." Her mother had told her the same sentence so much she could quote it. Her father never said anything about work. He worked; then he came home at dinnertime and a couple of nights during the week went back out with some of his buddies.

Cassie thought his evenings out might be what the fights were about but didn't know for sure. She had overheard many of them.

"You're going out, aren't you?" Mary accused, finding Paul in the bedroom.

Paul looked over the rim of the clean shirt he was pulling on. "Yeah, just for a few."

"It is never a few, and you know it."

"Meetin' the guys for just a few, Mary, and what do you care? I need a break."

"You need a break?"

The yelling started. Cassie knew to hide in her room. Her mother would rant and rave to her father about how she had to work her fingers to the bone at her job and no woman should have to do what she did every day and then come home and try to cook up some kind of dinner. How could he go out for a beer with the guys and leave her there with nothing to do? Cassie thought if her mother would stop yelling maybe her father would stay home more, or was her mother's yelling because he left all the time? Cassie thought there was no way she would be able to figure out grown-ups. She just did her best to hang on to her own happiness.

The following week on Monday morning Cassie woke with a start. "Cassie, get up and come out here. Your dad and I are leaving for work, and you don't get to sleep in every day, girl!"

"Let her sleep," Paul said.

Mary turned at his challenge.

Paul weakened. "We were up late last night fightin', Mary. She was bound to have heard us."

Mary ignored him. "Cassie, get up. We're leaving. Make sure you have your chores done before I get home." She looked at Paul as she walked out the door. He did nothing but followed her out and went to his truck.

Mary Marvin was not what anyone would call a delicate woman. She did not wear any makeup, and half the time her hair hadn't been washed in a few days. She did not take pride in the way she dressed either. She always wore jeans and a T-shirt with a logo or advertise-ment on it. "Why dress up all the time when all I do is work in that dry cleaners?" she'd say into the phone to some girlfriend she was talking too. Mary did not take pride in her home either, except for assigning the chores to Cassie. The ashtrays—the square, clear, glass ones from the dime store—were lying around the house often filled to the rim. Cassie emptied the ashtrays when she picked up the house. Cassie hated the way they smelled and promised herself she would never smoke when she grew up. Mary continued to act like she lived in a palace, yelling at Cassie to do this or do that. Every demand ended with "girl." Empty those trash cans, girl. Make up the beds today, girl. Put the groceries away, girl. On the phone, she acted lively to her friends. Cassie didn't recognize her own mother. She would laugh, smoking the whole time and saying bad words, Cassie would disappear into her room if she wasn't sent outside.

When Cassie was in her bedroom, she thought of her grandmother due to the gifts she had received from her over the years. Cassie kept everything. Her grandmother was good at sending books and drawing supplies for birthdays and Christmas. Sometimes for Valentine's Day or Easter she would get a new coloring book with that holiday theme.

Cassie did not get to see her grandmother often. Her mother never wanted her grandma to visit. "She's a plane ride away, Cassie. She can't come here on your every whim, and I don't like having company all the time." There was no grandpa. Cassie was told he'd left one day and never came back. Her grandmother raised the children on her own. She had two boys, Roy Jr., Mark, and Mary, Cassie's mother. Cassie could not remember meeting any of her uncles. Cassie knew they lived by her grandmother in Wisconsin. Cassie had never been there but she knew Wisconsin was north of where she lived.

The last time Cassie had seen her grandmother she was five years old. Cassie's uncles had given her grandmother a plane ticket to visit Mary and her family. Cassie's grandmother had not seen her since she was a baby therefore she was very excited to visit.

"Cassie, I am so glad I am here with you, honey; you are the sweet-est granddaughter any grandmother could have!" Elizabeth Lauren told Cassie again and again, hugging her and kissing Cassie's cheeks. Cassie loved the attention she was getting from her grandmother. The soft arms that hugged her and the sweet, perfumed smell that came with the embrace was a bonus to Cassie. Cassis let her grandmother hold her and cradle her all she wanted. It was the nicest feeling to Cassie, she never minded being detained as she walked by her grandmother for a few hugs and some kisses.

When her grandmother went home, Cassie laid on her bed and cried all afternoon. Cassie thought her insides were going to come out onto the bed she cried so hard. She had never cried that deep in her whole life. If a child could weep, Cassie wept. And it came from the very depths of her soul. She was going to miss her grandmother dearly. Elizabeth Lauren, the sweetest softest person Cassie had ever known, was going home and probably would not be back for a very long time. Cassie honestly did not know if she would be the same with her grandmother gone. Cassie wondered why families lived so far apart.

Elizabeth Lauren, when she arrived home from the airport, threw herself down on her bed and wept. She and Cassie reacted to each others absence in the same way. Elizabeth wished she did not live so far away from her sweet granddaughter. What troubled her most was the thought of Cassie being raised by Mary, her own daughter. Elizabeth was no fool. She knew Mary was not a good mother to Cassie.

Elizabeth would love to visit more often. Mary never wanted her there. Elizabeth did not know the reason. No one probably would. Plane tickets were hard to come by with Elizabeth's income so limited, and taking time off from her menial job was even harder. The boys helped her out as much as possible, but their jobs were not big money makers either. Elizabeth's boys had families of their own to raise. Elizabeth's last plane ticket had been a gift from her boys, and it was the nicest thing anyone had ever given her.

Elizabeth always looked back to the past, wondering where she'd gone wrong with Mary. *What in the world did I do to her?* Elizabeth would ask herself often. When her sons would talk about their sister, whom they had not spoke to in several years, Elizabeth would tell them, "At least we have Cassie," wishing the whole time they had Mary too. Elizabeth loved her daughter but didn't know what to do to help her anymore.

When Mary and the boys' father, Roy Lauren, had taken off, Elizabeth felt like Mary, who was only nine at the time, took it very hard. All of them did, but Mary handled it differently. The boys became the men of the house, feeling like they had to grow up and take care of their mother and sister.

Mary had become very angry with all of them, blaming each of them at different times. If the boys acted up, she would say things like, "See, if you didn't fight like that, Dad would never have taken off." Or she would say to Elizabeth, "What did you do to him, Mom? Why would he have left us? Were you mean to him?" Elizabeth never knew what happened to Roy except he took off with some waitress and their plans were to go out west. They wanted to see Las Vegas. That was the talk from the other waitresses that had worked with the girl named Becky— the "home wrecker" is what they called her. Elizabeth had to immediately get a job—two jobs to be exact—and the children grew up fast then. They had to; everything was different. She tried on a regular basis to reassure Mary it was nothing they did. Her dad was just blinded by a foolish dream and followed a woman. The only part Elizabeth knew to be true was her children did not do anything to make Roy leave, but Mary never seemed reassured.

Roy had been a decent father. He'd played with the children. He'd worked, paid their bills, and wrestled with the boys. Mary was his little princess, and he had treated Elizabeth well, his taking off was not a relief. It confused and hurt them all deeply. Elizabeth watched Mary grow up overnight. Her father was gone; he had left her and broke her heart in the process. What had concerned Elizabeth back then was how Mary's eyes grew hard every time she looked at her. It broke Elizabeth's heart to think her daughter somehow blamed her for Roy leaving.

After Mary graduated from high school, she moved out on her own. Rarely coming home for a visit, she met Paul and they headed south. They had no game plan. They just wanted to head south of Wisconsin. Both of Paul's parents were deceased, he had no reason to stay in Wisconsin. They ran out of money in Missouri, not having much to start with, they both took jobs and stayed.

No plans of having children were ever talked about. Mary just found out she was pregnant one day. Not much was said; there was not a lot of excitement from her about the baby coming. Paul was fine with the news. To Paul having a baby seemed pretty normal. On a day that started just like any other day, Cassandra Marvin was born in the late afternoon. The leaves were just starting to change color that October when Cassie was brought home from the hospital.

# CHAPTER 4

At the top of the apple tree, Cassie sat up on her perch looking down to the ground where Larissa and Samuel were beginning their climb up the branches of the apple tree. The beautiful apple tree with all its crooked and bent limps was in Samuel and Larissa's backyard. It was near the borderline of Cassie's backyard. When the children planned to meet there, Cassie usually arrived first. They had more fun climbing and playing games in the apple tree. Once in a while, they snacked on one of the, green, sour apples, but never for more than a taste. The green apples if eaten too much—they learned the hard way—could give them an awful stomachache.

"Hey, Cassie, that you way up there?" Larissa yelled out as she began her climb to the first big tree branch.

Larissa was a year older than Cassie, but they never noticed the age difference. They both acted like equals, even though in size they were opposites. Larissa was a head taller then Cassie; her long, red, waist-length hair made her look even taller. She was filled out more than Cassie too. Cassie's baby fat was limited to her cheeks and her hands. She had the cute full cheeks with dimples, and her hands were still dimpled and plump. All other areas were on the thinner side. Larissa had bright blue eyes and lots of freckles, which she would have loved to be able to rub off. When she told Cassie one day how she felt about her freckles, Cassie told her to not feel that way, that her freckles were pretty. "They are like kisses from heaven scattered all over your cheeks." Cassie said.

Samuel climbed up right after his sister. "Hi, Cassie!" he yelled up at Cassie. Samuel was eleven years old, going on twelve, and he was the perfect big brother to both Larissa and Cassie. Samuel took after his mother and had dark-brown hair and blue eyes. Larissa had her dad's red hair.

Samuel and Larissa had asked Cassie earlier before lunchtime if she wanted to play in the apple tree. They made up pretend games they could play in the apple tree together. The apple tree was a boat, or an island, sometimes a space ship, but never an apple tree. Just being an apple tree would be too boring for their imaginative minds.

"Hi, you guys. I just got up here a few minutes ago, and I was waiting for you," Cassie said from her comfortable position from a V in the branches. From way up high in the branches, Cassie could see all over. The view of the world looked different to her from up there. Cassie was drawn to the height. Only she used the top branches; Samuel and Larissa did not dare go so high up. When asked to climb higher, Samuel and Larissa told Cassie they got dizzy up there. The branches up near the top were thick and solid, so Cassie was safe. They could hold her weight.

"Do you want to play island and alligators, or do you want to play sharks and boats?" Cassie questioned them, ready to play.

They could play either game for hours, climbing up and down the branches, pretending to hang over and almost get bitten or eaten by the big and scary alligator or shark. Each would take their turns saving each other; the drama could go on and on for hours.

"Cassie, save me... save me!" Larissa called out, hanging from a branch. Larissa had huge alligators after her. They were ready to bite at her dangling feet.

Cassie and Samuel went right to work helping their companion on their island. "Larissa, here... reach for us here!" Cassie said, reaching out to Larissa and showing her where to put her foot to be able to climb or *swim* in their imaginative minds to the island.

Much later in the afternoon, Cassie looked at the sky. "Hey, you guys, I better get home before my mom does. I've got to set the kitchen table and stuff," Cassie told Larissa and Samuel as she began her climb down from the apple tree.

Jumping down, Cassie wiped off her hands on her pink shorts and then dusted off her white T-shirt with pink and yellow flowers on it. It was one of her favorite shirts—one reason being it was from her grandma; the other reason was the pocket looked like a flower. She didn't have anything to put in the pocket to actually use it, but Cassie liked the pocket. It was pretty to her and made the shirt different from her others.

Happy she hadn't gotten too dirty, Cassie told her friends Larissa and Samuel maybe they could play after dinner.

Cassie's friends were good at not questioning her about her situation, about her being home alone during the day and having to take care of herself or the times they had heard her mother yelling. They just accepted it because Cassie did... Larissa and Samuel never wanted to embarrass her, if they heard the yelling from the house, they pretended for Cassie's sake they didn't.

Only Cassie quietly experienced the embarrassment from her home. She would pretend nothing bothered her. When her mother would not calm down and the yelling would go on and on, Cassie could not help but look around to see who saw or who heard, wanting to climb right into herself and hide.

Jumping up and down, Larissa and Samuel tried to catch Cassie's attention as she was crossing her backyard. "Cassie! Hey, Cassie, we could play hide-and-seek in the garden later tonight!"

"That sounds good, you guys! See you later then after dinner!" Cassie shouted so they could hear her. Taking off on a run, Cassie hurried into the house, wanting to get everything done before her mother got home.

As Cassie was lifting the heavy lid off the garbage can, she turned because she heard something. Laying the lid on the ground so she could put the garbage bag in the garbage can, Cassie saw Mrs. Chambers from across the street walking up the driveway.

"Hello, Mrs. Chambers," Cassie said as she lifted the garbage bag to put it in the garbage can. Then returning the lid to the garbage can,

Cassie pushed it down tight to make sure it was sealed. Cassie then turned around again to smile at her neighbor lady, Mrs. Chambers.

"Well hello, Cassandra, how are you doing today, honey?"

Looking up, Cassie squinted against the sun and told Mrs. Chambers she was fine. She was cleaning up a few things before her mother got home. "Oh, and I played next door today at Larissa's and Samuel's! We played in the apple tree. We were on an island almost getting eaten by alligators," Cassie finished matter-of-factly.

Mrs. Chambers chuckled over Cassie's description. "Why, Cassie, you can make me laugh over the littlest things. My goodness, Cassie! Where do you children come up with all these ideas?"

Pointing to her head, Cassie explained, "Right here, Mrs. Chambers. It's all in here," Cassie told her, tapping the right side of her head. "I just get these ideas; then I tell Samuel and Larissa about them, and then we play the game. We have a lot of fun acting out them."

"You are a very talented little lady; you know that, don't you? Why, you can come up with all those acting out games and you can take care of yourself like a big girl. You even take care of your mother's home when she is not here."

Cassie just beamed because of the nice things Mrs. Chambers said to her, but she didn't think she was talented. They were just things she did, some she had to, and some she came up with because she was a kid and she wanted to play. It was all as simple as that to Cassie.

Mrs. Chambers told Cassie Mr. Chambers was sleeping so she was able to come out for a few minutes. "Just wanted to check on you, Cassie, so everything is okay?" Looking at her watch, Mrs. Chambers confirmed the time to Cassie. "It's almost four o'clock; your mother should be home soon."

Cassie liked Mr. and Mrs. Chambers and knowing she could run across the street if she ever really needed something was a comfort to her. They were like a security blanket to Cassie. She did not wear out her welcome at the Chamberses' home. She was told to leave everyone alone unless there was an emergency of some kind. Mary reminded her on a regular basis; this made Cassie feel if she did go around once too often, people wouldn't like her.

Quite often, Mrs. Chambers worried about Cassie. She wished Mary would take on a full-time babysitter for the child. Mrs. Chambers could not understand how a child Cassie's age could be left home all alone. Mrs. Chambers felt if anyone could survive being unattended this much, Cassie could. She thought Cassie was a wonderful child.

"Yep, I'm fine. I just set the table for dinner too. Momma wants me to do that every day, and I took out all the trash too..." Cassie said, shrugging her shoulders. "Thank you for checking on me." Cassie remembered to thank Mrs. Chambers. It was so nice of her to show she cared.

Mrs. Chambers thought for a moment on all the things Cassie told her. Not knowing what else to say to Cassie, she turned slightly and with a nod in the direction of her house asked Cassie, "Would you like to walk with me down to the street? And it's never a problem to check on you, Cassie. I look forward to getting out of the house sometimes. Just walk with me to the street, honey. Then you can sit on the front porch until your mother gets home. I can see you on the porch from my windows, I like knowing you're all right. Mr. Chambers likes to know you're okay too." Mrs. Chambers reached for Cassie's hand after saying her comforting words to her. Mrs. Chambers was thinking she would like to say something to Paul and Mary, but it wouldn't be nice.

. . . . . . . . . . .

Cassie skipped down the sidewalk after dinner to Larissa's and Samuel's house. Their home next door was not far away, but for a person Cassie's size, it was far enough to get in a few really good skips. Cassie loved skipping. She was energetic and her legs were strong enough to get her going fast, and on each skip, she went up high off the sidewalk. Skipping all the way to the front door, ready to play, Cassie knocked on the front screen door. Looking through the screen door, Cassie could see Mrs. Stockard at the kitchen sink cleaning the dinner dishes.

As Mrs. Stockard turned toward the door, her hands still in the soapy dish water, she smiled at Cassie. "Hi, Cassie! Come on in, honey; the kids are in their bedrooms."

Cassie reached up and pulled open the door. Stepping into the entryway, she said, "Thanks, Mrs. Stockard, I'll go find them." Then she rushed off down the hallway to their bedrooms.

Noticing how thoughtful Cassie was by stepping out of her slip-on tennis shoes and placing them together on the rug, Mrs. Stockard continued to clean her dishes. Mrs. Stockard was a neighbor who looked out for Cassie also. She was a Christian woman but did not think much of Cassie's parents. She knew from her children what Cassie had to put up with, and she also knew from personal experience what it was like to deal with Mary Marvin.

Many years ago, Mrs. Stockard, Barbara, had gone over to introduce herself to Mary Marvin. Mary being a new neighbor, Barbara thought it was a neighborly thing to do. Mary did not work at the time with Cassie being just a baby. Barbara had knocked on the front door and was told to come in. As Barbara entered Mary's home, Barbara had been appalled at the condition of the house. Everywhere she looked there were piles of clothes, magazines, and clutter. There was smoke in the house from Mary's cigarettes; one was burning in the ashtray when Barbara walked in and was causing a cloud so thick that it covered everything with its smoky film. Ashtrays on every surface were filled to the brim with cigarette butts. Dirty dishes were in the sink, and from where she stood, Barbara could tell that the pans that were left on the stove still had burnt food in them.

In the middle of all the chaos was Cassie. She was a very small baby at the time, but she looked like a colorful blooming flower in the middle of a rocky desert. So dry and lifeless were her surroundings, Barbara had wondered how a little flower like Cassie had gotten there. She was standing up in her playpen and smiling at Barbara. Cassie was holding the top edge of the playpen to help hold herself up, and she was jumping up and down very happily. Drool was coming out of her smiling mouth. It was hot outside, so Barbara thought that was the reason Mary had her daughter dressed in a diaper only, she was so cute and joyful that she looked like the belle of a ball.

Barbara fell in love with Cassie that day, and as Cassie grew up, Barbara's feelings toward her never changed. Cassie was still the little girl smiling and jumping up and down in the playpen, full of what her mother apparently did not have. Barbara's feelings toward Mary had only become worse over the years. As hard as she tried, Barbara did not like the woman, though she prayed for her because of Cassie.

Barbara recalled her experience on her first visit, she tried to explain to Mary as she stepped inside the door that she had stopped by to introduce herself since they were new neighbors.

Mary then proceeded to tell Barbara, "I guess that's nice of you and all, but I am a very busy woman with a baby, as you can see. I don't like people just stopping by. I know we live pretty close to each other, but I really don't want to be bothered with people coming over here unannounced."

Barbara was speechless. She had no idea how to answer someone who would talk to her like that. Having never been treated in such a way, Barbara was speechless for several long moments. "I am so sorry I bothered you then. You have the most beautiful baby," Barbara told Mary, nodding her head toward the playpen which held Cassie. "I'll be going now, but if you ever need anything, I am at home during the day."

As Barbara turned to the door, Mary said, "What in the world would I need?" Mary stared at her with one side of her mouth lifted up in what seemed to be a very cynical smile. The look from Mary challenged Barbara to say something.

Barbara opened the door and headed home as fast as her legs could carry her. *That poor child* was all Barbara could think about. She held her own children closer to her that day. Barbara was very thankful they did not have a mother like the baby next door.

Barbara got out the ice cream and strawberries for the kids' dessert. Barbara was so glad she'd waited to serve the dessert. Cassie could have some with them. Reaching for bowls for the ice cream, Barbara picked out the ice cream bowls she bought years ago. She forgot to use them most of the time because they were up on a higher shelf and she didn't see them. They were perfect. All were pastel colors, and the handles were shaped like an ice cream waffle cone.

"Kids, I've got ice cream and strawberries ready for you! Come on out and help me dish it up!" Barbara called, her voice filled with excitement.

With the patter of feet coming down the hallway, Barbara knew they had heard her.

"Go wash your hands, all of you, and then you get to help. Cassie, we are glad you're here. You and Larissa get to dish up the strawberries on top of the ice cream!" Looking at Samuel, Mrs. Stockard told him, "Samuel, you can help me with the ice cream."

"There are a lot of giggles coming from the sink. Make sure you all wash really well," Mrs. Stockard reminded them, giggling herself.

She waited at the kitchen table with all the goodies for the ice cream spread out. She had whipped cream and sprinkles for the ice cream, but she thought she'd leave that information for a surprise once they got started getting their ice cream ready.

Cassie loved being at Larissa's and Samuel's house; their mother was so nice, and Cassie thought she was so pretty too. Cassie believed Mrs. Stockard could be a movie star with her beautiful brown hair and bright blue eyes. Cassie thought Mrs. Stockard always smelled good too. Cassie loved the day Larissa showed her all the pretty perfume bottles on her mother's bathroom counter. The perfume bottles were displayed on an oval, mirrored tray. She and Larissa lightly touched every jeweled bottle. Cassie also noticed Mrs. Stockard's painted fingernails. They were always painted a pretty pink. Mrs. Stockard even let the girls play in her jewelry box. She encouraged them to try the jewelry on, and then they would parade around all sparkling with the costume jewelry. Cassie was made to feel very comfortable in their home; she was able to enjoy herself in every situation.

"Do you want sprinkles, Cassie?" Mrs. Stockard asked, holding up the sprinkles and spoon.

After spooning on the strawberries, Cassie had added the whipped cream to her ice cream bowl. "Oh, yes, please, Mrs. Stockard. That may be the best part!" They all laughed at that comment.

"What? What was so funny?" Cassie was focused on the extras for her ice cream, she just knew she'd missed something.

Larissa, already sitting down at the kitchen table, laughed. "Cassie, you are so funny! Your eyes got this big over the sprinkles!" Larissa said, forming a big circle with her hands.

Cassie, knowing Larissa was not laughing at her but she had made *her* laugh, said, "I know… I get so excited. The sprinkles just make it so much better!" She tried to giggle around a mouthful of ice cream.

On and on the fun went as they talked over their bowls of ice cream. Samuel told jokes from his joke book, and the girls giggled over each joke, which made him have a very responsive audience. Mrs. Stockard sat back and enjoyed the ice cream, but she was definitely enjoying the children more.

When they finished their ice cream, Mrs. Stockard told them to go on out and play; she would take care of the kitchen. Cassie put her dish by the sink on her way out of the kitchen and thanked Mrs. Stockard for the ice cream.

"You sure you don't need us to help you?"

"No, honey, you go out and play. You too, Larissa. You're going to play hide-and-seek, right?"

"Yep!" both of the girls said at the same time and then looked at each other and broke into giggles.

"Okay, you giggle boxes, go on out and play before it gets to dark. I'll come and sit in the backyard soon. Dad will be back in a few minutes; he'll be so sad he missed out on the ice cream," Mrs. Stockard said with a big smile to the girls.

"Where did he go, Mom?" Larissa just realized her dad was not there.

"He had to run over to Grandma and Grandpa's for a minute. Grandpa needed some help moving something in the garage."

Samuel opened the back door and peeked inside. "Are you guys coming out here or not? I have found some good... hiding places."

In unison, the girls said, "Here we come" and took off on a run to the great outdoors ready for hide-and-seek.

The Stockards' backyard had a huge vegetable garden, an apple tree, and lots of things to hide behind. Near the end of the summer, the corn rows were great to hide in. The kids were looking forward to their growth, having hid in the corn rows last year. Samuel had the advantage with his height over the girls, Cassie and Larissa had the advantage of being smaller than him. They could hide behind something smaller than Samuel, which gave them each a lot more choices. Each having an advantage made the game fairly equal.

Cassie sat there on the ground behind some of the grown plants in the garden. She was tiny enough if she scrunched down really low they couldn't see her. Hugging her legs to her chest, she waited. With no movement except her eyes darting from left to right to see if she was found out yet and her heart beating a mile a minute, Cassie was otherwise still. She heard Larissa scream, "Ah! Samuel, you found me!"

Cassie was next. Samuel would have to find her. Just the thought he was coming to find her made Cassie's heart leap up into her throat. Scrunching down lower, she waited. Samuel was on the other side of the yard, but it would not take him long to figure out she wasn't there.

"Cassie, Cassie, where are you?" Samuel sang, making the game funnier then before.

In the background, Cassie heard Larissa and Mrs. Stockard laughing at Samuel's song.

Cassie heard nothing now, so she waited. Then there was a crunch on the ground to her left. *How did he get over there so fast?* Cassie wondered.

With her heart beating in her ears, she wondered if when she sensed he was close should she jump out and scare Samuel or if she should sit and wait until he found her. There was another noise somewhere to her left and then nothing. Where was Samuel?

Then all of the sudden his voice was a couple of corn rows over. "Cassie, oh Cassie, where are you?" Samuel sang again.

*That's it!* Cassie thought; her heart jumped again with him being so close. Putting her hands to the ground to get leverage, she readied herself to spring up like a coil. She was going to change the game; she had to. Cassie couldn't take the suspense any longer. Cassie could no longer just sit and wait to be found. She had to come up with a plan to keep this fun and from not getting so scared. Keeping her head down, she waited for just the right moment. Holding her breath, she knew it was just a matter of seconds and Samuel would be close enough for her to scare him!

*Ready, ready,* she told herself. "Aah!" Cassie jumped up like a spring released into the air, screaming at the top of her lungs, waving her arms high up in the air. But her scream couldn't be heard over Samuel's. Samuel came around the corner just as Cassie jumped into the air. Not knowing she was there, he jumped high off the ground, arms flying, and let out a wail of a scream. "Oh my!"

Cassie had tears running down her face from laughing so hard. Samuel had looked like he was going to have a heart attack. His scream was so loud it had made them both jump. After stumbling back with his eyes as big as saucers and waving his arms to catch his balance, Samuel started laughing and could not stop. He had to bend from the waist and put his hands on his knees to catch his breath.

"Why, Cassie, you scared me to death! I think my heart popped out of my chest! I don't think I have ever had that much fun playing hide-and-seek!" Samuel exclaimed when he had caught his breath. Putting his arm around Cassie's shoulders, he said, "Come on, I can hear them laughing at me up at the house." They walked back up to the house, both laughing all the way.

"You should have seen your face, Samuel; it was really funny," Cassie couldn't resist one more comment, laughing as hard as Samuel.

# CHAPTER 5

Spending time with Mrs. Vashon in her flower garden was quickly becoming one of Cassie's favorite pastimes. Cassie stayed away on the weekend when her mother was home. If Mary knew how much Cassie went to the garden, she could make her stay away. Her time with Larissa was already limited when her mother was home. Cassie recently had stayed a little too long one evening.

"Don't you be goin' over there all the time. I don't want Miss Fancy Pants over there thinking I pawned you off on her. You hear me, Cassie." It wasn't a question. Cassie heard her.

"How much do you go over there anyway, hmmm?"

"Not as much as I would want to," Cassie replied.

"What the heck does that mean?"

"I don't go there much."

"Good, you make sure of that." Mary's silent threat was left hanging in the air.

Cassie made sure of it. Cassie also made sure it was not very long between her visits to the garden, and she enjoyed visiting with Mrs. Vashon too. Mrs. Vashon reminded Cassie of her grandmother, Elizabeth, whom she missed very much.

Mrs. Vashon's flower garden had come to life for her. It had been just a nice flower garden before Cassie. Having Cassie around now and enjoying the gardening with her was the new joy in Mrs. Vashon's life.

As Cassie pulled the water hose to unwind it, Mrs. Vashon hurried over to help her. Cassie was doing just fine, but Mrs. Vashon worried about Cassie overdoing it, probably because of Cassie's smaller size. She looked pint-sized but was strong and hardy.

Cassie laid the hose out along the flowerbed that she was going to water and then ran back to turn the water on. Twisting the dial halfway like Mrs. Vashon had told her, Cassie waited until she heard the water rush into the hose and then ran back to pick up the hose and start watering the flowers. Cassie was lightly spraying the flowers, giving them a misting, bending; she lightly sprayed at the ground to make sure the roots received their water for the day. So contentious and determined to do a good job, Cassie did exactly that. Every flower and plant received its daily water from her.

As she lifted the hose up, Cassie could see rainbows in the spray of water, "Mrs. Vashon! Come here, quick, look... There are rainbows in the water!" Looking through the water, Cassie loved what she could see. It was beautiful! She stood very still holding the hose up causing the sun to hit the water spray just perfect. Her arms were getting tired holding the hose still, Cassie never felt her arms tiring. She was so engrossed looking through the water.

Mrs. Vashon hurried over to Cassie and stood where she could see what Cassie was talking about. "Look through the water, Mrs. Vashon! Look how beautiful the flower garden looks. The flowers are covered with rainbows. Oh, look at all the colors together. I have never seen anything so pretty!" Cassie exclaimed in awe.

Mrs. Vashon stood and tilted her head to one side and then the other and enjoyed the beautiful waterfall that Cassie had created. "Why, Cassie, this is just glorious! You have made something here, my dear. I don't think I have ever seen this before!

"Here, Cassie, let me hold the hose for a while, and you just look; your arms have to be getting tired, honey," Mrs. Vashon suggested as she took over the water hose for Cassie.

Cassie gave Mrs. Vashon the hose, and the waterfall was even better. Mrs. Vashon could hold the hose higher and send the water spray farther into the air, she created a much bigger wall of water to look through.

"Don't you love it?" Cassie breathed, not needing a response because she was just enjoying herself and talking out loud.

Later, after turning the water hose off, Mrs. Vashon invited Cassie to sit on the porch with her and have some lemonade and cookies. Wanting to make their snack special, Mrs. Vashon put two small glasses on a serving tray with the lemonade pitcher and then put six cookies on a small blue plate. Mrs. Vashon used her hip to hold open the back door while she carried the tray with both hands.

Cassie jumped up to help her and held the back screen door. Mrs. Vashon had a table on the porch, which was placed between two wicker chairs that were painted white. It was there on the table she put down the tray and began to serve Cassie her snacks.

"Sit here in the chair, Cassie, and rest for a while. We can enjoy our snack together and visit while we are looking out at our beautiful flower garden," Mrs. Vashon told Cassie, looking forward to enjoying more of her company.

"Hmm... these are good cookies, Mrs. Vashon. Thank you!" Cassie exclaimed as she was enjoying her cookie.

"I am glad you like them, honey. I thought of you when I made them," Mrs. Vashon let her know. The cookies were sweet lemon-drop cookies, lightly covered in a powered-sugar frosting and then sprinkled with a crystal-like sugar.

"You did?" Cassie asked, looking very small in the big wicker chair, her legs sticking straight out in front of her.

"I sure did! I like to have something special for you, Cassie when you help me in the flower garden or just when you come and visit me. Do you and your momma bake cookies, Cassie?" Mrs. Vashon asked, taking another bite of her cookie.

Cassie thought for a moment, shaking her head. "No, I don't think she has ever made cookies. Probably because she has to work so much. That's what she says about dinner; she doesn't like to cook dinner. She does, but she tells my dad that she doesn't like it because she has to work all the time."

Mrs. Vashon could have already guessed the answer to her question but wanted to know just in case she had read Cassie's situation wrong. Not wanting to make an excuse for Cassie's mother, she still wanted to say something nice for Cassie's sake. "Well, Cassie, finding the time to bake sometimes is hard for moms who have to work outside their homes."

Cassie, enjoying her cookie, thought about what Mrs. Vashon had said.

"Nope, I don't think Momma would like to bake cookies either, even if she was home all the time." Looking up, Cassie smiled at Mrs. Vashon when she reached for her lemonade.

Mrs. Vashon was overwhelmed with Cassie; her heart swelled with love for the girl. She actually worried about Cassie's welfare. Mrs. Vashon's opinion was that Cassie was much too young to be taking care of herself. Mrs. Vashon didn't want to make trouble for Cassie, by talking to someone about it either. It was not against the law, Mrs. Vashon assumed, however what frustrated Mrs. Vashon was how Mary would not let anyone watch Cassie.

"No, she's fine on her own. She knows how to behave, and we don't have the money for a sitter, nor will I let someone do it for free and hold it over my head," Mary had told her once in the grocery store when Mrs. Vashon volunteered to help out at no charge.

Mrs. Vashon remembered Barbara Stockard, Cassie's next-door neighbor, had also tried to help out. She was told the same thing when Cassie was only five years old and on her own after school and during the summer months. The only person who Mary agreed about calling her at work just in case of an emergency was Mrs. Chambers. Mrs. Chambers still did not know how she was able to pull the request off years ago with Mary. She had approached Mary one day on the street while both of them were checking their mail. Asking for her work number, Mrs. Chambers in a matter-of-fact way told Mary someone needed to have a number to get in touch with her just in case Cassie needed her.

Much to Mrs. Chambers's surprise, Mary Marvin brought her work number over later in the evening. Knocking on the Chamber's back door, Mary said when Mrs. Chambers answered the door, "Well, here's my work number." Handing Mrs. Chambers the piece of paper with a number written on it, she added, "Don't call me unless it's an emergency. I don't want to get fired." Then Mary turned and walked away.

Mrs. Vashon brought her thoughts back around to Cassie. Cassie was enjoying herself, Mrs. Vashon smiled and quieted her worrying thoughts. She needed to just enjoy her time with Cassie.

Sitting in peaceful silence and admiring the flower garden, Mrs. Vashon and Cassie continued to sit in the wicker chairs while finishing the last of the cookies and having another glass of lemonade.

"Cassie, I had so much fun with the water earlier. I don't think I'll ever water the flowers again without remembering how beautiful the experience was. We probably won't ever have the sun reflection on the water spray exactly like that again; it was just perfect."

"It was so pretty, wasn't it?" Cassie agreed, wiggling in her chair.

Mrs. Vashon tried to think of a place where she could compare the water experience too. "Yes, it was very pretty, almost heaven-like."

Looking out at the garden, Cassie continued in a whisper, "You know, when I was little, I found those." Cassie looked at her like she had the biggest secret in the world, like she had found a secret treasure or something.

"What, honey? What did you find?" Mrs. Vashon's curiosity had her interrupting.

"The rainbows... the colors of the rainbows. I would get a drink from the water hose in our yard or spray the yard with the water, and sometimes I sprayed myself when it was really hot." Cassie turned and looked at her with a dimpled smile. "That was when I found I liked looking through the water. I told God I was glad he made water see-through just the other day. Anyway." Getting back on track, Cassie continued. "I like how you can see through to the other side, the other side of the water. But looking through the water changes things; it makes everything pretty somehow. I like how it wiggles and sparkles, and it is really pretty when you see the rainbow, the colors. I've even held my breath under the water in Larissa's splash pool. We've laid on our backs and held our breath. Then we open our eyes. It makes our eyes burn a little from the water, but you can see everything—the sky, the trees… and Samuel. He was standing by the pool looking down at us. That was funny."

Cassie smiled up at Mrs. Vashon again after finishing her story, and Mrs. Vashon thought her heart melted right there, pooled right out on the ground and not from the heat of the day but from Cassie.

"You have taught me something new, Cassie. I have never looked through the water before, but I will from now on. I will look for the rainbows too," Mrs. Vashon promised as she gave Cassie a smile full of the love she felt for her.

In all her innocence, Cassie replied, "Oh, I know you will now; you won't be able to stop yourself."

Mrs. Vashon had a hard time keeping her chuckle to herself.

As the afternoon wore on, the heat index continued to rise, and the thunderhead clouds rose in the western sky.

"Cassie, I want to walk you over to Mrs. Stockard's house and see if they're home. It looks like a storm is coming, and I don't want you home by yourself. I don't have a basement, so it's not safe in my home either. I know they have a partial basement, I would feel better if you were there when this storm hits."

"I've been home by myself in a storm, Mrs. Vashon."

"Were you afraid, Cassie?"

"I wasn't in the beginning. I liked watching the storm from the windows; then the wind and lightening got really loud, so I went under my bed. Then I was afraid," Cassie told her with big eyes.

"See, you need to be with others so we know you're fine. I need to know you're taken care of, Cassie. Let's go see if Barbara's home."

Taking Cassie's hand in hers, Mrs. Vashon started walking down the street. In the distance they could hear the thunder.

"If we do get a bad storm , where will you go?" Cassie wondered, worry making her frown.

"Oh, I will be fine, honey; don't worry about me. I have a small fruit cellar in the pantry. I can still climb down in there."

# CHAPTER 6

The afternoon grew still and quiet except for a car traveling down the road and the thunder in the distance. Mrs. Vashon couldn't help but walk faster, hoping Cassie could keep up and not notice that she was being dragged along at a quicker pace.

Cassie was all smiles, not sensing the impending storm or the fear of Mrs. Vashon.

"Do you want to stay with us, Mrs. Vashon, and then we don't have to worry about you?" Cassie asked, thinking she would be at the Stockards' home during the approaching storm and Mrs. Vashon shouldn't be alone either.

"Oh, honey, thank you for asking, but let's get you situated, and then I'll go on home and watch over my house. Then we will all check on each other later, okay, Cassie?" Hurrying up the walk, Mrs. Vashon was glad to see it looked like Barbara was home. Sighing with relief, Mrs. Vashon, still holding Cassie's hand, approached the front door.

The western sky was getting darker by the second. With the thunder in the distance and the wind picking up, most of the people near Tipton, Missouri, knew a storm was heading their way. Radios were being turned on, as well as televisions. Mrs. Stockard had already gathered up Samuel and Larissa. They were in the house when Cassie and Mrs. Vashon knocked on the door.

"Well hello, ladies, come on in; a storm is brewing out there," Barbara said, letting them both in the screen door.

Leading Cassie in the door, Mrs. Vashon stepped into the entryway. "Hello, Barbara. We are so glad you're home. Cassie was spending the day with me in the garden; then we saw this storm coming. I thought you wouldn't mind if she stayed with you just in case you might need to go to the basement."

Cassie had gone over to the living room floor and sat down with Samuel and Larissa. They were putting a puzzle together, so Cassie joined in.

"Of course, Suzanne; she is more then welcome, and I would have preferred it. I was just getting ready to run next door and get her."

Mrs. Vashon whispered, "I just love that little girl, and it's getting mean out there. Thank you, Barbara. I just needed to know she was being looked after. I can't imagine how her parents work all day and have no idea what's happening with her and especially with a storm coming."

Barbara turned and looked over at Cassie, wondering the same thing. "I know, Suzanne; it breaks my heart sometimes. I'll take good care of her. Now with the wind picking up, you go on home. Let's touch base after the storm, okay?"

"Yes, I am sure we'll be fine. I better get going." A little louder so Cassie could hear her, Mrs. Vashon continued, "Cassie, you stay inside and listen to Mrs. Stockard, and I'll see you soon."

"Bye, Mrs. Vashon!" the three children all chimed in, looking up from the puzzle that had their concentration.

"Thanks again, Barbara." Mrs. Vashon gave one more relieved look to Barbara.

"No problem! Now be careful and get home!"

Grabbing the screen door, Barbara had to pull hard to get it to close. The wind had really picked up. Looking off to the west, the sky had almost become black now. The storm was still miles away but approaching with power and speed. Several lightening bolts had lit up the black clouds and struck the ground. Over their area, the sky was still blue with some sunshine peeking out from behind the big thunderhead clouds.

*How fast a summer storm can sneak up on you if you aren't watching the whole sky*, Barbara thought.

"Mom, Dad's on the phone; he wants to talk with you!" Samuel yelled from the front door.

"Be right there, honey. I was just watching Mrs. Vashon walk home." Barbara went running in.

Bob Stockard was at work just out of town; being closer to the storm he could see this was going to be a bad one. "Hello, Barb, you and the kids inside?" he asked the moment she answered the phone.

"Yes, Bob, I got Samuel and Larissa in a while ago, and I've got Cassie here now too. We are going to go downstairs soon. I think that's best. It's starting to get really dark to the west."

"Okay, good, it's getting bad out here. It's as black as coal outside just west of us, it's definitely coming our way. We heard a tornado touched down with this storm earlier, so it's got some gumption. That was in Oklahoma, but you never know. Honey, get the flashlights and get down there in the basement. I'd feel better if you went down now," Bob said.

Barbara didn't need to be told twice. She got off the phone and hurried around the kitchen for supplies. The kids were busy with their puzzle so she could get some things together without causing alarm. Taking her gathered items downstairs, Barbara got everything ready before gathering up the kids and heading to the basement.

Entering the living room, Barbara could see out the front window. The sky was darkened now in their area and was turning a weird pea green below the blackened clouds.

"Okay, kids, let's go. The storm is coming, and we need to get downstairs now. Just in case, grab a cushion off the couch, each of you; you never know if we may need something to put over our heads."

Turning to look back at her mom, Larissa asked, "Mom, are we going to be okay?"

Patting her head, Mrs. Stockard told Larissa, but the words were meant for all the children, "Honey, that's why we are going downstairs. That's the safest place just in case this storm wants to get nasty. We can make it an adventure, and our cushions are part of our fort."

Cassie put her arm around Larissa and said, "We'll be all right, Larissa; you'll see."

Samuel helped get the girls in the cubby area under the stairs and put a cushion around each of them. Then he and his mother climbed into the space that was left, and there they sat. They had a little light from the basement's small windows, and they had the flashlights in case of an emergency.

Outside the storm was barreling down on Tipton, Missouri, with a vengeance. The winds had started to get severe. They were blowing in their cool air on the hot day. The whole area of the town of Tipton was darkened like someone had turned off the light switch. The clouds had darkened to a blackest black and were hanging over Tipton in big cone shapes. Each cloud looked like it wanted to reach down and touch the ground. Underneath the black clouds, the sky that had turned a pea-green color became very bright all of the sudden. It didn't look natural. The few people who were still looking out their windows or standing on their porches decided now was the time to run and hide from this monster of a storm.

Without blinking an eye, the winds stopped altogether. An eerie calm settled over the local area. Cassie and those in the basement with her saw the weird green color through the basement windows. It made the basement walls look green, like there was a big green monster out there and he was hovering over the house. She didn't want to watch anymore, but she couldn't peel her eyes away from the windows. Not saying a word, the four people in the cubby under the stairs in the Stockard home just waited, listening.

Mrs. Stockard was silently praying, and the children were holding hands, trying to be brave. Cassie and Larissa were practically on each other's laps they were sitting so close. Samuel was fighting to be brave for all of them since his dad was not home.

Then without any warning, the winds started up again, sending the marble-sized hail from the storm like bullets into whatever it could hit. It sounded like a machine gun was pointed at the house and had opened fire.

"I kind of wish I could see this," Cassie said from her huddled position.

The lightening was whipping across the sky—not in single bolts of lightening but lighting up the entire skyline. There was enough electricity in the air that the lightening was causing a strobe-light effect. Some of the electrical wires in town were standing on end and dancing in the blue light that was surrounding them with pure electricity.

"I know it gets your curiosity up, but down here is a lot safer, honey," Mrs. Stockard whispered.

They could hear what sounded like trees breaking in the distance. "I hope that's not the apple tree," Cassie said. Larissa started crying, and Cassie hugged her tighter.

The wind had roared for what seemed like forever; and then the rain, hail, and wind just stopped. "Do you think there was a tornado out there?" Cassie asked Mrs. Stockard.

Not sure, Barbara said, "I hope not, Cassie, but it sure sounded like something was out there. I'm surprised the house it still over our heads." She looked up to the basement ceiling just to double-check.

Releasing their holds on each other and trying to relax, each of them took their turns stretching out their stiff limbs. "The color is more normal coming through the windows now, Mom," Samuel said.

Rising, Barbara told the kids, "Stay here and let me go check."

Larissa, still shook up from the storm, said, "Mom, you be careful!"

Barbara gave them all a hug before leaving. "I will, honey. I'll call down if it's over, and if it's not I'll be running right back down."

Barbara had assessed the situation outside from the front living room windows and then had gone back down and gathered the kids out of the basement. It looked like the worst was over. The town had taken a severe beating. Trees were down everywhere; their branches were scattered like broken toothpicks, and a few chimneys were toppled over on several houses. It looked like most of the homes were still intact. This was a very good sign. Everyone was safe and had survived the storm.

Once the children reached the top of the basement stairs, they took off to see if everything was still intact. The apple tree was the first thing they ran to check on. The apple tree was fine; none of its branches looked like they had been touched. They straightened up the patio furniture that was tossed into the backyard. The children took off then to Cassie's house. Everything looked like it was still where it should be. It was a miracle with the winds and rain that had just beaten the area.

As Cassie entered the house, she could see she needed to go around the open window ledges and wipe up the rain water that had come in onto the ledges and the surrounding floors. The side back door had been left open too and must have blown in with the storm because the floor in the back door area was really wet.

"I'll be right back out. I have to get a towel and wipe up the water!" Cassie called to Samuel and Larissa.

Waiting out on the porch, they told her that was fine and that they would wait for her. Samuel and Larissa would have gladly gone in and helped Cassie, but no one was allowed in the house, and Cassie obeyed her mother's rules about that. Cassie found a bath towel in the bathroom that was used and hurried around the house cleaning up the water the storm had left behind. Then she put the towel in the washing machine to be washed, almost hiding it from her mother, not knowing if she'd be in big trouble leaving the house like she did with the door and windows open. The house was so hot though; Cassie was sure she would not have thought of closing the windows even if she was home.

By now most of the neighbors that were home were coming out of their homes to talk with the other neighbors and look for any damage. Looking around the neighborhood, they all thought they had been lucky. It looked like something scattered twigs and leaves everywhere, but for the most part, there was not any huge damage. Two of the neighbors were going to need their chimneys put back together; there were tossed bricks on their roofs and in their yard. Thankfully none of those bricks had damaged anything else. The people north of the town of Tipton was without power someone said, and two barns had been damaged; the roofs were blown right off of them. No one had seen a tornado, but with the winds and the damage north of town, it made them wonder if something didn't touch down for a few moments and bounce its power around in destruction.

Barbara had called her husband, Bob, and let him know they were fine. He had told her they had watched the storm for a few minutes before seeking shelter, and he told her it looked like a hurricane on land and that they were all lucky.

"I'll be home early, Barb; we are closing up shop. We don't have power here, so there is no sense in staying. After seeing that, none of us can get our minds back to work."

Barbara smiled. She loved it when Bob acted lively about something. She laughed to herself, hanging up the phone. It took almost a tornado to get Bob excited about something.

They all wanted to check on Mrs. Vashon, so they headed toward her house. Cassie walked ahead of everyone else. She wasn't aware of it, but she was just in a hurry. She had grown very fond of Mrs. Vashon and wanted to make sure she was fine and survived the storm.

As they hurried through the garden, Mrs. Vashon was bending over and picking up some stray leaves and smaller twigs that had blown into the yard.

"Oh, I am so glad you walked over. Thank goodness we all survived!" Mrs. Vashon said. "I was just on my way over to check on all of you!"

"That was some storm, huh?" Cassie asked, smiling up at her.

"Yes, it was Cassie. My goodness, I did not know if the house was going to stand through it all, but look around. The garden looks good. A few leaves and some small twigs blew in here, but nothing has been damaged." Mrs. Vashon took in the surrounding area in surprise.

Cassie walked over to the garden angel statue, pointing. "This here is the garden angel I told you about, Samuel and Larissa. See, Mrs. Stockard, this is the angel Mrs. Vashon got for the flower garden, and I bet she watched over it today and would not let the storm hurt anything. It's a good thing you got her, Mrs. Vashon," Cassie finished, looking over at Mrs. Vashon with a nod of her head.

Barbara looked at Suzanne and was warmed by what Cassie had just said. Samuel and Larissa went to check out the garden angel.

"Oh, she is pretty!" Larissa told her.

Barbara whispered, "Suzanne, you got the garden angel for Cassie, didn't you?"

Mrs. Vashon smiled at her. "You caught me."

Cassie gave them a tour of the flower garden like it was the botanical gardens in some big city and they were paying customers. The petals of the flowers looked untouched by the storm that had just passed through, a big miracle for the garden angel. The only evidence of the past storm were a few raindrops still clinging here and there on the petals gleaming in the sunshine. The flowers were standing tall, reaching for the sunshine. The daylilies were stretching. The rainbow-colored plumerias and the hibiscus looked beautiful in the light. With the dark clouds still in the east and the sunshine in the west, it made an unusual lighting in the garden. Cassie pointed out that the lotus flowers in pink and white were exactly what would grow in a Japanese garden.

"Wow, Cassie, where'd you learn all the names of the flowers?" Samuel asked, very impressed by their tour of the garden.

Cassie looked up at Mrs. Vashon like a proud student. "Mrs. Vashon has let me help her here, and she has taught me a lot about the flowers and how to take care of them."

Mrs. Vashon was just as proud of Cassie. Not every child would take such an interest in gardening.

"Well, you are a very smart girl, Cassie, and it has been my pleasure showing you all you need to know about maintaining the garden." Looking over at Samuel and Larissa, she continued. "Don't be fooled, children. Cassie has been a great help to me too."

"Well, I am impressed, Cassie. I think you are a natural around flowers!" Samuel said like a proud big brother.

Larissa laughed. "Samuel, now we know where she's disappeared to when we wanted to play!"

# CHAPTER 7

Last night had not been a good night for Cassie. She got a belt whipping from her dad. Several lashes across the back of her thighs, and the few of them that hit her buttocks would be considered a lucky strike, but lucky was not the tender skin that took the whipping. Cassie's mom made her dad do it. Mary stood at the door and told him what to do and when it was okay to quit.

"She ate my Popsicle, Paul! Did you hear me? She ate what was mine. She had no right to eat it!"

"Mary, it's hot outside. She does nothing but sit here in this heat, and no one is home with her all day. It's only a Popsicle, Mary!" Paul yelled back, trying to reason with her.

"You whip her, Paul, or I am!" Mary stood firm, her eyes blazing. There was a craziness there that made Paul decide he'd do the whipping.

Cassie was lying on her bed waiting, both hands held on tight to the spindles of her headboard. *I am not going to cry*, Cassie kept saying over and over to herself. *I won't cry. I won't let her see me cry. I didn't do anything wrong. I didn't mean to do anything!*

Cassie knew the whipping was coming. They always did. Her dad never won with her mom. He tried to stick up for her, but it never worked. No matter what, when Mary wanted her whipped, she got whipped. As she braced herself, she thought of defending herself but knew it would not work. The Popsicle really wasn't Mary's, not really… Cassie had brought it for her from the ice cream truck man with her own money. Mary had never eaten it, so Cassie thought she could eat it and then replace it the next time the truck came around. She wasn't trying to do anything bad. It was just so hot, and she was so thirsty that the Popsicle was a huge temptation to her. If only the ice cream truck had come around again she wouldn't be gearing up for this whipping right now and her knuckles wouldn't be turning white on the spindles.

Paul said, "Cassie, don't eat your momma's Popsicle anymore, you hear?"

"Yes, Daddy."

With her arms folded across her chest, Mary watched as the whipping started. Cassie gripped harder so she wouldn't cry. Something rose up in her. She did not want to give her mother the satisfaction of seeing her cry anymore.

"You make sure you make them sting, Paul!"

The whipping went on until Cassie's legs were pink, and in a few places the skin was raised from the welts.

Paul, getting sick to his stomach from the craziness of it, was silently hoping it would be enough for Mary, and he hoped soon he could stop.

Turning from the doorway, she had enough. Mary said, "Okay, Paul, that's enough."

Paul looked up at Mary and then at Cassie. He looked transfixed in his eyes. They were glazed over with what? Sadness maybe? Then he turned and left Cassie's room, saying nothing. What could he say? He had no words. Cassie lightly relaxed her hands, flexing out her fingers from the death grip they were in and just laid her head down on her pillow. Her lips were quivering. She wanted so much to cry. Her bottom and thighs stung so badly, but she didn't want to focus on the pain. She wanted to try to relax every muscle. Maybe it wouldn't hurt so badly if she could relax her body. As Cassie reached back to feel the burning skin, she could feel the rising welts on her skin. She quickly looked back at her legs to make sure she wasn't bleeding, in her mind the pain equaled blood. Thankfully there was no blood. The welts would bruise, but there was no blood. The knowledge somehow made Cassie feel better; she had survived.

· · · · · · · · · ·

Cassie had fallen asleep on her bed some time in the early afternoon. Maybe it was the heat or last night's belt whipping, but some time after her peanut butter and jelly sandwich, Cassie couldn't keep her eyes open. With her bedroom window open, a nice breeze blew through and brushed over her; it had lulled her to sleep. Cassie had slept the afternoon away and was woken up by her mother. Mary must have come home from work in an angry mood because she started banging the dishes around in such a way it was a miracle they didn't break. It would seem like Mary's agenda was to wake anyone who could be sleeping because the banging seemed extra loud that late afternoon. Cassie lay still and readied herself to go out into the kitchen. She hadn't set the table yet and was sure to be in trouble. Taking a few deep breaths and rubbing her tired eyes, she thought of what she should say to her mother. Maybe saying nothing was best.

After washing up in the bathroom, Cassie headed to the kitchen.

"The table's not set. What have you been doing?" Mary demanded when she saw Cassie in the hallway, accusation dripping with every word. Her face crinkled up into to something that wasn't pretty.

"I'm ready to set it now, Momma. I laid down and must have fallen asleep. I slept through. I'm sorry," Cassie tried to explain, looking at the ground. All Cassie could think of was, *Why in the world did I sleep so long? I knew better.*

Mary raised her hand and then lowered it and snapped the kitchen towel she was holding into the air.

"Fine, set it now. Maybe you're growing, Cassie, or maybe it's this heat…" Mary went on to herself as if trying to explain why Cassie may have needed a nap and why the table wasn't set. It made her so angry when things weren't done the way she wanted it. Mary felt like she could break something. She had wanted to hit Cassie but thought better of it when she saw Cassie flinch.

As Cassie set the table for dinner, she thought she was lucky. She'd seen her mother raise her hand and knew she was going to get hit. What made Mary change her mind, Cassie didn't know, but she was thankful.

Sitting on the back porch, Cassie was glad for the fresh air. The kitchen was hot, and with her mother frying up the meat, the smell was getting to her. The grease and heat hung in the air like a dirty cloud. Cassie felt like she couldn't breathe in there. Cassie almost jumped off the porch when the door slammed behind her. Mary had come out to have a cigarette. Lighting her cigarette, Mary squinted and blew out her smoke, throwing her match to the ground.

"It's so hot in there. You hungry?" Mary asked Cassie.

Looking up, Cassie thought about it. "Yeah, kind of," she told her mother.

"Well good. It should be done soon," Mary said, looking out to the backyard. Watching her mother puff on her cigarette, Cassie was actually shocked but happy her mother was outside talking to her. Her mother was usually on the phone or not in the mood to talk.

Mary wasn't giving it much thought. She just wanted to be out in the air, and Cassie just happened to be there on the porch. Mary was uncomfortable talking to Cassie, but not trying to say something to Cassie was even more uncomfortable to her. Mary felt bad sometimes when she would see Cassie looking at her. Cassie looked at her like she wanted something, and Mary could never figure out what Cassie wanted.

Mary always said to herself, *I am what I am, and I just can't be any more.* Mary never tried to be anymore then what she was. Mary didn't want to try.

Cassie knew it was hard for her mother to be there with her. She knew her mother was not comfortable.

"What are you making, Momma?" Cassie asked, hoping to keep this conversation going for even a few minutes with her mother.

Looking back at Cassie, Mary said, "What? Oh, I'm making goulash. You like goulash, don't you?" Grounding out her cigarette, Mary jumped up the steps, went around Cassie, and went back in the house.

"Yes, Momma, I like goulash," Cassie said, but her mother was already inside, and Cassie doubted her mother had heard her.

After dinner, Cassie was in her bedroom drawing when her dad came in her room.

"Come on, Cassie, you come with me. I need to go to the store to get a few things."

He stood waiting at her door, fidgeting with his truck keys.

Cassie sat up from her stretched-out position on her stomach.

"Okay, Dad, where are we going?" Cassie asked, not totally understanding what was going on. Her dad seemed to be acting strange to her.

Paul thought it was best to get her out of the house for a while. Mary was throwing a fit out in the living room. She was saying Cassie slept all day. She didn't do anything around the house. Maybe she shouldn't be able to eat dinner the next night for punishment. How Cassie didn't hear all of this was unbelievable to Paul; maybe she had just tuned it out. He wished he could. But he needed to get out for a while, and there was no way he was leaving Cassie here. He didn't trust Mary tonight. She seemed fine at dinner. Not one word of this was spoken; then she started going off after a few beers.

As Paul and Cassie were leaving, Mary called out, "Yeah, get her on out of here." Mary laughed. "What do you think I'd do, Paul?" Mary grabbed her cigarettes and lit one. Blowing out the smoke, she continued to laugh at Paul's expression.

"Cassie, let's go. I have some errands to do, and you are coming with me."

Sensing the trouble, Cassie followed her dad out to his truck.

"You might as well go with him, Cassie, but I'm still thinking about no dinner for you tomorrow for sleeping the afternoon away. You've got to earn your keep to eat." Mary stood in the doorway, smiling through the smoke.

As Paul was driving to town, he looked down at Cassie sitting next to him in the front seat. She looked so little sitting there. She had to crane her neck to see over the dashboard.

Sensing her dad looking at her, Cassie turned her big eyes on him. "I'm sorry I slept through the afternoon, Dad. I was so tired, but I didn't mean to sleep all the way through and not set the table."

"Cassie"—Paul sighed—"that's okay. Once in a while everyone needs a nap, honey. You're growing. Your mom just doesn't believe in breaks, Cassie. Your mom thinks she has a hard life, so everyone else has to have one too."

Cassie nodded her head, trying to understand. She turned and looked back out the window, her legs dangling from the big seat and her hands calmly folded in her lap. "You know what I need to do, Dad?" Cassie asked.

"No, honey, what do you need to do?"

Cassie looked up at him like she had some kind of a brainstorm. "I need to set the table early on, in the morning, right after Momma leaves; then I'd be all set. I wouldn't be late doing it or forget to like I did today!"

"You are a very smart girl, Cassie. That may be just the best idea." Paul smiled down at her, wishing things were different for Cassie with Mary.

Paul was overwhelmed at how he was very concerned with Cassie's welfare all of the sudden. Could Mary hurt her? He knew Mary's love as a mother was lax when it came to Cassie but had always thought it had more to do with Mary not Cassie, but now he wasn't so sure.

Pulling into the local bar, the tires of the truck crunching over the rocks that made the parking lot, Paul thought he'd run in for a quick beer. Cassie was reaching up, trying to see where they were.

"What are we doing here, Dad?" Cassie looked worried. This was the bar where she had stayed on the floor of her mother's car many times while Mary went in and argued with her dad. Mary had gathered her up late at night before and hid her on the floor and told her to stay put, that she had to go in and try to get Paul to come home. Cassie only remembered being scared. She could hear people talking outside of her mother's car, and she always wondered if they knew she was there or if they could see her. A long time would go by before Mary would come back. Cassie remembered she was too scared sitting there curled up in the dark to go to sleep.

Looking uncomfortable, Paul said, "Uh, I've got to go in there for a few minutes, honey. You just stay here. I will be right back, and then we'll go for an ice cream. You'd like that, right, honey?"

Paul knew this wasn't right, but he still needed a drink. He was sure he would burn in hell one day but could not stop himself. Mary could get under his skin in such a way only a few beers would numb him to what he felt.

"I'd like to just stay with you, Dad," Cassie said, looking around unsure. She didn't like this place, never had, never would. The building was painted a light green, and the paint was chipped in spots all over the building making it look very old and rundown. The neon lights in the windows were blue and red, and some of them blinked on and off trying to get your attention. The words *open, spirits,* and *welcome* blinked all day long in the windows from the neon lights. The stairs going up to the bar's door didn't have a railing. Cassie thought they should have a railing because she heard many people fall down those stairs. She never looked from her spot on the floor of the vehicle she was in, but by the bad words, Cassie knew they fell down the stairs and probably hurt themselves. There was always a lot of laughing too, but Cassie never knew what was so funny.

Paul thought, *I need my time too.* "Well, you can't come in there, Cassie, just wait out here, and I will be right back."

Opening the door of the truck, Paul stepped down, got out of the truck, and hurried into the bar. The closing of the door, the sound of it, metal against metal, felt like a lid of some kind came down on top of Cassie.

Cassie knew she'd been had. He was going to be in there a while; she just knew it. She climbed down off the seat and sat on the floor as close to the door as she could. She didn't want any of those people out there to see her. It wasn't only embarrassing to her, but she was scared to be sitting out in the parking lot alone. She wished she had stayed home and gone over to Larissa's. She could be having fun with her and Samuel right now. Bored, thirsty, and hot, Cassie started playing with the sand on the floor. She swept it into a pile with her finger and started creating pictures with it. At least she had the dirt on the floor to keep her busy. As her pile of sand grew, she smiled. Lightly humming to herself but making sure she was quiet, Cassie tucked herself underneath the dashboard of the truck out of sight.

It was dark by the time Paul came back out. Cassie had fallen asleep on the floor of the truck next to her sand pile picture.

"Cassie, wake up, honey. We are going now," Paul said, not looking at her. The guilt was getting to him. The beers he drank—he lost count of how many—wouldn't numb his common sense. And his common sense told him he'd stayed in there way too long and shouldn't have left Cassie out in the truck in the first place. Was she really safer with him? Paul didn't know at the moment.

As they drove to the ice cream stand, Paul hated himself even more. He probably took too long, and the ice cream stand would be closed. Looking over at Cassie, Paul noticed how hard she was trying to wake up, probably looking forward to the ice cream he promised her. Those thoughts made Paul feel even worse.

When he got to the ice cream stand, he could see all the lights were off, and the small parking lot was empty. The flowerpots that were on each side of driveway gave proof to how hot their summer was. The flowers that were once colorful and beautiful were now crinkled-up, brown twigs. The owner of the ice cream stand had good intentions adding those flowerpots to the entrance but must have given up bringing water out to the flowerpots a long time ago. In this kind of heat, most people tended to give up keeping anything green. A burnt light brown was the usual grass color by this time in the summer.

Pulling into the parking lot, Paul felt like the heel he was. Cassie's face fell. No ice cream for her. It didn't matter now anyway. *I am too tired to enjoy the ice cream*, she told herself.

"I'm sorry, Cassie. Boy, they don't stay open very late. On these hot summer nights, they should stay open later, you know?" Paul said, trying to make the situation seem better at least for Cassie.

"Its okay, Dad. I'm tired anyway. Maybe some other time."

Pulling into the back, Paul pulled the truck up to the fence and got out. "Where are you going, Dad?" Cassie asked, now alarmed that he was leaving her again.

"I have to take a pee," Paul said as he walked over to the fence behind the building. Cassie could hear him unzip his pants. Then Cassie could hear the liquid hit the ground. She squirmed in her seat and hurried to look the opposite way. She wanted to put her hands over her ears. She felt so embarrassed to be there while her dad went to the bathroom outside. The sound of him doing his business was so loud in the quiet night. Cassie could feel her cheeks burn hot pink.

Cassie ran to her bedroom when they got back to the house and threw herself under her covers. She was tired and could not believe what a horrible evening she'd had. She was very uncomfortable with how the evening went with her dad and did not want a repeat any time soon. She hoped her mom and dad would not fight tonight; she just wanted to sleep. Staring out her window, Cassie tried to think of anything that would remove the evening she just went through from her head. Nothing was working. Over and over again, she remembered how she felt when her dad went to the bathroom outside the truck in front of her.

*What was he thinking? He wasn't supposed to do that in front of me, was he?* Cassie thought. Cassie hated what she felt. *Is it bad to think these things? Doesn't Dad know better?* Cassie sighed in pure embarrassment and hoped sleep would come.

Looking out her window at the night sky, Cassie said good night to God. She only wanted to think on good things. She whispered, "Good night, God. You made everything special; even the night sky is pretty. If you're up there, please watch over us and take care of my family." Then she blew him a kiss good night and closed her tired eyes, praying for sleep.

# CHAPTER 8

Cassie skipped all the way to Mrs. Vashon's house with Larissa. They were going to check and see if she needed help watering the garden. As the girls skipped down the sidewalk and entered the flower garden, Mrs. Vashon looked up. She was already outside watering the plants and flowers. In the heat, it was best to give them their water early before the sun was up and overhead.

"Hello, Mrs. Vashon!" the girls called, excited to be there. They giggled as they caught their breath. Their mood was contagious, and Mrs. Vashon broke out into a big grin.

"What are you girls up to? You both are so happy this morning!" Mrs. Vashon asked with the now-contagious excitement.

Cassie had caught her breath, she answered first. "Nothing really. We wanted to come help you, and then Larissa's mom is making us lunch today and is filling the splash pool right now for us to use later!" Cassie exclaimed.

Larissa was still trying to catch her breath and just kept nodding her head in agreement with Cassie. They all started laughing because it was just a plain "happy funny" in the garden that morning, and Larissa, not being able to catch her breath enough to talk, helped make the mood even funnier.

"Well, I am more than happy to have you both help me this morning. There is always a lot to do," Mrs. Vashon declared as she looked around the garden to see what all the girls could help her with this morning. She loved their company and loved having them help her. Mrs. Vashon had bought some garden gloves at the hardware store for Cassie. Since Larissa was helping also, Mrs. Vashon thought Larissa could use her gloves. She didn't want the prickers on the weeds poking the girls. The flowers grew and bloomed beautifully in the garden, but the weeds were hardy too.

"Here, girls, I have some gloves you could both wear. Would you like to pull any weeds you see?" Mrs. Vashon asked. "Here's a pail you could put them in. There shouldn't be too many of them. Then you could help me water the flowers if you like while I go get us some tea, and I think I have a few cookies in the kitchen too." Mrs. Vashon finished with a conspiratorial smile.

Both girls ran to her to get their gloves and the pail they were to share. The gloves were big but would work for the job of pulling the weeds.

"They are so big, Mrs. Vashon!" Cassie giggled, pulling the gloves on.

Larissa, giggling too, explained, "Well, Cassie, we are a kid; that's why. These are for grown-ups!"

"That's right, girls. They are made for bigger hands than yours, but they will protect your fingers so you don't get any slivers from the prickers," Mrs. Vashon said, laughing.

While Mrs. Vashon got the tea and cookies ready on the back porch, the girls filled their pail with the unwanted weeds. Pulling the weeds and then smoothing the ground, Cassie and Larissa went about making the garden even more beautiful. The sun was already making the morning hot, it didn't take long to work up a sweat. The girls were looking forward to the ice tea and cookies.

Running up to the back porch with Larissa, Cassie showed Mrs. Vashon the weeds. "Look, we filled the pail! Some of them weeds were hiding, but we found them!"

"Thank you, girls. Now come and cool off and enjoy the treat I have for you," Mrs. Vashon said as she pulled the chairs out from around her table on the back porch.

Both girls talked like magpies. Mrs. Vashon had a hard time keeping up with their conversations. The girls couldn't sit long. They gobbled up their cookies and wanted to get right back to their work in the garden.

"I know watering is your favorite part, Cassie. Do you want to water the flowers some before you leave?" Mrs. Vashon asked as she gathered up the glasses and plate that held the cookies.

"Yes, I will water! Could I spray from the hose and show Larissa the rainbows?" Cassie asked politely but hopefully.

Surprised, Mrs. Vashon said, "Well, of course, Cassie! You can spray the water hose anytime you want, honey."

"Thank you, Mrs. Vashon! Come on, Larissa; this is really pretty in the sunshine. I'll show you!" Cassie said, already on the run to get the hose out.

Larissa took off, trying to keep up with Cassie. Running as fast as she could, she was still trailing behind Cassie.

"Wait up, Cassie! What are you going to show me?"

Cassie had stretched the hose out to the big flower garden and then ran back and turned the water on. Out of breath but excited, Cassie gathered up the hose and got a good grip on the spray handle. Before pushing the handle in to spray the water, she looked at Larissa.

"Okay, come over behind me, Larissa, and look what I can make with the water and the sunshine!"

The anticipation was contagious. Larissa positioned herself to Cassie's right and stepped behind her so she could see what Cassie was seeing.

Raising her arms up as high as they could go, Cassie pulled on the spray handle to release the water. "Okay now... Look, Larissa! Do you see the rainbows in the water? Look through the water to the other side, Larissa. Doesn't it make it pretty?" The excitement and joy on Cassie's face was as bright as the sunshine outside.

Larissa could not believe the beautiful picture Cassie had created. "Oh, Cassie, that is so pretty! How did you ever figure this out?"

Cassie, caught up in the moment, wiggled the hose and said, "Larissa, look now at the pink flowers. They have rainbows over them!" Cassie continued to lightly spray the air, creating a beautiful water mist using the garden and all its colors as her backdrop.

Larissa sat on the ground and just watched the beautiful water display. As the flowers were getting their much-needed water they were thirsty for, Cassie and Larissa was experiencing something so beautiful and tranquil neither wanted it to stop.

After several wonderful minutes, Cassie's arms got very tired. After stopping the spray of water, she plopped down on the ground beside Larissa. For several moments, they both just looked at the flowers with the droplets of water dripping off their petals.

"That was so pretty, Cassie! Looking through the water..." Larissa said, still in the tranquil moment. Sitting very still and not wanting to move, Larissa was mesmerized by the simple beauty of the water and the garden. Larissa remembered, "That's what you do in the splash pool when you open your eyes?"

"Yep, but you just see the blue sky, maybe a cloud or two, so the garden is prettier," Cassie confirmed.

"Cassie, you are so funny sometimes," Larissa said. "How'd you ever come up with this, this looking through the water?"

"You know, I don't know." Then she laughed.

Larissa lightly pushed on her arm. "Well, you are one funny friend. You come up with some of the best things!" Larissa smiled at her friend, wishing she could be more like her. Larissa was always bored. She never could come up with any ideas on her own of something to do, but Cassie always could. Cassie could make up a game for all of them to play. Cassie was never bored, and she always found something to do. Larissa envied her friend for that, but in a good way. Larissa was glad Cassie was her friend, and she kept her busy with all her wonderful ideas.

"You know summer would be so boring without you, Cassie," Larissa said matter-of-factly, lounging back on her elbows.

Following suit, Cassie leaned back on her elbows in the grass too. "No, summer would be *so* boring without you, Larissa." Cassie turned to her friend with a smile.

"Well, I am glad we have each other then."

"Me too, Larissa."

# CHAPTER 9

Racing up the stairs of the front porch, Cassie flew into the house to find her bathing suit. She and Larissa were going swimming in Larissa's splash pool! The heat in the Missouri summers was stifling without something to help cool off, so Cassie and Larissa always looked forward to an afternoon in the splash pool. It felt hotter in her house than outside, so Cassie went around and checked to make sure the windows were all open and letting in what little breeze might come by.

After changing into her bathing suit, Cassie placed her clothes in a neat pile on her bed. She decided not to grab a towel. It was so hot she would be dry in just a few minutes after swimming. She didn't have to make herself lunch today either. Mrs. Stockard invited her to have lunch with Samuel and Larissa. All smiles, Cassie went into the kitchen and placed the dinner plates, paper napkins, and silverware on the kitchen table. Just in case the time got away from her, she wanted some of her chores done. Cassie took out the garbage can from under the sink and went around to all the ashtrays. She didn't want ashes from the ashtrays to blow all over in case they got the much-needed breeze in the windows. That's all she needed to happen, to come home and have to clean up ashes blown everywhere.

Taking a last look around, Cassie ran out the door, excitement bubbling up for the fun she knew she would have with Samuel and Larissa. Her bare feet padded down the sidewalk to their home.

. . . . . . . . . . .

Holding her breath, Cassie lay flat on the bottom of the splash pool. She was short enough to fully spread out. She lay there and looked through the water at the sky and clouds for as long as she could. Turning her head toward Larissa, who was lying right beside her, she started laughing under the water, sending thousands of air bubbles into the water. Sitting up and wiping her eyes, Cassie continued to laugh. Larissa had looked so funny under the water with her cheeks full of air and her eyes wide open.

"Oh Cassie, you should see your face under there!" Larissa sat up, laughing.

"Mine! You should see yours!"

"That was so funny! Want to bob for dimes now?" Larissa asked, reaching for the dimes on the ground beside the pool. They both loved bobbing for the dimes. They threw them up in the air so they landed in random places and then dove under the water to find them.

"Yup, sounds good!" Cassie agreed.

Their lunch was settling so their stomachs were ready for all the pool fun. Mrs. Stockard had set up lunch out on the picnic table. She had grilled hot dogs and made potato salad. Potato salad was one of Cassie's favorite dishes. Mrs. Stockard had cut up a fresh bowl of strawberries to enjoy for their dessert. Now with her stomach full, Cassie was so content. The afternoon couldn't get much better for her.

Rolling over unto their stomachs, Cassie and Larissa searched for the dimes. Bobbing up and down in the water, they played the game several times before tiring of it.

"Hey, Cassie, what are all those marks on your legs?" Larissa asked.

Knowing what she had seen, Cassie thought maybe she could share her secret with Larissa. "Um…"

"Did you hurt yourself?"

"I um…"

Larissa was really wondering now. "What happened?"

"Those marks are left over from the belt whipping I got."

"Belt whipping? Whatever did you do, Cassie?" Looking at the marks, Larissa noticed the yellowing stains a somewhat healed bruise would leave.

"Nothing really. I ate a Popsicle that I had bought for my mom. Remember when the ice cream truck stopped? I got her that 7-Up Popsicle? She never ate it. So I did the other day, and when she looked for it after dinner and she found it gone, she asked me. I admitted eating it and told her I would get her another one when the ice cream truck came by again. She got really mad. *Really mad.* Then she made my dad whip me," Cassie said slowly, waiting for Larissa's reply.

Putting her arm around Cassie, Larissa whispered, "Oh, Cassie, you shouldn't have gotten the belt for eating the Popsicle."

The girls just sat there for a few moments. Cassie was enjoying the comfort. At least her friend knew and understood. She never talked much about what went on in her home. It was nice someone knew. She had wanted to tell her grandmother in the past but didn't want to worry her. Her grandmother lived too far away to do anything about it anyway.

"Don't tell your mom, okay, Larissa?" Cassie's face had burst forth in color; the shame and embarrassment would be too much if people knew. It was all right for Larissa to know because she was Cassie's best friend, but for others to know? Cassie didn't want to think about it.

"No, I won't say anything, Cassie. But if you ever get scared or anything, talk to my mom. She loves you, Cassie. You could always talk to her."

Cassie felt safer knowing that. She really liked Mrs. Stockard. There were times she wished Mrs. Stockard were her mom, and then she would feel guilty at her thoughts.

"It feels better just telling you, Larissa. You're my best friend," Cassie said with a smile and leaned into Larissa.

While their fingers and toes were becoming wrinkled, Cassie and Larissa continued to just sit in the splash pool lost in their own thoughts. Larissa wished Cassie was her sister; then she could protect her. Larissa would share her room, her parents, and all she had with Cassie with no problem. Larissa knew even at her young age an injustice was being done to Cassie somehow. Cassie did not deserve her home life. She was so sweet and kind. Larissa wanted more for her but didn't know how to get it for her.

Cassie was having a quiet moment thinking how nice it was right then sitting there in the backyard in the pool with Larissa. She turned her head and looked over to her yard. Looking at the house made her stomach tighten and twist—something she noticed now all the time. Her stomach didn't like some things now. It would tighten and burn in pain all on its own. She thought of cringing at night in her bed listening to her parents fighting. Just looking at the house made her feel very sad. She realized she didn't like it there. Cassie frowned.

Shaking those thoughts off, Cassie smiled and looked over at Larissa, trying to think on something better. She leaned back and dunked herself under the water. Smoothing her hair back over her forehead and bobbing back up, Cassie felt better. At least she was going to try. She didn't like staying focused on those other thoughts. They didn't make her feel good.

"Hey Cassie, you want to baptize each other?" Larissa asked, the idea just coming to her as she jumped up to her knees in the pool.

"Baptize each other?" Cassie looked at her, wondering what she was talking about.

"Yeah, I can baptize you here in this water. At our church, they baptize people in this pool thing that looks like a bathtub but bigger," Larissa said, excited. "Almost every Sunday someone is getting baptized. It's fun!"

Cassie remembered her grandmother talking about it before. She told Cassie that when she was older she needed to get baptized to show she was a Christian.

Sitting up on her knees too, Cassie replied, "Do they dunk the people all the way down in the water?'

"Yep, they do."

"What do the people wear, Larissa? They can't wear their clothes, can they?" Cassie wondered at all the details about baptism. *How does someone go about doing something like this?*

"Oh no, not their regular clothes. We have a room they can change in, and we have robes they wear."

With the sun scorching and high in the afternoon sky, going down in the water a few times sounded like a good idea to the girls.

"I can start. I will be the preacher and baptize you, Cassie. Then you can do like I do and baptize me!"

Cassie thought it was a good idea. She didn't know the first thing about baptizing someone. She would definitely need to learn; with Larissa going first this would help. Larissa would show her what she needed to know and do.

"Okay, baptize me, Larissa! What do I do?"

"Okay, stay on your knees because the pool isn't deep enough for us to stand up and then turn this way." Larissa twisted Cassie around so she could get a good grip on her for the dunking. "Now I am going to pray over you and ask you some questions. Then you plug your nose, and I will dunk you down under the water."

"I'm ready!" said Cassie, getting excited. She'd never been baptized before.

"Now, fold your arms like this," Larissa explained, showing Cassie how to crisscross her arms so she could plug her own nose.

"Do you, Cassie, accept Jesus Christ into your life as your personal savior?" Larissa asked in a deep voice.

"Yes, I do."

"Do you, Cassie, know he died for your sins and you are a sinner and are you sorry for all your sins?"

"Yes, I know Jesus died for me, and I am sorry for all my sins," Cassie declared, suddenly very serious sounding.

"Okay then, I baptize you in his name. I baptize you in the name of Jesus!" Larissa proclaim as she dunked Cassie down backward under the water.

As Cassie was lifted back up in Larissa's arms, she opened her eyes wide under the water. Coming back up through the water was one of the most beautiful things Cassie had every experienced. She could see Larissa smiling through the sparkling diamond-like water, and behind her was the most beautiful blue sky. A peace came over Cassie, which settled on her like a cool cloth. The sun seemed brighter. The colors seemed brighter everywhere she looked. An intensity of light and color seemed to settle over Cassie.

"Your sins are forgiven, child. Thank Jesus for all he has done!" Larissa shouted out into the yard as she pulled Cassie back up out of the water.

Cassie was so touched by the experience she did start thanking Jesus for what he had done. "Thank you, Jesus!" Cassie proclaimed out loud, wiping the water from her eyes.

"My turn now; you get to baptize me!" Larissa turned to get ready for her dunking.

Cassie hurried to get into position to be the preacher but wished she had a few moments to gather her feelings on what she just experienced. Whatever it was, it had felt so special to her.

"Your turn now, Larissa," Cassie said, trying to remember all she would need to say in Larissa's baptism.

They continued to baptize each other into the afternoon, but try as she might, Cassie did not experience a repeat of the feelings that happened to her from the first dunking. She knew somehow the first baptism of hers was something special.

Mrs. Stockard got a kick out of the girls baptizing each other out in the backyard. She could hear their proclamations of, "Thank Jesus for all he has done; your sins are forgiven!" *Well, they have definitely been baptized and are definitely washed! They are looking like prunes!*

Barbara continued to watch the girls, loving the idea Cassie was getting some church experiences out there in the splash pool. Mary would never let Cassie go with them to church. In the past when Barbara had asked Mary if Cassie could go to church with Larissa, the answer was no. Mary had said, "Cassie has no need for church. Church never does anyone any good! No, no good at all! All those preachers just want your money!"

Mary let Barbara know in no uncertain terms Cassie would never be going with Larissa, ever, so she shouldn't ask again. Larissa and Cassie were very disappointed. Their faces fell when they got the news from Mrs. Stockard. Cassie wanted to go to Sunday school with the kids. It sounded fun to her. She had an interest in learning about God, and her parents wouldn't tell her anything. Cassie liked talking about God. She had told Mrs. Stockard on several occasions about her talks with him.

Barbara could picture God up there listening to Cassie and thinking she was one of his special dear ones. She was so cute and innocent in her perspective of things; it just had to melt God's heart. Some people in this world really knew God in a special way, and Barbara thought Cassie was one of them. She could see the simple things of this world as the beauty of the creator. Cassie knew nothing got here by accident. Someone very special created everything. This was what she told her mother when she got into trouble for Barbara coming to her about Sunday school. Mrs. Stockard felt horrible when Larissa told her Cassie got yelled at when she came home that evening.

Barbara felt horrible for Cassie again as she remembered what Larissa had told her. Larissa had said Cassie had really feared her mother was going to hit her. She had thought Cassie might have put Mrs. Stockard up to asking about Sunday school.

Barbara smiled at how the ugliness of Cassie's home life did not touch the beauty that came from the child. Her heart broke, wondering what really went on over there inside the walls of Cassie's house. Barbara promised herself she would get a hold of Cassie's grandmother if she heard of Cassie getting hit again by her mother. If only Cassie's grandmother lived closer. Barbara remembered her to be a wonderful woman who had looked very apologetic for her daughter's behavior.

Elizabeth Lauren, when she visited Tipton, Missouri, was very kind and enjoyed Cassie, taking her on walks to meet all the neighbors. Mary never came on any of the walks, nor would she stop to talk on the sidewalk to anyone. Elizabeth made up excuses for Mary to the few neighbors and to Cassie. Elizabeth would tell the neighbors or the business owners downtown that Mary was busy doing something in the house and that was the reason why she was never with them on their adventures outside the house.

Her explanation was always met with a smile from the workers at the ice cream store. They knew Cassie was always in their store alone without Mary but would never say a word to this sweet lady who was trying to make what was an unusual situation to her look normal.

# CHAPTER 10

Cassie was not feeling well in the morning. She did not have much energy, and her leg hurt her again. Over the past few weeks, Cassie would wake up with leg pain. She had told her mom about the pain in her leg. It was a dull ache, which bothered her most of the time in the morning and then again at night after being active all day. Mary kept telling her it was just growing pains and to quit complaining.

Rolling her eyes, Mary was very frustrated when Cassie had complained about her leg.

"All it is, Cassie, is growing pains. How many times do I have to tell you, huh? How many times?" Mary snapped. After letting out a muttered sigh, Mary would go on watching TV or whatever she was doing when Cassie had tried to get her attention. Mary never stopped to look at Cassie's leg just to make sure there wasn't something else going on. She was never truly concerned that there could be anything else. This morning, though, the ache in her leg made Cassie just want to go back to bed for the day. She curled up on her side and rubbed her calf muscle, which helped some, but it did not give her the energy back that the pain was robbing her of.

*Growing up is hard to do*, thought Cassie. From the pain in her leg to the pain in her stomach, Cassie thought this getting bigger and growing up thing was difficult sometimes. She was hungry but didn't have the energy at the moment to get up and fix a bowl of cereal. She looked around her room wondering what day it was. It must be Saturday because her mother didn't normally let her sleep in. Mary always got her up when they went to work. There were very few days Cassie woke up in peace.

After a little thinking, Cassie realized it was Saturday! She could lay there and take her time getting up. Most Saturdays Cassie was up before her parents, so she went into the living room and watched TV with the volume low, almost turned down all the way. She would laugh quietly through the Saturday morning cartoons. She had to strain to hear the cartoons, but she never wanted to take the chance of waking her mother and father up.

Just lying in her bed sounded the best to her. Cassie kept stretching out her right leg, thinking that might help the pain. The ache in her leg was throbbing this morning. Curling up on her left side and lightly rubbing her leg was all she had the energy to do. Closing her eyes, Cassie fell back to sleep.

Waking up an hour later, Cassie stretched out her legs and realized she felt good enough to get up for a bowl of cereal. She lay there listening to see if anyone else was up, but all was quiet. Pulling back her coverlet, she slowly climbed out of her bed. Before she left her room, she made up her bed and put her doll and stuffed animals up against her pillow. Her grandma Elizabeth had gotten those toys for her. Cassie loved to display them. That way every day she could remember the one who gave them to her. It had been two long years since Cassie had seen her grandmother in person. She was fearful she would forget her—what she looked like and her wonderful smell.

Tiptoeing out to the kitchen, Cassie poured cereal and milk into a bowl as quietly as she could and then went into the living room, hoping she did not miss all her favorite cartoons. Sitting on the floor in front the coffee table, Cassie ate her breakfast, which consisted of a bowl of *Lucky Charms* cereal, and watched *Bugs Bunny* on the TV. Cassie laughed quietly at all the antics the *Bugs Bunny* characters were acting out in the cartoon. She noticed she was feeling better as she jumped up to run into the kitchen to answer the telephone. Cassie had to jump up on the wooden chair, which was placed right under the telephone on the wall, to answer the telephone.

Grabbing the phone quickly before it woke up her parents, Cassie said a whispered, "Hello, the Marvin residence."

"Cassie? Hello, honey, it's Grandma!" Elizabeth said with a grandmother's excitement at finding her granddaughter on the other end of the telephone line.

"Grandma!" Cassie whispered again, her whisper full of the happiness she was experiencing.

Aware of the whisper from Cassie, Elizabeth asked, "Are your parents sleeping, Cassie? Is that why you're whispering?" Elizabeth hoped it was true; then she could talk to Cassie. If Mary answered the phone, Elizabeth would not have been able to talk to Cassie for much more than a hello.

Cassie jumped down from the chair and then tiptoed over to the back door and pulled the phone cord so she could reach the back door landing. Cassie then answered. "Yes, Grandma, they are still sleeping, but I am at the back door now in the landing, so I can talk to you now!"

Elizabeth was very glad she had a smart granddaughter. But at the same moment, she felt such sadness Cassie had to be aware of such things. A young girl as sweet as Cassie should not have such knowledge or be aware of such things. The only way she could talk to her grandmother was to sneak and whisper in a back door landing. Elizabeth's heart broke a little for her granddaughter. Elizabeth wished Cassie did not have to live in such a way because of Mary. Cassie knew she would be in some kind of trouble talking to her.

For most people, when they did not have the same thinking in their mind as someone like Mary, it was very hard to understand where they were coming from. Even in their wildest imaginations they couldn't figure out the "what and why" of their thinking. Cassie just knew by past experiences. If she was lucky to be home and answer the phone when her grandmother called, then she'd say everything she could in that phone call!

The smile on Elizabeth's face was evident in her voice when she said, "How have you been, honey?'

Cassie sighed into the phone. She'd missed her grandmother's voice so much. "I'm fine, Grandma. I miss you! I wish you were here with me again."

Elizabeth thought she might just cry. She took a huge breath to calm herself and started blinking back the tears.

"I know, honey. I miss you so much too! We will see each other soon, huh? I will try and make plans soon to do just that. How are you enjoying your summer, Cassie? Are you okay during the day? Do you play with your friends?" Elizabeth stopped, hoping she didn't overwhelm Cassie with all her questions.

"I hope you come here soon, Grandma. I have a beautiful garden to show you. I have made best friends with Mrs. Vashon, the lady with the flower garden. We have a garden angel statue in the garden too. She watches over it. Mrs. Vashon bought her and asked me to help her find the best place to put her, Grandma. I placed her in the perfect spot so she could see the whole garden!" Cassie was out of breath telling her grandmother about her garden. Thanks to Mrs. Vashon, Cassie felt it was her garden too.

"My goodness, Cassie, you are one busy girl! I can't wait to see the garden and this statue. It sounds really nice, and gardening is a wonderful hobby for you to learn," Elizabeth said, so happy at the interest her granddaughter had in things.

"I love it, Grandma. I am learning a lot about flowers," Cassie confirmed.

"What about your friends next door? Do you still play with them, Cassie?" Elizabeth questioned, trying to picture her granddaughter's day in the neighborhood.

"Yep, Larissa and I are best friends! Samuel, of course, is my friend too, Grandma. Mrs. Stockard is so nice to me. She is really pretty too. You remember?

"Yes, I remember them."

"I have lunch sometimes there, and we swim in the pool in their yard. Oh yeah, a few weeks ago, we had a bad storm. I stayed in their basement with them. Mrs. Stockard took good care of us. I had to be brave for Larissa. She almost cried!"

Elizabeth, almost afraid to ask, said, "How's your mom and dad, Cassie?"

A moment of silence was a moment of thinking for Cassie. How could she answer the question? She didn't want to worry her grandmother, and somehow Cassie knew if she told the truth, the plain truth, her grandmother would worry about her. Cassie, not wanting to ever lie to anyone and especially her grandmother, was thinking, *How do I tell her the truth but not worry her?*

Was everything okay? Was the yelling okay? Was staying on the floor of her dad's truck because she was afraid while he was in the bar for hours okay? Was the belt whipping over a Popsicle okay? Cassie felt shame at all of the flashes that went through her mind. The actions of her parents embarrassed her, and she thought somehow she must be to blame.

"Its fine, Grandma. I'm all right, Grandma," Cassie said with conviction because that was true to Cassie. She was fine. She didn't want her grandmother to worry about her. There was nothing she could do anyway so far away. Cassie knew of nothing to be done anyway. She would have liked to have her grandmother closer, to have another place to be able to retreat to when her home life got uncomfortable for her. What she felt was uncomfortable for the most part. Cassie never felt comfortable in her own home. She squirmed a lot in her seat, not knowing what was going to happen next.

Elizabeth, knowing the truth, knew Cassie was not being fully honest with her. Her blessed granddaughter didn't want her to worry. Also, Elizabeth noticed Cassie never mentioned how her mother and father were doing. Elizabeth experienced a real heart-crushing moment. "Cassie, my sweet Cassie, I know you're fine, but if ever you need me, Cassie, you will call Grandma, right?"

"Momma won't let me call you, Grandma, or I would. She says it costs too much money to call you, so I wait till you call me. I am glad you called me, Grandma!"

"Oh, I am glad I called you too, honey, and I know your mother doesn't want to spend the money, but if you ever need me, you call, Cassie, and I will pay for the phone call. Don't hesitate to call if there is a need, Cassie, an emergency. Okay?" Elizabeth was trying hard to get the point across to Cassie. It was important to Elizabeth. She needed Cassie to understand that an emergency changed everything.

Cassie didn't know how to answer her grandmother. Cassie knew she would not defy her mother. If she looked up her grandmother's phone number in the phonebook her mother kept in the small drawer right below the phone on the wall and found her grandmother's phone number, she would still never make the call. Creating a situation with her mother that would be hard to explain would not be worth it to Cassie. Cassie's thoughts also included her grandmother. She would never want to make her mother mad at her grandmother. Then for sure Mary would keep her away, and it had been too long now since Cassie had seen her. Cassie was having a hard time remembering her, which frightened her. Cassie did not want to forget anything about her grandmother. She wished she could remember her smell and wished she could conjure it up right at the moment. Cassie knew she loved the way her grandmother smelled. Her smell was like warm flowers—if there was such a thing. The way a flower smelled in the sunshine was what her grandmother smelled like to her.

"Okay, Grandma. You would not believe how I have grown since we last talked! I am getting taller. I can reach things now I couldn't just a while ago!" Cassie told her proudly. She had wanted to change the subject. She didn't want to waste her precious time with her grandmother talking about things that were making her uncomfortable.

Talking about her mother made her have feelings she did not understand. She was so torn on the inside when she thought of her mother. She wanted so much more from her mother. Cassie wanted to hug her but was afraid to. Mary never touched Cassie except when she lost control and slapped her. Even though the only type of attention she got from Mary was lacking, Cassie was her daughter, and she still looked for the comfort of a mother from Mary. She still hoped she could do something that would change her mother. If she showed kindness just one more time, maybe Mary would change and love her, touch her.

Elizabeth, hearing the excitement in Cassie's voice, exclaimed, "Oh, Cassie, I bet when I get off the plane, I won't even recognize you at the airport. Why, you may have to hold up a sign that says, "Cassie Marvin" so I know who you are!"

Giggling, Cassie snorted. "Oh, Grandma, you are silly! You'll know who I am. I haven't changed all that much, just a little taller!"

Elizabeth, not wanting to hang up the phone, but knowing it would be the best for Cassie, told her, "Well, honey, I should let you go now so you can get ready for your day. What were you doing when I called?"

"I was watching the cartoons on TV and having a bowl of cereal when you called, Grandma. *Bugs Bunny* was on."

"Oh, I love *Bugs Bunny*! Cassie, you should go back to watching your cartoons before your mom gets up. I will call her back later. Just tell her when she gets up I called and I will call back later. Tell her I did not want to wake her up, all right, honey?" Elizabeth did not want to get off the phone, but one never knew with Mary. How would she take even a simple thing as a phone call with Cassie?

The pain of saying good-bye settled in on Cassie; she even felt tears flood her eyes. She started blinking and swallowing so she could talk. Cassie did not want her grandmother to know she might start to cry.

"Grandma, I love you, and I miss you. I'll tell Momma you called." She took a few deep breaths, hoping her grandmother could not hear the tears in her throat changing her voice. Cassie cleared her throat and continued. "Call me when you can, Grandma. Oh, I almost forgot. I colored some real pretty pictures. I am saving them for you."

Elizabeth smiled at the returned excitement in Cassie's voice. It was refreshing to hear the child in Cassie back again.

"I love you, Cassie. You are my angel, and don't you forget it! Also keep making me pretty pictures. I need more to fill up the front of my refrigerator. See you soon, honey. Bye now. Grandma is hanging up."

"Bye, Grandma, love you to the moon," Cassie whispered back, concentrating on being quiet.

"Bye, honey, I love you to Jupiter," Came her grandmother's reply on the click.

Tiptoeing back into the kitchen from the back door landing, Cassie jumped up on the wooden chair so she could hang the telephone back up. Forgetting the cartoons were on the TV, Cassie went into her room to color another picture for her grandmother. After talking to her on the telephone, Cassie wanted to make a drawing for her. Maybe if she asked her dad to mail a few of the pictures to her grandmother he would.

Her pile of colored drawings for her grandmother was getting very big. Cassie sat down and drew a picture of her on the telephone; at the end of the curly cord was Cassie's grandmother talking to her. Cassie's drawings were very detailed and bright with color. She'd hide this one from her mother. She didn't want Mary to figure out she'd talked to her grandmother on the telephone for a long time.

Mary could never understand and would get very angry if Elizabeth wanted to talk to Cassie. "You should be calling here to talk to me, Mother!" Mary would shout into the phone if Elizabeth asked to talk to Cassie. Elizabeth had to space out asking to talk to Cassie.

Nothing was said if Elizabeth asked to say hello to Cassie in a phone call here and there. Mary would then hand Cassie the telephone and let her say hello to her grandmother. Cassie and Elizabeth were only able to talk for a few minutes though, and then Mary would end it. Mary would grab the phone right out of Cassie's hand and tell her, "Okay, that's enough talk. Let me have the phone now. Grandma calls here to talk to me."

Elizabeth would be so disturbed by Mary's behavior but did nothing to stir up any more jealousy with Mary over Cassie. She felt like a coward every time she hung up the phone from a conversation with her own daughter, but how could she combat someone like Mary? Elizabeth knew she should try to enable this kind of behavior from Mary but also knew she couldn't. Cassie would pay for anything Elizabeth tried to do.

There were several things Elizabeth and Cassie shared. Their love for one another was one and their embarrassment over Mary's behavior was another. Though they never shared their feelings on this. It was something they had in common. Cassie was actually a lot like her grandmother; she looked like her too. Cassie definitely had Elizabeth's features and coloring. They shared the same hair color—the nice brown with a shiny copper color running naturally through—and their eyes were the same shade of brown in color. Elizabeth was almost all gray now, but as a younger girl, her hair was the same as Cassie's. The thick, very long eyelashes came genetically from Elizabeth too.

# CHAPTER 11

Cassie didn't like the weekends except for the Saturday morning cartoons. The weekends meant her parents were home and there was a lot of fighting and yelling. For the most part, anything Cassie asked to go do, the answer was no. During the week, she could come and go as she pleased, but on the weekends Mary wouldn't let her do anything except the things Mary wanted her to do. Very rarely on the weekend did Mary forget Cassie was at her beck and call. Cassie would accept this and try to make the best of it. This was when she would draw in her room or play quietly by herself outside in the backyard. Cassie learned early on if she could play quietly enough her mother would almost forget she was there. Being forgotten made Cassie's life easier. If Mary kept Cassie in her constant thoughts, then the day would be very hard for Cassie—from the endless chores assigned to her to the yelling about each thing that hadn't been done right. The nit-picking was just an excuse for Mary to vent. Cassie was already very meticulous for the age of seven. When she did something, she did it right.

After rolling out of bed on Saturday morning, Cassie's parents looked like they aged ten years. The drinking and smoking was taking a toll on their bodies. Cassie had still been sitting on the floor before the coffee table watching her cartoons when they came out into the kitchen to make coffee.

Mary looked into the living room and noticed Cassie sitting there. "I hope you already had some breakfast, Cassie, and weren't waiting for me because I'm not cooking this morning," Mary muttered at her, looking all disheveled.

"I had cereal, Momma. Grandma called earlier. She didn't want me to wake you up. She said she would call you back later," Cassie explained, waiting, her eyes watching the entry into the kitchen.

All was calm from the kitchen, which was a good sign. Maybe Mary would just accept it with no problem.

"That's fine. She calls too early anyway." Then as an afterthought, she added, "Did you talk to her long, Cassie?"

Feeling the loaded question, Cassie took a moment to think of her answer. "I told her you were sleeping, Momma, and I was watching cartoons. So no, I didn't get to talk to her as long as I would have liked to. She said she'd call you back," Cassie finished, hoping it would be good enough for her mother. Sitting there on the floor, Cassie crossed her fingers behind her back and made a nervous wish it would stop there. No more questions.

All was quiet. Cassie waited, and then she heard her mom laugh a bitter laugh to her dad.

"Well, it's her fault she doesn't get to talk to me. She calls too early, Paul." Then the normal sounds of making coffee and getting a coffee cup out of the cupboard was all Cassie heard. Hoping her mother was done with her, Cassie got up and turned the TV off and headed down the hallway to her bedroom.

Cassie took a quick look around her room to see if there was anything out of place. She had made her bed and put her pajamas away in the bottom drawer and picked out a cute red shirt with yellow daisies all over it and yellow shorts to match. Cassie could match up her clothes all on her own. She had an innate knowledge of what looked good with what or what shirt would match her shorts. With her fashion talent or color talent, Cassie really looked cute and put together when she left the house.

· · · · · · · · · ·

Saturday during the day was uneventful. Saturday night was a different story. Cassie was able to keep to herself most of the day. She played in the backyard and waved through the yard at Samuel and Larissa several times. They were helping their dad mow the lawn. Saturday was the day for chores for most of the neighbors. Everyone seemed busy in his or her yards earlier during the day before the sun came up high in the sky. Because of all the shade trees, the neighbors still had grass. With the heat and no rain, most of the grass would be burnt up if not protected by the shade of the trees the neighborhood provided. So there was still grass to mow and yard work to do.

As Cassie was watching Samuel and Larissa helping over in their yard, she thought of her special garden at Mrs. Vashon's. She would love to be there right now watering the flowers and helping Mrs. Vashon. Her mother told her to stay around their yard; she wanted her close just in case she needed her help with something, and she didn't want Cassie to wander off so she would have to go looking for her.

Cassie had gone in earlier to make herself a peanut butter and jelly sandwich. Her stomach was growling, reminding her she hadn't eaten anything since her bowl of cereal.

Her dad was lying on the couch watching some sport's event on TV and already drinking a beer, and it was only lunchtime. Her mother was folding clothes at the kitchen table but did not pay any attention to Cassie. Cassie got the sandwich supplies out of the refrigerator and cupboard. She quietly made the sandwich, afraid to look at her mother. Usually she would have to fold the towels or match up the socks, but her mother never said a word.

Cassie had put everything away and then slipped out the back door to eat her sandwich. Chewing slowly and carefully because she didn't have anything to drink, Cassie wished then that she had put the peanut butter on a little thinner. The sandwich tasted good, and Cassie was silently thanking God for her unusually quiet day. *Thank you, God, for my telephone call this morning from Grandma. I am so glad I was up and Momma wasn't. Is it wrong for me to think like that? That Momma wasn't up? I love my grandma, and I miss her. I am having a hard time remembering everything about her. I really liked the way she smelled, God. They are awfully quiet in there today, Momma and Dad. Even so, I like it better out*

*here talking to you. I should have gotten something to drink. This peanut but-*
*ter is really thick. I put it on too thick, but Momma won't let me bring a glass*
*outside anyway. She says I'll break it. I wonder if Grandma will be coming*
*soon to see me. Please take care of her.*

Looking up at the blue sky, Cassie continued. *I wish I was in the*
*garden right now helping Mrs. Vashon. The flowers are so pretty there. I love*
*helping her; she likes my help. Thank you for making the flowers such pretty*
*colors. When I water the flowers, I love how their color shows through. As I*
*look through the water, it's like a wall of glass with rainbows floating in it. I*
*like it. I wish I could step in. The clouds are so pretty in the sky today, fluffy.*
*Did you make them that way, or do they just form like that on their own?*
*How do you make the birds fly? Why can't I fly? I wish I could fly! Hmmm…*
*well, I guess that's all for today. I don't want to bug you. This is Cassie, down*
*here in my backyard.*

· · · · · · · · · ·

As Cassie sat outside and the afternoon ticked by to evening, her stomach started to rumble from hunger. She didn't know if she should enter
the house or wait until one of her parents called for her, telling her that
dinner was getting ready. Maybe she should go in anyway and set the
table. Cassie could not decide which was better: stay outside or go inside
and see what it got her.

The coffee table in the living room was now lined up with empty
beer cans. *Pabst Blue Ribbon Beer* was the beer of choice for her parents. The house stank of smoke and beer. Not a pleasant smell, especially when mixed together. The smell that reeked from her parents' skin
when they drank all day made Cassie wrinkle her nose up, and it turned
her stomach. Their breath was bad, and their clothes smelled worse. The
ashtrays were full of cigarette butts and ashes. They were spilling over
the edges onto the tabletop. The stinking beer cans on a hot day made a
real unhealthy atmosphere for a young girl like Cassie.

As she entered the house to see if dinner was cooking, she wondered
if she needed to set the kitchen table. Cassie was shocked at the condition of the house. Seeing the house trashed again was like a bad dream.

Her dad was out, sound asleep and lightly snoring. A cigarette was still burning in the ashtray. Cassie looked for her mother but did not see her anywhere. The kitchen was quiet. There was no dinner started on the stove or any signs of anything cooking. Cassie looked at the clock on the stove. She was pretty sure it read that the time was almost six thirty, way past dinnertime for her stomach. Cassie could not believe how many hours had passed, and all she'd done was sit in her backyard. *Well, what am I supposed to do now?* Cassie thought, looking around the quiet house.

Cassie decided to tiptoe to her room and find something to do there until she found out what her parents were going to do. As she passed by her parents' bedroom, she saw her mother sound asleep on her bed.

Her stomach growled. Cassie went back into the kitchen and opened the refrigerator door slowly. Grabbing a piece of cheese, she went over to the breadbox and took out two pieces of white bread. Taking a paper napkin out of the plastic wrap they came in, Cassie made a makeshift plate with the paper napkin and quietly headed back to her room. Alone back in her bedroom, Cassie wondered if this was going to be the extent of her dinner. This was different than the norm. They always had dinner. Something as simple as hotdogs, but at least they had hotdogs.

After settling down on the floor next to her bed, Cassie realized with a sigh she hadn't got herself something to drink, and she was very thirsty. Placing her napkin with the food on the floor, she hurried back out to the kitchen for a glass of milk. There was a plastic blue cup in the strainer that she slowly pulled out and poured only a half of cup of milk so she wouldn't spill any as she walked back through the house. The floors squeaked as Cassie walked back down the hallway. She heard one of her parents stir. Her heart pounded so hard she almost spilled her milk. With the milk sloshing around in the plastic cup threatening to spill, Cassie hurried back into her bedroom.

The noise she heard was her dad getting up from the couch. He was heading to the bathroom. Cassie sat on the floor quietly eating her emergency meal. Her dad did not close the bathroom door while he relieved himself. Cassie hunkered down, trying to pretend she did not hear. Cassie thought he should definitely close the door for privacy. Her parents' lack of it always made her feel uncomfortable.

The nerves in Cassie's stomach started to jump. There was no reason for them to be jumpy. Nothing she knew of, but they had started getting all jumpy just the same. It was like an inner sense told her trouble was brewing. Trouble was in the house. She felt like hiding under her bed. Looking around her bedroom, Cassie looked to see where she could hide.

As she listened, she could hear her dad talking in her parents' bedroom. For some reason, the tone made her stomach clinch. The sounds of their voices were getting clearer. Her dad woke her mother up.

"What you gonna do, sleep all day? What are we going to have for dinner?"

The voices were loud and clear now. "I'll make something in a minute. What time is it? Why didn't you wake me up?"

"It's not my job, Mary, to keep you on your schedule. I was sleeping too, so it really doesn't matter, but get something going now for dinner. I'm starving."

As an afterthought, Paul said, "Cassie needs something to eat too, Mary." Blame filled his voice.

That did it. Reminding Mary of her motherly duties seemed to change the whole scenario. What could have been tension caused from lack of food and grouchiness after waking up from a nap now became something totally different for Mary.

Jumping up from the bed, Mary yelled, "Cassie! Where is she? Cassie, have you set the table?"

With a finality that weighed too much for her, Cassie realized her quiet afternoon had come to an end. Rising off the floor, Cassie answered, "I will set it now, Mom. I was waiting for you and dad to wake up from your nap."

Hurrying out to the kitchen, Cassie got there after her mother. Mary was already slamming the kitchen cupboard doors.

"You should have woken us up, Cassie!" Mary slammed a big boiling pot down on the stove. "Now, in this god-awful heat I have to make spaghetti. That's all I have!"

"I like spaghetti, Mom." Cassie said without thought.

"I don't care what you like, Cassie!" Mary turned and looked at Cassie.

Turning in fear and hurt, Cassie went to the dish drainer and pulled out three plates and began setting the table.

After pouring the tomato sauce in a pan, Mary added some spices to the liquid. Each spice container survived the slamming they received on the side of the metal pot and were put back into the cupboard. *They didn't do anything*, was all Cassie could think while placing a paper napkin and silverware next to the plates on the kitchen table. The thing was that Cassie was too young to understand they didn't have to do *anything* to be the brunt of Mary's wrath. Yes, those spice containers were innocent of any wrongdoing, but they were the tools to show the world how mad she was.

Paul, hearing Mary banging things around in the kitchen, prepared for a fight. When he had drink in him and a lot of it, which was often lately, he was a bolder man, an angry man. Something rose up in him that could not be pushed down. A voice in his head warned him no matter what he said, there was going to be a fight. Everything she touched now had violence to it. It was a good thing Cassie was setting the table. The dishes would not make it through Mary's temper. Paul was getting sick of her temper. Paul was getting sick of a lot of things.

Cassie shivered involuntarily when her dad came into the kitchen. Something was going to happen. She didn't know what, but something was going to happen. The kitchen was hot already with the two burners going on the stove, but all of the sudden, it seemed hotter. Cassie opened her mouth and took in a deep breath for oxygen or to calm her racing heart; she didn't know. She just needed a big breath of air. Moving slowly to the other side of the table, Cassie readied herself for the worst.

Paul just stood there staring at Mary, willing her to look up at him during her tantrum. The leftover beer in his system was making him feel bold, mad. *This woman's crazy, nothing but crazy!* What he normally put up with from Mary was making *him* crazy that evening. Paul usually did nothing, said nothing, or he just left the house when she was like this. Unstoppable. That was what Mary was. Unstoppable. He felt mean; he had to lash out. He had to.

Finally Mary looked up, her face shiny from the heat.

"What are you lookin' at, Paul? You'll get your dinner."

*My God, she loves this. She loves causing this much trouble. She loves making us miserable,* Paul thought and realized with a blow to the gut, *She's sick; something is wrong with her.*

*Don't say it. You will put her over the top.* But he could not stop himself. The anger in Paul had to come out.

"What? Spaghetti again, Mary? Is that all you know how to cook?" Paul mocked. He didn't have to get creative in finding something to say that would get a dig at her. Anything mocking would do the trick, and Paul knew it. From past experience, Paul knew it didn't take much to push Mary over her edge. She teetered at the edge most of her days.

Mary stared at him. She started to boil like the water in the pot for the spaghetti noodles. Cassie watched in fear mixed with curiosity. *What is she going to do?* Just watching the scene unfold, she knew Mary was going to do something. Cassie pushed herself up against the wall in an effort to get as far away as she could without leaving the kitchen. She needed to see just what was going to take place between her parents.

Cassie thought her dad was crazy to stand there near her mother with that water boiling on the stove. *She wouldn't fling that pot of boiling water at him, would she?* Cassie trembled as the thought crossed her mind. Cassie shook her head, trying to remove the awful vision of that from her head. Cassie waited. Time seemed to stand still in the Marvin kitchen.

"Why, you stupid—I'll give you spaghetti!" Mary yelled as she hurled the pot of spaghetti sauce.

All Cassie could think was, *Thank God it is not the boiling water!*

The spaghetti sauce hit everything in its sight. Mary had grabbed the handle and started to hurl it sideways. The sauce started at the side of the refrigerator, hitting the back wall and then the side wall, going as far as Paul's chest and then past him to the edge of the kitchen table and unto the floor. The sauce was hot. Not as hot as the pot of boiling water, but hot enough for Paul to hurry and pull off his white T-shirt, which saved his skin from most of the heat.

Cassie stood there wide-eyed at the mess in the kitchen, silently praying her parents' fight was over. Even though her stomach was still growling for some much-needed dinner, she was no longer hungry for spaghetti or anything else for that matter. As Paul removed his shirt, Mary ran out the back door.

Paul moved quickly and shut off the burners on the stove and then turned to go get cleaned up.

"Cassie, don't go near any of this. This stove is too hot. Maybe you should go to your room now," Paul said with pure exhaustion lining his voice. "I will clean this mess up and get you something to eat; just go on in there and play or something. I'll bring you something to eat in a minute, Cassie."

He did not want Cassie cleaning up Mary's mess. If left alone, he knew she would. Cassie would jump to it. She would immediately think it was something she should do, clean up the mess her mother made. The thought made Paul sick to his stomach. He just didn't know how to fix it, to fix things for Cassie.

"Okay, Daddy. I'm not that hungry though," Cassie replied with uncertainty.

"We've got to eat, Cassie. I'll be done in a minute. Just stay in your room until I get this mess cleaned up," Paul said as he headed for the bedroom to get another shirt.

. . . . . . . . . .

Later, Cassie and her dad had peanut butter and jelly sandwiches with some potato chips. Cassie also had two glasses of milk and one glass of water; she was so dehydrated. Now with some food in her belly and the stress of the evening, Cassie could hardly keep her eyes open.

"Let's get you to bed, Cassie. It's been a long day."

Cassie got up from the chair and agreed with her dad. "All right, Daddy. I am getting tired. Where do you think Momma went?"

Paul thought about that for a minute. "I don't know, Cassie. Probably to a friend; she'll be home soon. Now don't you worry about that."

"Are you gonna go look for her?" It was the weekend, and the week-end meant late nights at the local bar. Cassie just hoped he found Mary or he was home before she got back. Cassie did not want to be left there at home by herself at Mary's mercy if she came home.

Paul felt guilt wash over him at Cassie's look. *This child was smarter than both he and Mary,* he thought. "Yeah, I guess I will. I'll tuck you in first, though, and then go out for a while."

Fear at being left alone at night swept its ugly hand over Cassie.

"It's dark outside now, Daddy. How will you find her?" Cassie said, hoping he would just stay there so she could go to sleep and not be afraid. She did not like fear. She was always alone. During the day, it was sort of okay. But at night, well, night became a different story for Cassie. At night, her imagination worked overtime. With the summer heat, every window and the front and back doors were left open, anyone could come in and get her. Cassie didn't want anyone *getting* her!

Paul's mind kept changing about going out. But he just lied to himself and said it was to look for Mary. He did need a drink. He needed a few, but that was not the reason he told himself why he would leave this child who was staring up at him. It was clear she wanted him to stay with her.

Lying again to himself and Cassie, Paul spoke with difficulty. "It will be just for a little while. I promise, honey. I'll be back before you know it, and I will come in and check on you. You'll be sound asleep and not even know I've left." Paul had to look away. He saw she knew the truth, and he felt ugly and naked before her.

Cassie gave up. Her dad was leaving her alone for the night, so if she heard anything that didn't sound right, her plans were to hide under her bed. She had to have a game plan. If her mother came home in the same mood as she left, Cassie didn't know what she would do then. She'd cross that bridge when she got there. She liked having a plan, but sometimes she couldn't come up with one, she learned that if she listened long enough, God would tell her what to do. Many a time, Mary had come into her room yelling about something, and Cassie felt something tell her just to pretend she was sleeping, to let her mother yell away but lie still and not react. She would go away soon and leave her alone. It worked. Mary would leave Cassie's room after a while, and all Cassie suffered through was a nervous stomach. A nervous stomach was bad enough for a child of seven, but in Cassie's estimation, it could be a lot worse.

Cassie was on the floor under her bed when she woke up to the noises. *When did I crawl under here?* was her first thought. She realized she must have done it in her sleep as she heard the whispered voices of both her parents were home. They were in their bedroom, and they both sounded drunk. Her stomach clinched. Were they fighting? Cassie looked out from under the bed down the hallway. Their bedroom door was open. There was a lot of shuffling around; then Mary actually giggled. Giggled? That was a far cry from what had happened in the kitchen.

Cassie crawled out from under the bed. She waited, hoping they were not going to fight and keep her up all night. Cassie did not recognize the sounds coming from her parents' room, but they made her very uncomfortable. She came to the conclusion they were not fighting. Cassie quietly stepped away from her bed and closed her bedroom door. She did not want to listen anymore to what was going on in her parents' bedroom.

# CHAPTER 12

Later Monday morning Cassie raced to Larissa's house. It took the whole morning to clean up from the weekend. It had been a rough one on the house—from the stinky beer cans everywhere, dishes, and the ashtrays that looked like volcanoes had erupted. Nothing had been picked up or cleaned up from her parents. They stayed in bed together most of Sunday. They said they were tired.

*Yeah, fighting, drinking, and staying out until early morning will make most people tired*, Cassie thought when they said that to her, but she didn't say the words.

Not knowing much about the adult bar life, Cassie was smart enough to figure out some things all on her own. No one had to tell her. No one had to tell her that her parents must have made up after "making up" the night before. Cassie was sure they had made up at the local bar. They must have stayed out drinking until the early morning hours, which was the reason they were useless on Sunday. No dinner for her on Saturday night but a peanut butter and jelly sandwich. Sunday was worse. She found some cheese and crackers in the kitchen.

Leaving Monday morning for work, neither one of her parents noticed the condition they left the house in, or if they did, they did not care. Cassie cared. The garbage was piled high in the kitchen and bathroom that it was spilling over onto the floor. The ashtrays everywhere were worse. Cassie knew when she grew up she would never smoke; she absolutely hated the smell of them.

Happier than ever to be out of the house, Cassie pounded away at Larissa's front door.

Mrs. Stockard yelled out, "Come in!"

Those two words sent such relief and happiness coursing through Cassie. Mrs. Stockard opened the door and saw that it was Cassie. "Why, Cassie, it is so good to see you! My goodness, I have missed seeing you this weekend."

"Boy, Mrs. Stockard, have I ever missed seeing Larissa, Samuel, and you!"

"Well, the important thing is you're here now. Larissa is in her room setting up the dollhouse. I do believe she hoped you'd be here soon!" Mrs. Stockard honestly replied.

Off on a run to the back of the house, Cassie said, "Thanks!"

So quietly that Cassie did not hear her, Barbara said, "You are more than welcome, my little Cassie." Barbara's eyes filled with heartfelt tears as she quietly began to pray for Cassie. *Dear Lord, that sweet girl is an angel from you! Cover her with your protection. Continue to take care of her in her situation. Turn all that she goes through for a purpose. Strengthen her angels today. May they protect her and guide her through all she does.*

Barbara had to stop, or she would break down into a fit of tears, such was her burden for Cassie that morning. Believing on ending on a positive note, she started to hum a tune. She started to hum "Jesus Loves Me." Barbara felt if she filled her home with God, then while Cassie was there, she would get some God too. Barbara did not consider herself religious; she just had simple faith.

Cassie and Larissa played for hours on the floor with Larissa's dolls and all the accessories that went with the dolls. They set up what looked like a whole town, from a grocery store, which consisted of fake plastic food of all varieties; a toy store; and two complete home sites, one for each of the girls. When Barbara looked in on the girls, they were brushing their dolls' hair, pretending both were at the beauty parlor. Both girls were talking in made-up voices.

"Oh my, Cassie, you look beautiful in your new hairdo!"

"Why, thank you, Larissa. I come here all the time and get my hair done. They do a good job, don't they?"

Barbara quietly went back down the hallway so the girls could play uninterrupted. She laughed to herself. It looked like everything Larissa owned was out on the bedroom floor. The girls probably took as much time pulling the toys out as they were going to get to play.

The girls played on into the early afternoon. Barbara had served them sandwiches, potato chips, and ice-cold lemonade picnic style in the center of Larissa's room. Barbara had found a small square cloth in the hallway closet and spread it out in the middle of the room. The girls had cleared a small spot for her to do this. What a fun surprise the "picnic in the room" was for both of the girls. They giggled at the special treatment they were getting.

"Later, when Samuel gets home from Bobby's house, let's walk downtown, and I will buy you all an ice cream. Does that sound good to you girls?" Mrs. Stockard asked before she left the room.

Samuel would be home soon. He played at Bobby Tucker's house two streets over. He and Bobby had been friends since kindergarten, and they had a lot in common; so getting along had never been a problem with the boys. Both of the boys loved baseball. Every chance they got, they organized a neighborhood ballgame, which was their plans for that morning. By lunchtime, Samuel and Bobby would have worn out every baseball player within blocks with their continuous baseball game. Their baseball games never ended. They played baseball until everyone was too tired to play anymore or too thirsty and hungry to play anymore. Samuel had run out the door that morning. "Bye, Mom!"

"Be back around noon. I will have lunch ready for you then. Don't be late. You can always go back to the field. Plus, those other children will need a break to keep up with you and Bobby," Barbara had reminded him.

Larissa and Cassie both jumped up and started jumping up and down, saying, "Yay!"

With Barbara just watching them because they were so cute, they both calmed down, trying to behave themselves and act more grown-up.

"Yes, Mom, that would be great!"

"Yes, Mrs. Stockard, I would love to go to town and get an ice cream," Cassie pleasantly said.

Barbara started laughing at their attempt at being grown-up and proper. "Oh, you two!" She laughed as she waved her dishtowel at them.

. . . . . . . . . . .

Cassie rushed in the front screen door, which slammed hard behind her. She was home with time to spare. She was happy remembering the fun of skipping into town with Larissa for an ice cream earlier. Cassie and Larissa had skipped the whole way holding hands and laughing while Mrs. Stockard and Samuel followed them into town. All of them had looked forward to a sweet treat on the hot summer day. The town was busy with people shopping and enjoying their day. The meat shop was a friendly place that afternoon. A lot of the customers were treating themselves to an ice cream after placing their meat orders with Mr. Winters. While the employees were getting the meat packaged in the white freezer paper, most of the customers moseyed over to the ice cream counter and ordered their ice cream.

Cassie felt very special when Mrs. Stockard told her to order whatever she would like. Cassie ordered a small orange sherbet on a cone, and it felt like gold to her. She felt important when Mrs. Stockard looked at her and said, "Cassie, honey, what would you like to order today? Any flavor, honey, and any size you think you might be able to eat."

Mrs. Stockard looked at Cassie like her choice was a very important decision. Her eyes couldn't get any kinder. The day marked a very special day for Cassie. Cassie thought right then and there, looking at Mrs. Stockard, she wanted to be just like Mrs. Stockard when she grew up. Cassie wanted to be kind to children like Mrs. Stockard and not just the children she hoped to have one day when she grew up. Cassie wanted to be kind to all children.

Something began to take a root in Cassie. She knew in her heart she was not alone in her feelings. Children like her were everywhere, and they needed someone like Mrs. Stockard to be kind to them. It made a difference. Mrs. Stockard made a difference.

Whatever it was Cassie felt from those kind eyes that told her she was important enough to pick her own ice cream flavor and size, whatever it was, Cassie wanted to pass it on to others when she grew up. She had felt very important all of the sudden like she knew her purpose here on this earth. On that warm summer day while waiting for her ice cream cone, Cassie felt chills go up and down her arms.

. . . . . . . . . .

Remembering the chills that went up and down her arm earlier, a confirmation to what she had been feeling, the chills returned to her again. Cassie liked what she felt. She knew it was something special. Getting ready for her parents to return home from work didn't seem like such a dread for once. She didn't feel guilty for thinking those thoughts either, which was something new for Cassie. The shame, the guilt that had piled up on her in the past for her feelings toward her home life were huge. Too much of a burden for a child Cassie's age, but it felt lighter today; she felt older, wiser.

Cassie did not see herself as an "old soul," but others did. She touched others and did not know it. She made others dig deep. Cassie could make others analyze their life and want to be a better person, and she did not know she had the power to do such a thing. She was too young to know such things, which made her even more special to those who knew her.

Cassie sat on the front porch humming a tune she'd made up. Leaning back on her hands, she started to swing her legs to her tune. With all her dinner chores done, all she had to do was wait for her parents to come home from work. The only evidence of her wonderful day with Larissa was a small spot of orange sherbet on her yellow top. One big drip of ice cream had made the orange-colored spot. Cassie decided not to tell her parents what she did during the day. Her mother could end days like this for her by prohibiting her going anywhere during the day. Cassie knew if she shared how the day had made her happy or she had fun, Mary would end it. She would come up with some excuse why she couldn't do it again. She would say something so her true reasons weren't obvious, but her reasons were obvious to Cassie.

Mary did not like any of their neighbors. She did not want any of the neighbors to know their business. Cassie having fun with any one of them or doing an activity with them could be done away with if Mary knew any of her privacy was threatened. Cassie would not say anything and ruin her chances of having things to do with nice people such as the Stockards.

Cassie would not lie to her mother about anything. It helped that Mary didn't over question Cassie. It was as if Mary never thought about anything except what pertained to her. If she left a list of chores for Cassie, she would question her about those, but usually not anything about Cassie personally. Cassie hoped leaving out her daily activities was *not* lying to her mother because her mother never concerned herself with asking. As she sat on the front porch figuring all this out, Cassie wondered why she had to figure this out anyway. *"Why do I have to work all of this out in my head anyway?* Cassie thought. She knew the answer. Stay ahead of what Mary may be thinking.

Paul, Cassie's father, pulled his truck up in front of the house. He parked where there used to be grass, but now it was just a patch of dirt. Mary did not want him parking in the driveway and blocking her in. Nor did she want to have to go out and move her car in case she was blocking him in. Mary had Paul create another driveway on the extension of their front yard. When Paul first griped about it, Mary told him plain and simple, "Well, at least you're not in the street, Paul."

"But the grass, Mary, it will ruin the grass out front," Paul argued weakly.

Mary looked up at him and rolled her eyes. "I don't give a lick about the grass, Paul, and I am not going to be blocked in. It's not my fault we have this small driveway, now is it?" Her look told him it was final and he was to blame for the situation.

Paul walked up to the house with his metal lunchbox, covered in grime and sweat. His white T-shirt was no longer white and looked to be holding a gallon of sweat from Paul's body. He still smiled at Cassie though. The grimy conditions at work didn't seem to change him during the day.

"Hey, Cassie girl!" Paul said with a smile.

"Hi, Dad!" Cassie was glad he arrived home first. They could have a few minutes together. Cassie's dad seemed "normal" to her before he drank and before Mary was home. The rare moments with him before the beer started or before Mary started were the best for Cassie.

"So how's my Cassie girl?"

"I am doing good, Dad. How was your day?"

"Long and hot, but it's good to be home now. Looks like I beat your mother home."

"You *look* like it was real hot in there!" Cassie giggled out her reply.

Paul sat down on the porch next to her; he was enjoying this rare moment also. "Why, Cassie, it is over one hundred degrees in the factory every day. We drink water all day long and never pee. Our bodies just sweat. Some of the men can't take it and drop like flies."

Cassie was picturing everything in her imagination and could imagine what it must look like to see a man drop like a fly.

"Can you put a fan on you?" Cassie asked, thinking maybe it would help.

"Oh, there are huge fans everywhere; it doesn't help, it just stirs the hot air around," Paul told her. Hoping to describe the factory to her, he continued, "The machines alone in the factory make enough heat we would never have to have a furnace on in the winter. They run all day and spew their hot air and fumes into the building. It seems to just settle there like a cloud up in the ceiling. The hot metal we work with boils to temperatures that heat the building all on its own. Forget the heat coming from the machines running; then consider the outside temperature in the summer, and you have what we call 'devil hot,' hot as Hades."

Paul looked down into those liquid eyes looking up at him with such admiration, and he wished he had more time. Mary had just pulled her car into the driveway.

"Thank you, Dad," Cassie said, knowing their time was done.

"Whatever for, Cassie?"

"For telling me all that. I like to picture where you work."

As Paul rose from the porch, he marveled at how Cassie's words cut to his heart. Had he never spoken of his work before? Had he never taken a few moments to share his life with her before? He had to think on this. He did not want to forget to think on this again.

Looking down at Cassie, Paul stretched out a hand. "Let's help your mother bring in those bags, Cassie. Looks like you stopped at the store, Mary."

Mary grabbed a bag from the backseat. "I stopped for a few groceries. Can you get the rest? I will start frying up the hamburgers."

That was all she said, a good sign to Paul and Cassie.

# CHAPTER 13

Cassie was sitting at the kitchen table drawing. She drew pictures with mountains, flowers, and trees most of the time. She had never been to the mountains. She had never seen them with her own eyes, but in her imagination she knew what they looked like. Pretty streams flowing, birds singing, green valleys, and the hillsides covered with greenery. She imagined God visiting her there. He would run along the hillside and meet her at the water. She felt no fear there. When she was there in her imagination, Cassie could feel the beauty, could feel the peace there.

After finishing a very colorful picture of her mountain place, Cassie had something Larissa told her on her mind. The story had saddened her. Cassie wasn't sure she wanted to think about it, but she couldn't get it out of her mind. Larissa told her the story with Mrs. Stockard filling in when Larissa couldn't get her words right. Cassie had asked Larissa what her Sunday school lesson had been the previous Sunday. She always asked Larissa about her church lessons. That was when she got the whole story, the story of how Jesus had died for her. With those details still vivid in her mind, Cassie began to draw.

Cassie wasn't there. The event had happened long before her birth. She had only the details that Larissa and Mrs. Stockard had given her, but a picture was vivid in her mind. It was so clear it was like she *was* there.

The sky was cloudy, dreary, like even nature itself did not like what happened on that day. Calvary—the place was Calvary. The word seemed very important to Cassie. There was a hill, so she drew it. As Cassie remembered the story told to her, she added the details. She put Jesus on the cross made of broken and cut-down trees. As Cassie drew in every nail, she spaced them perfectly around his body. As she drew, she felt every nail. Somehow this became very personal to her. Her eyes filled with unshed tears as she wondered at who did this to him.

Why would those people be so mean to him? Would she have allowed such a thing as this? How could one human being do this to another? Why did he die for her? That is what Larissa told her. He died for her. Why did he have to die like this for her?

Cassie had to wipe at her eyes as her heart filled. Her drawing took up a lot of her time during the evening. She made her details so very clear. She drew Jesus's mother kneeling at the bottom of the hill and someone kneeling beside her helping to hold her up. Cassie felt she would have had to be held up so awful must have been the day for the mother. As Cassie filled in the color of her drawing, she felt her heart being filled in with a love for this man who died for her. A love like his was more then she could handle at the moment. Cassie swiped many more times at the fresh tears flowing down her cheeks.

As Cassie drew looking through her tears, she had a thought come to her. *What do you see through your tears, Cassie?* Cassie thought about it for a minute. *I see Jesus on the cross through my tears.* Cassie blinked several times to clear her tears, but they kept filling up her eyes. As she looked at her picture, a sudden revelation came to Cassie that made the moment seem extraordinary! *I can see through my tears! I can still see my drawing. Looking through the tears, I can still see him!* An overwhelming peace settled on Cassie. She actually looked around the room to see if she was still alone. She was all alone, but Cassie didn't feel alone anymore. She felt as if the man on the cross had shown her something very special. Maybe he could see her drawing and wanted her to know he liked it. The thought warmed Cassie's heart.

When the drawing of Jesus on the cross was finished, Cassie signed her name in the bottom right-hand corner. She wanted to put the sun in the upper corner like all her other drawings, but she did not think the sun shone that day. *It wouldn't be right,* Cassie thought as she took a look at her picture.

Cassie was very proud of her drawing. She made the story that was told to her come alive on the paper as well as in her heart. Mary entered the kitchen as Cassie was examining her finished drawing.

Mary went over to the counter near the sink and finished washing up a few dishes from earlier. As she looked out at the backyard from the kitchen window, Cassie watched her mother, wondering if she should share her picture with her. Cassie would love to show her mother the drawing, but in the past, she never took an interest in what Cassie drew, so Cassie honestly didn't know if she should or not. She could get into trouble since the picture was something about what she learned from Larissa and the information came from the forbidden Sunday school. Looking at the drawing then and back at her mother, Cassie decided not to show her mother the picture. She would tuck it away and keep it safe, and then she could show her grandmother or Mrs. Stockard or Mrs. Vashon. She knew they would like it. Before she could gather the drawing and her pencils and crayons up, Mary walked over and grabbed at the picture.

"What you drawin' now, Cassie?" Mary examined the picture for just a few moments. Then she burst out laughing. "My god, Cassie, look where you put those nails. You put one right in the center of his legs. You put a nail in Jesus's crotch!" Mary thought it was really funny. Cassie didn't. Cassie did not know what she meant by it, but she knew it was not funny.

Mary laughed at the drawing as she walked away. "That drawing is a good excuse for a break! I need some fresh air. My god that is funny." She laughed even more outside while having a cigarette. Her laughter came back into the house like a whip, lashing through the air trying to connect with something, the backlashes trying to reach Cassie. The laughter was directed at her.

Cassie, devastated she may have done something wrong, looked at her picture drawing again. *What does she mean? Where did I put a nail?*

Cassie wondered, hurt. Nothing she did got a kind word from Mary. Mary's laughter was as bad as her being uninterested in the past, maybe worse.

Cassie didn't see anything wrong with her drawing. To Cassie's eyes, nothing was wrong. She measured out perfectly the nails around the body on the cross. To Cassie, if there were nails, then they had to be perfectly placed. She had placed them every so often around the entire body in her drawing. One nail happened to be at the center of his legs.

Cassie, being as young as she was, still did not understand what her mother was laughing so hard about. What she did understand, though, was her mother did not like her drawing and thought it was stupid. It had to be bad in some way to get her laughing so critically at it. Cassie didn't care. She would keep the picture. To her, it was a very nice picture. Something was wrong with her mother. Cassie didn't think anyone could look at her drawing and laugh. Laughter was not the response that made any sense to Cassie. She hurried to her room and hid the picture. If her mother thought it was so funny, maybe she would throw it away as she had Cassie's other drawings.

In the past, Cassie had made pretty drawings for Mary. She had given them to her mother as gifts. Mary never made a big issue over any of Cassie's drawings. Much of the time Mary did not acknowledge them. Cassie could be going on and on about what she drew, what it meant, or tell the story behind the drawing, and Mary would still not give her enough attention to even look at what Cassie was holding up to her. Once in a great while, Cassie got a "that's nice." But anything from Cassie ended up in the garbage pail in the kitchen.

Cassie's illusion her drawings would be something her mother wanted to keep was quickly replaced by reality. The reality was "give anything to Momma, and it will be in the garbage pail soon after." It was not a keepsake; it was not special. Cassie hid everything that was special to her in her bedroom. Mary never came in to tuck her in bed at night and never came in to clean her room, so Cassie's room was a safe haven for her personal things.

Cassie remembered one time in particular when it was Mary's birthday and Cassie had made a picture card out of several sheets of colored paper stapled together. The card was a birthday wish for her mother, a very sincere poem Cassie had written herself, and then she drew the pictures, which acted out the words on the several sheets of paper. Cassie remembered handing it to her mother on her special day, and Mary placed it down on the coffee table, telling her she would read it later.

Cassie kept going by the living room to see if Mary would say anything about the card. Nothing. Cassie noticed on the many trips by the living room the card had not left its spot. It was still lying there unnoticed. Cassie had not known what to do.

*Should I remind her it's there? No, she'll read it when she's ready,* Cassie counseled herself.

After exhausting herself with many attempts and excuses to go by the living room to see if her mother had read the card yet, Cassie almost gave up. She went by one more time to get a drink of water. Slowly she walked down the hallway that led to the opening between the kitchen and living room. As she looked inside the living room, she felt a burst of anticipation. The card was no longer on the coffee table.

*She's read it; she has it somewhere! Oh no, I wonder if she liked it.* Cassie looked for her mother. She heard her on the phone out back. Mary had gone outside to have another cigarette. She and Paul smoked in the house, but if the weather was good enough, Mary preferred to smoke outside. A cigarette was a good excuse to get out of the house to her.

On the way to the back door, Cassie spotted her card in the garbage pail. It was covered in something Mary had thrown out from the refrigerator no less. Cassie glanced up quickly and saw her mother's back through the screen door. She hurried and grabbed her card up from the liquid, greasy mess. As quickly and as quietly as she could, she took the kitchen rag to the paper and wiped off what she could.

Mary had never read the birthday card Cassie had made for her. Cassie knew it; she was sure of it. Mary tossed the birthday card into the garbage pail just like she'd toss out the garbage. Cassie could not let her mother see her or let her know she saved the card. It might have meant nothing to Mary, but it meant something to Cassie.

As Cassie wiped the card off the best she could, she watched the back door, her heart beating a mile a minute in her chest. She could not get caught! Cassie could hear the pounding in her ears; it was deafening. Everything around her sounded as if she were thirty feet under water.

The pounding in her ears and the pressure was a drowning sensation. She needed to save the card. It was a mess—a wet, greasy mess. Cassie had wanted this to be something special to her mother, but it meant nothing to her Cassie now knew. Her hopes of giving something nice to her mother were just thrown into the garbage pail.

Cassie felt she meant nothing to her mother as she looked out the back door at Mary laughing on the phone and smoking her cigarette. Cassie cradled her card close to her heart and went back to her bedroom. Cassie hid the card, feeling sorry for her mother.

# CHAPTER 14

Later in the evening Cassie received a handful of coins from her dad. He came into her bedroom and put out his hand, a warm smile on his face.

"A little something for you, Cassie girl." His palm was full of coins. He turned as he reached the bedroom doorway and added, "Don't spend it all in one place, Cassie girl."

Cassie, surprised at the gesture, grabbed at all the coins in her dad's hand. There were so many Cassie could hardly hold all the coins with both of her hands.

"Thanks, Dad!" came the excited but puzzled reply. Her dad gave her his quarters once in a while for some candy, but all these coins had to be a lot of money!

Alone in her bedroom, Cassie spread the coins out on her bed. Lining them up according to size, Cassie handled every coin. She felt she had a treasure touching each coin.

"I must be a millionaire!" Cassie said as she examined all of her coins.

Cassie picked up a silver fifty-cent piece. The right side of the face was worn off smooth and shiny. As she rubbed her thumb over the smoothed-off edge of the coin, Cassie wondered how many people had touched this very coin. As she looked at the wear of the coin, the coin became something more special to Cassie. The history behind this coin made Cassie wonder if other children just like her had received this very coin from their fathers. What did they buy with it? Did they save it for a while and then have to spend it? Did they feel the history behind the coin and want to save it or spend it on some candy?

Cassie was still kneeling by her bed holding the coin, thinking. Had this coin been in the pocket of a nervous person and they'd rubbed it until the decoration imprinted into the metal had been worn off? Where has this coin been? Cassis wondered. Maybe if she rubbed hard enough it would reveal to her some of the most beautiful places in the world that the coin had traveled to. Cassie closed her eyes and made a wish, hoping such a thing could be true. Maybe the coin held some kind of magic. Maybe it could show her what she desired to see. Nothing happened. Cassie couldn't conjure up anything.

Cassie had never left Tipton, Missouri, she was sure this coin she held was a world traveler. She was sure this coin had seen so much more of the world than her. As her thumb rubbed over her special coin, she knew she could never spend it. Cassie had to keep this coin. It made her a part of something bigger than her world. Looking around her room, Cassie looked for the best hiding place for her coin. She needed to find a good spot because maybe in the future she would be able to add more special coins to her "just started" coin collection.

As Cassie continued to browse through her coins, she found seven more special coins to add to her collection. Two pennies were dated in the 1940s. Their age made them so much more special to Cassie. The perfect coins did not stand out to Cassie, but the worn, world-traveled ones did. Those were the few she would save. The other coins she could have fun spending downtown, or if the ice cream truck went around again, she could treat herself to an ice cream.

With all the coins, Cassie was sure to have enough for when the ice cream truck would come around again. Many times the ice cream truck would go by with Cassie sitting on the front porch wishing for an ice cream, all she could do was wish. Cassie fought embarrassment watching the other children run to the truck with their money or a parent in tow.

Cassie remembered one day Larissa and Mrs. Stockard came out of their front door on a run to catch up with the ice cream truck, and they both yelled, "Cassie, come get an ice cream!" having seen her on the front porch. Cassie had not run out that particular day because she was all out of silver coins.

By the invitation and Mrs. Stockard waving her to come to the road, Cassie knew Mrs. Stockard would buy her an ice cream. But embarrassment or pride stopped Cassie from getting off the porch.

Cassie said, "Thank you! But I am okay. I don't want an ice cream today." Her shoulders sank down an inch for the fib she felt she just told… and to her best friend and her mother.

Larissa, not believing Cassie didn't want one, said, "Oh come on, Cassie. Come pick out an ice cream!" To her mother, she added, "Will you buy one for her, Mom? Cassie may not have any money."

Sensing the situation and not wanting to push or embarrass Cassie, Mrs. Stockard told Larissa, "Of course I will buy her one, honey. I just don't want to embarrass her." Then to Cassie, she added, "Are you sure, Cassie? It's my treat today. I am buying all the kids an ice cream."

Cassie wanted to say yes and jump down and join her friend picking out an ice cream but couldn't. "No, thank you, Mrs. Stockard… but thank you!" Cassie said, feeling sad.

Why couldn't she join Larissa and get an ice cream? Cassie felt miserable. Under most circumstances, taking a gift or free food from Larissa and her family had never been a problem. But Cassie remembered on that afternoon it was.

Whatever caused Cassie to stay seated on the porch and not be her usual self also caused a very hurtful tightening within her chest; she felt her heart being squeezed. She hated the look of question Larissa gave her from the road. Even the whole front yard away, Cassie could see it clearly. She was saddened again by the look of understanding Mrs. Stockard had given her. She was acting weird even for her. She knew it, but she could not stop herself. Her generous neighbors just finding her there caught unaware in her circumstance on the porch was too shameful for Cassie.

· · · · · · · · · ·

Cassie put the coins to spend in the purse her grandmother, Elizabeth, gave her two years ago for her birthday. It was pink with sewed on beads and had a metal mouth clasp to close it. It was dainty, cute, and sweet, just the thing Elizabeth would buy because it had reminded her of her granddaughter. Cassie used the purse to store her coins and a few other items. She never took it out of the house. She didn't want it to get dirty. If Cassie went into town, she took out some of her money and put it in her pants pocket. The purse stayed safe in her room. It was too pretty for Cassie to want to carry it around. She feared something would happen to it.

Cassie didn't have much, what she did have, she took care of. Items in her room she tucked away were not because of any material greed Cassie had. She held on to things and took care of them. She did not want to forget the experience of getting them. If an item became old or worn out and she had to throw it away, Cassie feared she might forget the memory that went along with it. Like an *out of sight, out of mind*, and Cassie did not want to forget some of the special memories in her life.

With all of her coins tucked away in their safe places, Cassie jumped in bed; then she jumped right back out realizing she had not taken her bath or brushed her teeth. She was still in her shorts and T-shirt. The house was quiet. Cassie thought about just putting on her pajamas and going to bed, maybe letting all the cleaning up go for tonight.

*Do my teeth have to be brushed every night?* Cassie wondered. *Grandma Elizabeth says they do.*

Cassie walked silently to the bathroom. She hoped no one would hear her and she could just get this done and go to bed. Peeking around the doorway and down the hall, she heard nothing, she quickly rushed to the bathroom and brushed her teeth. She decided against a bath and went back to her bedroom.

Cassie put her pajamas on and jumped back into her bed. She'd made it without anyone seeing her. She hoped for a quiet night on the home front. She was tired now and just wanted sleep—peaceful sleep in a quiet house. As Cassie closed her eyes and relaxed, she told God good night. *Good night, God. Do you sleep? I wondered about that. Take care of Larissa and Samuel and their parents. Especially Mrs. Stockard; she is so nice. Take care of Grandma Elizabeth. Do you think she will visit soon?*

*I hope so. I miss her. I can't really remember what she looks like; it has been so long. I don't want to forget, so can you help me always remember? Help my mom and dad. Help me be a good girl, and thank you for the quiet house tonight. Please help it stay that way.*

Ending on a very long yawn, Cassie went to sleep. The house stayed quiet, so Cassie was able to sleep.

# CHAPTER 15

C assie had fallen back to sleep after her parents left for work. She had lain down on the couch in the living room for what she told herself would only be a few minutes. Cassie actually slept a few more hours. The course fabric of the couch had left its weaved imprint on her cheek. As she stretched and yawned, Cassie looked out the front living room window at another beautiful sunny summer day. The temperatures were already rising outside and inside the house.

Her cheek felt funny, Cassie went into the bathroom to see why her cheek felt funny. As Cassie looked closely in the mirror, she could see the imprint on her cheek. To her it looked like weaved lines. With a little thought, she figured out what had happened and started laughing because her face looked like the thick fabric of the couch.

Cassie rubbed at her cheek to get the imprint to go away, all she did was make her face more red.

"Hopefully these lines would go away soon or... no, maybe they will stay for a while and I can show Larissa," Cassie thought out loud. She felt she definitely had a show-and-tell thing here on her face.

Fully awake now, feeling hungry, Cassie thought about what she wanted for breakfast. Cereal and toast were the usual choices, sometimes one of those choices was all gone. Looking at the kitchen counter, she could see a loaf of bread. Peanut butter toast sounded good to Cassie.

"Hmmm… I wonder if we still have some peanut butter."

Pulling over one of the kitchen chairs, Cassie climbed up to look in the small cupboard her mother kept the peanut butter in. There was a jar of peanut butter almost out of Cassie's reach. Reaching, Cassie said, "Good, peanut butter toast it is!"

After eating her breakfast, Cassie set the table for dinner and cleaned up the counters in the kitchen. She had already made up her bed earlier, after hanging up the towels in the bathroom—she found them damp, one thrown over the shower rod and one thrown over the tub—she took off for Larissa's. Cassie lightly touched her face, hoping the line marks from the couch imprint were still there. She wanted to show Samuel and Larissa.

"Do you see it, Larissa? I had lines there that looked like the couch material."

Going over to the mirror, Cassie and Larissa were double-checking her cheek to see if the imprint was still there. "I don't think I see anything, Cassie."

"Oh well, it was there. I should have come over and shown you sooner, Larissa." Cassie frowned.

"How'd you get it?" Larissa asked, wishing she could see something, any evidence of what Cassie was talking about.

"I laid on the couch after mom and dad left this morning. I was still really tired, and when I got up, my whole face looked like the couch!" Cassie laughed as she finished.

Larissa started laughing, picturing what Cassie had described. "You are so funny, Cassie! Only you could sleep on a couch and then wake up looking like it!"

"Well, if it happens again, I will come over and show you sooner."

Larissa and Cassie were playing dolls in Larissa's room when Marty Coleman from a block over stopped by. Marty wanted them all to stop by her house after lunch to swim in her new pool.

"Hello Mrs. Stockard. Could Larissa and Samuel swim in my new pool today after lunch?" Marty beamed with her excitement; she'd been waiting all summer for this day.

"Oh, how exciting, Marty! Your pool is all ready then?" Mrs. Stockard said.

"Yep, Dad got all the chemicals right last night, and it is ready!" Marty could not hold in her enthusiasm.

"That will be fine. Cassie is here with Larissa, Marty. Were you going to invite her also?"

"Yep, I was just going to run next door and invite her too!" Jumping up and down, Marty couldn't stand still any longer. "Okay, tell them right after lunch! My mom wanted to wait till then." Turning, Marty started to run back home. "Oh, and Mrs. Stockard, you're invited too!"

The Coleman's had installed a real, upright pool. It was an above ground pool and was three and a half feet deep. It even had a ladder to climb to get in it. To the children it was really fancy and the only one Cassie and Larissa knew about. They had never seen a pool like that in person, much less swam in one. A prior invitation by Marty to swim in her new pool, when it was done, was very exciting for the children. Marty's dad wanted to have it installed and ready at the beginning of summer, but the company who installed it for them was very busy during the first part of the summer, and later in the summer was when they could fit the Colemans in their schedule. Mr. Coleman had told most of the neighbors it wasn't something he wanted to put up himself; he didn't know the first thing about installing a swimming pool. In the end they had to wait for the pool company's schedule. The company was from another city and had to travel to Tipton, so late summer was better then no summer at all!

Watching Marty take off down the street, Barbara had to laugh.

"Thank you, Marty! We will all be there!" she shouted after the running girl. Marty was running so fast that Barbara thought she was probably running home to eat lunch in a hurry, trying to make the time go faster so it would be pool time.

Marty was a sweet girl. She was going into third grade the coming fall and was finally growing into her freckles. Marty had the biggest blue eyes you've ever seen. Her mother kept her hair really short and cut straight-across bangs because it was "easiest," Mrs. Coleman had told Barbara once.

The unique thing about Marty was her freckles; she was covered with them. When she was younger, she looked like one big freckle, but now that she was growing, the freckles seemed to be spreading out.

The day was getting better and better for Cassie. She was happy Marty's pool was all ready and even happier she was invited to go swimming with her friends. Cassie liked going to Marty's house. Cassie thought Mr. and Mrs. Coleman were very nice and that they really loved their only child, Marty.

Marty had told her she wanted a brother or sister, but her mother told her, "God has blessed us with you, Marty!" Apparently Mr. and Mrs. Coleman had waited twelve years for her, and they didn't think there would be any more children coming. Their joy of having Marty was apparent; they did everything they could with her. They bought her everything they could. But no matter what they did, Marty never acted spoiled. Nor was she spoiled. Marty was "just loved," which was the overall consensus of anyone who would have had given an opinion.

Back in her bedroom, Cassie opened her dresser drawers looking for her bathing suit. She would need a towel too, she supposed. After gathering everything up, she ran to the bathroom to put her bathing suit on. She would take one of the damp towels she had hung up that morning.

Mrs. Stockard had asked Cassie to eat lunch with them, but Cassie told her she would eat a sandwich at home. Mrs. Stockard already did so much for her. Cassie did not want to wear out her welcome. Mary's voice was always in her head. "Don't wear out your welcome at people's homes, Cassie. You don't want them to have to tell you to go home when they are sick of you."

Too excited to be hungry, she still thought she'd better eat so she didn't get hungry later. Cassie made a bologna sandwich. She liked it with just mustard. Cassie poured orange juice in a glass and stood at the kitchen counter and ate her lunch. She gobbled her lunch so fast it felt like a brick when it hit her stomach. Drinking her orange juice, Cassie hoped it would help the bologna and bread go down. Something sweet sounded good too. Cassie hoped they had some cookies in the pantry closet. There were some Oreo cookies left in the package. There was a line and a half left in the package, so taking four cookies would not make a difference. Her mother would not notice. No one ate the last of Mary's cookies.

Standing there eating her third cookie, Cassie saw a paper bag on the floor by the plastic garbage pail. It looked full of air. Cassie wondered if it would pop if she stepped on it. Raising her right foot up high, she stomped on the bag. It did not pop. But what it did do was send several sharp pokes into Cassie's foot. Cassie slightly yelled out loud being caught off guard. "Ow!" Then she hopped around on the uninjured foot.

Sitting down on the floor, Cassie grabbed her foot and twisted it around so she could see what in the world happened to it. The pain finally started to really reach her brain. Her foot was bleeding. Cassie was in shock. Between the pain and not knowing what happened, she sat there in a confused state for a minute. Her foot seeped blood. Cassie hobbled up and grabbed some paper napkins, and then she opened the paper bag to see what was inside it.

The top of the paper bag was bunched up and folded shut. As she lifted the paper bag, it was very heavy. It was not an empty bag after all. Lying on its side, it had given the impression it was an empty bag to Cassie. This was why she thought she could stomp on it and make a popping noise as the air rushed out. As Cassie opened the bag, she could not believe what she had done. The bag was full of nails. No wonder her foot was now injured!

She needed to clean herself up fast and get back over to Larissa's. Cassie didn't want to miss out on the swimming. Larissa would have never left without her, but Cassie did not know that. Cassie hoped her foot would stop bleeding soon. Hopping into the bathroom and holding her foot in the paper napkin, Cassie went to work on her foot, wiping it with wet tissue paper. Cassie put six Band-Aids across the bottom of her foot hoping that would help. She would take them off before getting into the pool. She did not want them to fall off and float around in the water of the new pool. Band-Aids would not stay on in the pool for long. Cassie knew that from a past splash pool experience. Cassie hoped she would be all healed by the time she got to Marty's house.

All bandaged up, Cassie limped over to Samuel's and Larissa's. Mrs. Stockard was out in the garage getting a lawn chair down from one of the hooks on the garage wall. Seeing Cassie, she called out, "Just in time, Cassie. I am going to bring a chair for me just in case. I want to sit by the pool and watch all you children in the pool."

Out of breath, Cassie told her, "I hurried as fast as I could!"

"Did you eat lunch, Cassie?"

"Yep, I had a bologna sandwich," Cassie told her, leaving out all the other happenings. Her foot hurt, but she didn't want Mrs. Stockard worrying over her or thinking she should not swim.

"Okay, good, sweetie. I don't want you going hungry. The kids just finished up and are getting their swimsuits on. Let's go on in and get them."

Barbara set up her chair out by the pool so she could enjoy watching the children and play lifeguard. Mrs. Coleman had a patio set on the small cement patio by the back door of their house, but Barbara wanted to be closer to the pool and sit in the sun.

The entrance into the pool was a ladder, so up the ladder the kids went. Marty led the way. Behind her the others lined up, trying to patiently wait their turn. The Colemans added plastic floating toys to the pool. They were dotting the surface of the water. They did not fill the pool all the way to the top with water, so all the kids could get in, and there was no worry the water would be too deep for any of them. Samuel, taller than all the children, stuck out of the water like a pole. Samuel and Larissa knew how to swim, they were busy showing Cassie and Marty what to do. Cassie and Marty were swimming in a matter of minutes.

Barbara was actually very impressed with this. "Cassie, Marty, you amaze me! How are you already swimming around?"

Both of the girls stood up and jumped up and down, hugging each other. Cassie explained, "I think I just needed a pool deep enough, Mrs. Stockard!"

"Me too. I didn't know I could swim, but it's easy!" Marty confirmed, still jumping up and down.

"Well, I am so impressed with you girls. You learn quickly!" Barbara said, surprised. It sure seemed harder to swim than what these girls were performing.

Cassie, up on her tiptoes looking over the edge of the pool, told Mrs. Stockard, "Marty and I had really good teachers." Looking back at Samuel and Larissa, she added, "Samuel and Larissa taught us really well!"

Samuel laughed and made a bow in the pool. "Thank you, thank you."

"I helped too!" Larissa reminded him with a pout on her face.

"Okay, you two. Cassie and Marty were taught by two good teachers, but remember, they were the ones who learned to swim in just a few minutes." Barbara laughed at her two children taking all the credit.

Rebecca Coleman came out onto the patio with a pitcher of Kool-Aid and some cupcakes placed on a plate.

"You won't believe it, Rebecca! Marty and Cassie are already swimming!" Barbara told her proudly.

"You're kidding!" Rebecca exclaimed, not quite believing that the few minutes she was inside getting the food ready that her daughter was already swimming. *Didn't you need lessons to learn to swim?* Rebecca thought as she stared open-mouthed at the pool.

"No, Samuel and Larissa showed both of them a few quick tricks to how they learned, and they were both up and swimming! I am still amazed, but I saw it with my own eyes."

Setting the plate and pitcher down on the patio table, Rebecca went over to the edge of the pool and watched her daughter and Cassie swim. Sure enough, they sailed across the water with both of their legs kicking out behind them. Neither one of them touching the bottom of the pool, they both looked like they had been swimming for years.

Rebecca turned to Barbara and said, "Well, I'll be."

The shocked look on her face was priceless. Rebecca was a beautiful woman. She had strawberry-blonde hair and with age had grown into her freckles. Marty definitely got her freckles from her mother. Now standing there looking completely shocked by what the two girls had already accomplished, she looked ten years younger than her forty-one years.

Both of the ladies started laughing. "I do believe we gave birth to fish, Rebecca," Barbara said, still laughing.

Cassie was having so much fun in the larger pool she thought they could stay in the pool all day and never leave it. The girls went under the water, plugging their noses and then opening their eyes. Looking at each other under the water made them all surface, laughing in a million bubbles. None of them could stay down underneath the water looking at each other for long without laughing and releasing tons of bubbles into the water.

Cassie would go under and make faces at the others, wiggling her head and opening her eyes. She made a funny sight.

"You crack me up, Cassie!" Samuel burst out as soon as he reached the surface.

"What's so funny?" Barbara asked, knowing something funny just happened.

Samuel quit laughing long enough to tell his mother. "Cassie is making funny faces under the water, and she looks so funny."

Cassie jumped up out of the water. "Samuel, Samuel, I have another one! Let me show you!" Cassie went back under, holding her breath. Then she proceeded to show off her new funny face under the water. Cassie could stay under now without plugging her nose. Then she would open her eyes and cross them all the while lightly blowing air out through her nose. With the bubbles floating up in front of her face and her cheeks full of air making her look like a chipmunk with her eyes crossed, Cassie was so funny looking that all the kids started laughing, bobbing back up in the water in tons of bubbles.

They all popped back up laughing and slightly choking on the water their laughter had caused them to intake. Wiping off their faces, all the kids tried to catch their breath.

Barbara called out, "Okay, my little prunes, break time. Mrs. Coleman has some Kool-Aid and cupcakes for you."

Not wanting to get out of the pool, Marty said, "Can we swim some more, Mom, after we eat our snack? Please?"

"Yes, honey, it is still early afternoon. Come have a treat; then you can swim some more before we get ready for dinner."

Turning to Barbara, Rebecca laughed. "They *will* shrivel up like prunes if they don't take a break."

"I think they could stay in there all day if we let them. And thanks again, Rebecca, for inviting us on your opening day," Barbara said sincerely and thankfully.

"You are more than welcome. And remember, we need friends to share this with or it would not be as fun for us, Barbara," Rebecca stated kindly.

"Oh, I know, but thanks just the same. This has been wonderful," Barbara said as she took off her floppy hat and fluffed her hair.

"Barbara, you look like a movie star in that hat. What in the world are you doing in Tipton?" Rebecca remarked with a chuckle at she sat down to sip her Kool-Aid. Barbara had bought the light-pink straw hat at the drug store downtown. She thought it was cute and somewhat fashionable. She had no idea how nice she looked in it. She brought it to keep the heat at bay.

"I'm in Tipton because this is where we grew up, Bob and I. You know, it's funny, Rebecca; we never thought of leaving." Barbara laughed and clearly ignored the movie star part of the comment. Barbara never dreamed of Hollywood; she had only wanted children and a family. She had no desire still to this day to work outside the home.

The kids stretched out on their towels in the sun. Their nylon bathing suits were dry in a matter of seconds. Cassie was in heaven. Lying on her towel with her eyes squinted, she yelled over to Marty, who was on the other side of Larissa, "Marty, thank you for inviting me here today! This is so much fun! I can't believe we learned to swim on the same day! We won't forget this, will we, Marty?"

"Nope, we surly won't, Cassie. We can swim! Yippee! Mom, can we get back in now?" Marty jumped up and asked her mother.

"Yes, you can; go ahead. I think you all look somewhat normal again!" Rebecca told them, laughing.

The kids swam for another hour before the ladies decided it was time to start dinner. About halfway home, Cassie became aware of her foot with all the holes again. As she walked and put pressure on it, she began to feel the pain again. She smiled to herself, though. Because of the good time in the pool, she had forgotten all about her injured foot.

Slightly limping to take pressure off her foot, Cassie didn't want it to start bleeding again. She walked home content with the Stockards. Her cheeks were slightly pink from all the sun, and she was happy.

"What a wonderful day!" Cassie proclaimed out loud.

"Yes, it was!" Larissa added in agreement.

"One of the best! I have to agree, Cassie!" Samuel added.

"It sure was, Cassie. I had a wonderful day watching you children in the pool. I wish now I had dunked under a few times and saw the silly faces you made, Cassie!" Barbara said, smiling down at Cassie.

"Oh, they were funny, Mom!" Larissa giggled. "I wish I could cross my eyes like Cassie, but mine won't cross."

Samuel laughed too, looking over at Cassie like a big brother. "Cassie, you are so funny. You had me laughing; that's for sure." Samuel showed his affection by messing up her hair.

Barbara hated to see her go, but it was time for Cassie to go home. Cassie was still laughing at Larissa's comment.

"I think they're crossed, Larissa. We just can't tell because your eyes are almost closed from you looking down. Well, I better get home." Cassie realized they were standing in front of the Stockards' home.

"See ya later!" she said, turning toward her house, not knowing how much time she had. "Bye, Cassie!" Larissa, Samuel and Mrs. Stockard all chimed in.

Cassie jumped up the stairs on the front porch. Stepping lightly on her right foot, the pain was back fully, reminding her of what she had done to her foot earlier. Cassie hurried in to change back into her clothes.

Looking around the house, Cassie was pleased. Everything was ready for her mother to come home, and she hoped she would not have any complaints from her. Cassie went out on the front porch to wait. She liked waiting outside instead of being in the house busy doing something and allowing her mom to take her unaware. Cassie wanted no surprises.

Mrs. Chambers from across the street was out front pulling weeds from her almost-dead flowerbed.

"Hello, Mrs. Chambers!" Cassie called out.

Mrs. Chambers stood up and waved. "Hello, Cassie. How are you, honey?"

The weeds she was holding in her hand were dead and brown, a sign the flowerbed definitely needed water. The soft fat on her upper arm lightly shook while she waved at Cassie. Her hair was nicely teased up today, and her smile was big for Cassie.

Cassie thought Mrs. Chambers was cute standing there like a grandma. Cassie smiled and said, "I am doing good, Mrs. Chambers! I learned how to swim today in the Colemans' new pool. It's deep and comes up to here." Cassie stood and put her hand under her chin to show Mrs. Chambers how deep the pool was.

Mrs. Chambers walked closer to the street so she could be heard without shouting. "Why, Cassandra, I am so proud of you. You learned to swim in one day?"

"I sure did. Larissa and Samuel showed Marty and me all the things to do to swim, and we both did it. We swam right up there on top of the water!"

Impressed, Mrs. Chambers told Cassie, "Well, again, young lady, I am so proud of you; that is quite an accomplishment! Swimming is not easy, and it is a good thing to learn. You know, Cassie, I have never learned to swim. I have a certain amount of fear where water is concerned. I hate to admit it. I do believe it is from never having been around water most of my younger life."

Cassie, feeling bad for Mrs. Chambers and her confession about not knowing how to swim, told her, "I could teach you one day if you like, Mrs. Chambers. You just let me know if you ever want to try."

Mrs. Chambers said, "I will, Cassie. If I ever get brave enough, you will be the one I ask to teach me to swim."

Cassie sat back down on the porch with a smile and waited. Mrs. Chambers was so touched that Cassie had offered to teach her to swim.

*What a wonderful, sensitive child*, thought Mrs. Chambers. She waved back at Cassie as she went into her home to check on her husband.

"Come on over and say hello to Mr. Chambers soon, Cassie."

"I will, Mrs. Chambers," Cassie promised.

Cassie sat there on the steps. Her hair was still damp and tangled from her afternoon of swimming. Her cheeks were pink with a slight sunburn, a total giveaway to what she may have done all afternoon. But when Mary pulled in and got out of her car, she didn't even look at Cassie. Mary climbed the front stairs going into the house and walked right past Cassie.

"Hi, Mom..." Cassie spoke, unsure. She hated how nervous her mother made her. Should she say something? Should she not?

Mary looked down; she had just realized Cassie was there.

"Oh, hey." Mary walked in the house. "You bored like this all day, Cassie? Don't you do a thing? You look so bored. My God, you need to do something to stay busy…" Mary went on and on as she walked into the house, her voice fading as she went farther away from Cassie.

No answer was necessary. Cassie was just very happy she didn't have to tell mother of her day. She would have liked to tell her mother she learned to swim. But then she thought better of it; maybe her mother would not be as excited as she was. Maybe she would get in trouble for having gone to the Colemans' new pool. Maybe her mother would put a stop to further visits to Marty's house, and Cassie especially didn't want that to happen.

*Nope. Going to Marty's is more important than Mom and Dad knowing I know how to swim now*, Cassie thought. Her achievement of being a swimmer must stay a secret. *Maybe I could let Grandma know somehow. Oh, I can tell Mrs. Vashon! She will be excited for me!* Cassie sat there plotting about who she could tell. She was still busting at the seams with happiness about being a swimmer. She had to tell someone. She just had to.

# CHAPTER 16

Cassie began tossing in her sleep. *What is that noise?* was the thought she woke up to. Sleepy, she rolled over and fell back to sleep, hoping it was just a dream. It was not a dream; there was the noise again. Cassie tried blinking. Sometimes that helped the wake-up-out-of-a-dead-sleep process. There were definitely voices, and they were coming from within the house. Cassie lay there and listened, hoping to make sense of what she was hearing, but the voices were muffled.

*Should I get up and check, or should I try and go back to sleep? Maybe they will leave me alone.* Cassie wondered what she should do. Sometimes it was a no-win situation for her. If she stayed in her room, her mother would get her up so she could see her no-good father in action. He came home drunk sometimes and would start or finish the fights with Mary—so drunk, though, all Cassie heard were slurred words, nothing making any sense.

In the past, if she got up and tiptoed out into the living room and Mary saw her, then she became the focus of Mary's comments to Paul. "There's your little precious, Paul. She needs to stay out here and see how grown-ups fight. She needs to see the real world, Paul! Stay here now, girl, since you're so nosy."

Curiosity won out. There seemed to be a few different voices; maybe her parents weren't fighting. Cassie, awake now, pulled the cover back and crawled out of bed. She opened her bedroom door and listened. There was a woman talking and crying in the kitchen. Not her mother. Who could it be? Cassie then heard her mother.

"You can stay here tonight, Julie, on the couch; can't she, Paul?" Mary looked at Paul for a confirmation but had already decided. Cassie had never heard her mother sound like that, like she cared. Now Cassie was very curious.

Leaving the safety of her bedroom, she tiptoed down the hallway to the corner wall that met the hallway opening to the kitchen. Looking around the wall, Cassie saw a very pretty lady. She was wearing short pants to her knees in a green color with a white shirt still tucked in her waistband for the most part. She had on white tennis shoes. But the most noticeable things were that her hair was really messed up and her face had bruises on it. There was some blood on her skin near her mouth. It looked liked she tried to wipe it off. It was smeared, and her lip was still bleeding.

"Yes, Mary, of course she can stay here," Paul answered and then turned to Julie. "Julie, does Don know where you are? I don't want any trouble with him," Paul said with some concern. Paul knew Don Daniels as a pretty calm man, but Paul had heard some talk before of Don putting his hands on his wife, Julie, and not in a good way. Paul always wondered if women with men like that drove their men to it. Did they push too far at something and their man just couldn't take it anymore? It still didn't justify what Paul was looking at in his own kitchen right then. Paul knew in the past it was always best to leave when he and Mary went at it.

Julie just sat there. "Julie?" Paul asked again.

Looking up at Paul and Mary, Julie answered, "No, Paul, Don would think I went to my mother's, but he wouldn't call her until tomorrow, it being so late and all."

Mary patted Julie's hand. "You're fine here, Julie. I'll make up the couch for you." Rising, Mary started for the hallway closet to get sheets and a blanket out for Julie.

"That's so kind of you both, Mary, Paul. I didn't have the strength to drive to my mother's, and I hate to disturb her so late in the night."

Cassie, in a state of shock at her mother's tone, just watched, trans-fixed. Mary reached up into the hallway closet and grabbed a pillow, blanket, and some sheets. Then Mary went into the living room and started making up the couch.

Leaning over the couch, Mary asked, "Julie, can we get you any-thing? You want some water or a beer?"

Paul got up from the table and asked, "You want a beer, Julie? I think that sounds good right about now." He walked over to the refrig-erator to get a beer, looking back at Julie for her answer.

Julie lit a cigarette and let out a puff of smoke before answering. "Yeah, Paul; thanks, Mary. A beer sounds good."

"Grab me one too, Paul. Julie, this is actually comfortable. I'll make Cassie sleep out here and give you her room—"

Julie interrupted her. "Oh no, Mary, I wouldn't want you to do that. The couch will be fine; believe me. I am just glad your lights were still on, or I would have driven on by. I parked down the street under a tree just in case. My car should be unnoticeable. But Don's passed out; I am sure. He was drunk, very drunk. This is what I get when he is drunk." Julie gestured to her face.

Julie knew Paul and Mary from her husband, Don. Don and Paul worked together and were sometimes drinking partners. The couples met for bowling groups and some cookout parties from work. The owner of the factory put on huge pig roasts for the employees in the summer. The factory owner believed the events raised the morale at the workplace.

Mary and Julie talked on the telephone often, mostly complaining about their husbands, wondering where they were, why they weren't with them. Mary had a weakness when it came to drink and would actually like to have been included on some of the drinking nights with the guys. Paul would go off by himself to get away from Mary; half the time he didn't want to include her on his nights out. In the past, if he took Mary, there was always a fight. Something would be said, and that would start her off. The so-called good evening out was then over.

Cassie could not believe the kind, concerned lady in the living room making up the couch, tucking in the sheets, and fluffing the pillow was her mother. Why was it that only Cassie seemed to think a stranger was taking the place of her mother? Cassie ducked back behind the corner as Mary walked back in the kitchen and sat back down in her chair at the kitchen table.

Mary picked up her beer that Paul had taken out of the refrigerator for her and took a long drink, like she was dying of thirst, and then she lit a cigarette. Taking a long drag on her cigarette, Mary sighed.

"Julie, do you need some help cleaning up your face? I have some medicine, I think, in the bathroom that may help with the cuts."

"Yeah, after I finish this beer I will borrow a washcloth if you don't mind."

"I'll get it." Paul stood with a stretch and answered before Mary could. "I'm gonna go to bed. I'll lay the towel in the bathroom for you, Julie. Lock up the front and side doors, Mary. I don't want any trouble."

"There won't be any trouble, Paul." Mary said. Looking at Julie, Mary added, "This is no trouble, Julie."

"Oh, it's all right. Paul's right. No sense in asking for trouble. Thanks again, Paul, Mary."

"You want another beer, Julie?" Mary asked. "I'm gonna have another one."

Julie decided to join Mary in one more beer and conversation. Cassie hid in her bedroom while her dad went to bed. Once he was in his room, she crouched at the corner of the hallway again listening but couldn't make out much because her mother and the Julie lady were whispering now. Cassie observed such kindness on her mother's face. It looked like she really liked Julie and was concerned for her. Cassie had never seen this behavior from her mother before. Cassie had never witnessed this side of her mother. As they continued to talk in whispers, Cassie stayed hidden hoping to learn more about her mother.

Julie cried. Mary sat listening to her; then she reached out and patted Julie's hand. The next moment, Mary lit a cigarette for Julie and handed it to her. Even that action was laced with compassion from Mary. Cassie yawned from her spot on the floor but could not make herself get up and go to bed.

Who was this woman sitting in the kitchen in her mother's body? Cassie did not know this woman. She looked like her mother, but there was nothing else recognizable. This curiosity kept Cassie pinned in her spot. *Who is this Julie woman?* Cassie wondered. *Who is she to Mom that she gets treated so well? Mom must really like her.* Cassie knew then her mother did not like her. She had never touched Cassie like that... ever.

The feelings that were swimming around in Cassie at the moment made her feel sad. She felt sad for herself, and she felt sad for her mother. She would probably never have what she knew somehow was possible with a mother and a daughter. She would never have what she was witnessing between her mother and her friend. Her own mother cared more for her friend than she did for her own daughter. The revelation was not a surprise to Cassie, and it actually came as a relief. What Cassie was watching made her wish she was on the receiving end of the kind hand from her mother, but it also helped her know she wasn't imagining things. Her mother did treat her differently. It was not a figment of Cassie's imagination. This made Cassie feel better somehow.

Her mother and Julie continued to talk and smoke cigarettes long into the night. Cassie had seen enough. She got up quietly and went back to her bedroom. Cuddling deep into her covers, Cassie prayed for sleep. She wanted to sleep and forget what she'd witnessed in the kitchen. She did not want to envy this stranger for the tenderness her mother showed her. This woman needed someone to be kind to her. She was just beat up by her husband so Cassie was glad someone was being kind to her. Witnessing this exchange between her mother and the stranger left Cassie feeling very confused.

*I have tried to be a good daughter. What else can I do?*

Cassie cuddled down even deeper, hoping to drown out her thoughts. She wanted, needed to sleep. She felt so tired, and it would be morning soon. Pulling the covers over her head, she tried counting sheep.

. . . . . . . . . .

When Cassie got up in the morning and went out into the kitchen to see what was going on in the house, the pretty lady, Julie, was still sleeping on the couch. Her mother was standing in the kitchen by the sink drinking coffee. The brewing coffee had made the kitchen smell so good to Cassie. She loved the smell of coffee, but no one would let her drink any to see what it tasted like.

"I have company, Cassie. Julie is sleeping on the couch in there, so you be really quiet this morning," Mary told her with a quick look over her coffee cup.

"Okay, Mom. Who is she?" Cassie asked, even though she'd already figured a lot of the situation out the night before.

"Shhhh… she is a friend of mine," Mary snapped at Cassie, looking over at Julie to make sure they were not waking her up.

Cassie stood there looking at her mother. There were so many unanswered questions. Cassie's stare made Mary uncomfortable.

"Dad and I know Julie and her husband, Don. Dad works with Don; they're friends. Julie and I are friends. There was trouble at their house last night, and Julie needed a place to stay. I don't know why I am telling you any of this. Now go on and get dressed. Stay in your room for a while. No seven-year-old needs to butt their nose in any of the adult business around here," Mary muttered to herself as she refilled her coffee cup.

She needed a cigarette. As Cassie went to her room, Mary headed to the back porch.

Cassie didn't hurry getting dressed since she was pretty sure she should just stay in her bedroom. Cassie did some real muttering herself as she looked through her dresser drawer for something to wear. "Well, at least I get to stay in my bedroom. You didn't kick me outside with nothing to do like you usually do." As soon as the words were out of her mouth, a part of Cassie felt good letting that comment to her mother out. The other part of her felt like she was a bad girl for feeling that way.

Cassie heard the voices first and then smelled the aroma of eggs and bacon cooking. The morning coffee had already created a smell from the kitchen that made Cassie's stomach growl. Cassie opened her bedroom door wide so she could hear if her mother called for her. Then she waited by her doorway, hoping to get the signal to come get something to eat.

Her dad was leaving. Had he already eaten breakfast? Cassie wondered. Normally Mary didn't cook a big breakfast during the week— big meaning eggs, bacon, and toast. Cassie heard the door close with a good-bye from Mary and Julie. Her dad had left for work.

Cassie crept quietly to the corner of the hallway. Her mother and Julie were sitting at the kitchen table eating the cooked breakfast Mary had apparently cooked. Cassie swallowed the saliva that was in her mouth as it had watered from her hunger.

*Was she not going to tell me breakfast was done?* Cassie wondered. *She knows I am up. Did I not hear her call me?*

Cassie felt in a predicament. Now what was she supposed to do? Should she just walk out there? Mary got up from the table, reaching for the coffee pot, and refilled Julie's coffee cup; then she handed Julie the sugar bowl. Julie was pushing her toast around on her plate, wiping up the last of her eggs.

"Why, thank you, Mary. You don't have to wait on me," Julie said, looking up at Mary.

Cassie's stomach growled loudly.

"You're in my home, Jules. I don't mind. I called in and told my boss I'd be a few hours late."

"Is that going to get you in trouble?"

"No, I hardly ever take any time off. They can get by till ten," Mary said, looking at the kitchen clock on the stove. "I told him I'd be in by ten and work over if needed."

Cassie's stomach growled again, making her put one foot in front of the other. She headed down the hall, trying to look normal. *Maybe it isn't hunger*, Cassie thought. *The growling could be nerves.* Mary looked up at her.

Fighting back the uncomfortable feeling that just settled over her like a wet blanket, Cassie said, "Good morning," as she entered the kitchen.

Julie turned so she could see Cassie. She looked much better this morning. There was some light bruising, but the blood was all gone.

"Good morning. You must be Cassie. Why, I don't think I've ever met you before. I'm Mrs. Daniels, Julie Daniels." Then she put her hand out to shake Cassie's hand. Before Cassie grabbed her hand to shake it, she looked up at her mother. Mary just sat there watching the exchange.

Cassie, sincerely wondering what her mother was thinking, shook Mrs. Daniels's hand. "Hello Mrs. Daniels. I am Cassie."

Mary sat holding her coffee mug with no exchange with her daughter. Julie then added to the conversation. "Why, you must be hungry,

Cassie." Then turning to Mary, a little unsure of herself, Julie asked, "Mary, is there any breakfast left, or did I eat it all?"

Cassie waited. Was there some food left for her? Mary looked at her, the look saying, "You came out of your bedroom too early." Then she spoke directly to Cassie. "No, there's nothing left, but that's fine for Cassie; she usually has cereal. Don't you, Cassie?"

Cassie felt disappointment that all the cooked food was gone. She would have loved to have had some of the bacon she had smelled.

Cassie looked at Mrs. Daniels when she answered, "That's right, Mrs. Daniels. I make my own breakfast most mornings. I have cereal, and some days I have peanut butter toast."

That was not the answer Mary wanted her to say. It was a good thing Julie was there because Mary wanted to smack that comment right out of Cassie's mouth.

Julie, not sure of anything, did not sense there was a problem with the banter back and forth from mother and daughter. Cassie went over to the kitchen counter and put two pieces of toast in the toaster. Then she took a bowl out of the dish drain and went in search of a cereal box in the pantry. As she began buttering her toast, she looked over at Mrs. Daniels. Her mother's back was to her. Mary had never left her seat to help Cassie with her breakfast. When Cassie caught Mrs. Daniels watching her, she smiled. It was at that moment she saw that Mrs. Daniels understood her situation and had the decency to look down at her lap and not let Cassie see the pity that had just become very clear in her eyes.

But Cassie waited. She willed her to look back up. Finally Julie did look back up, and then Cassie smiled again at her, wanting her to know they had something in common. Her husband treated her badly, and Cassie understood. Cassie wanted her to know it was okay; she was not alone. Cassie's smile made Julie take a deep breath at what it said.

"I better be going, Mary. Thank you, and tell Paul thank you too for letting me stay."

Looking back up at the little girl across the room that seemed to read her very heart, Julie said with a small smile as to not let Mary see. "Cassie, it was so nice to meet you; you take care now."

Unsure, Cassie looked at her mother and then said, "Nice to meet you too, Mrs. Daniels."

Cassie never left the kitchen counter area. She ate standing up at the counter in front of the toaster. She quickly gobbled up her cereal and peanut butter toast. She needed to be done and quick. When Mrs. Daniels left, she was on her own again with her mother, and the outcome might not be a good one. Her mother did not look too pleased with her this morning. Spending any extra time with Mary was not going to be considered a smart move on Cassie's part. Cassie knew she should get a move on and get outside so her mother could get ready for work alone.

Cassie listened to her mother and Mrs. Daniels saying their goodbyes at the front door. Mary was telling Julie to be careful; she kept looking outside and down the street. She then asked Julie to call her later, and then they hugged. Cassie thought she had witnessed everything the night before, but when her mother hugged Mrs. Daniels, Cassie felt abandoned. Just watching the emotional exchange between the two friends made Cassie's shoulders slump in defeat. She was really all alone, wasn't she? Her mother was standing fifteen feet from her, but she was an abandoned child. Tears welled up in Cassie's eyes. She did not blink them away; they distorted what she was seeing enough so she really wasn't seeing anything anymore.

# CHAPTER 17

Cassie needed the flower garden. She watched her mother's car move down the street. When the blue four-door sedan turned left at the corner and disappeared, Cassie took off at a run down the street. Without even knowing what pushed her, she had to get to the garden and quick. She ran hoping nothing had changed there, hoping the familiarity would be there. She needed to breathe it in. She wanted to cover herself with the garden.

Calling out before reaching the yard, Cassie yelled out, "Mrs. Vashon!" Cassie had no idea if Mrs. Vashon was outside in the backyard. She just needed to yell out. When Cassie ran into the yard, she let out a sigh. She'd made it; she was there! She did not have to leave; she could stay for hours if she wanted. Cassie bent over, putting her hands on her knees, and tried to catch her breath. Breathing very hard, she wondered what had gotten into her; she felt desperate.

Looking around the garden was a comfort to Cassie. Mrs. Vashon was not outside Cassie noticed as she took in her surroundings. Taking another deep breath, Cassie walked around the flower garden. She needed to relax and calm her heart beat.

"I'll pull the weeds first," Cassie said out loud to no one.

Her pail was by the shed, placed there for her, always ready for her. Cassie liked that about the flower garden. It needed her and was always waiting for her.

As Cassie weeded quietly around her beautiful flowers, she looked at the garden angel.

"You're not alone are you?" Cassie said as she looked around the garden. "No, you're not alone. You have all of this to take care of and love. I am glad you're not alone, garden angel." Not liking how she was feeling but too young to be anything but honest, Cassie continued taking care of the garden, hoping her mood would change.

Mrs. Vashon was rubbing some hand lotion into her hands at the kitchen sink when she looked out her kitchen window and saw Cassie in the backyard. Smiling, she hurried to finish up. Mrs. Vashon had made a chicken casserole for her dinner later on in the day. She was just finishing up the dishes and putting them away. Cassie must have come over while she was busy cleaning up, Mrs. Vashon quickly turned and placed the casserole in the refrigerator.

She made a mental note to put the casserole in the oven around four o'clock that afternoon. Mrs. Vashon had nothing else planned that could not wait, she wanted to enjoy some of the day with Cassie.

"Cassie! How are you, honey? I am so glad you are here. Can you stay awhile?" Mrs. Vashon called out as she walked off the back porch.

What a sight she was for Cassie. Mrs. Vashon's light-brown hair, which was mostly gray at the temples, was nicely teased and hair sprayed. The curls were somewhat straightened out, causing soft poufs all around her head. She had a healthy, soft look to her, and she gave good hugs. Giving good hugs was important to Cassie. There weren't many people who could give a good hug, and Mrs. Vashon gave a good hug.

Setting her pail down, Cassie ran to Mrs. Vashon. Grabbing Mrs. Vashon around her waist, Cassie held on tight.

"Mrs. Vashon, you're here!"

Surprised but delighted by the greeting she was getting from Cassie, Mrs. Vashon said, "Why yes, Cassie, I am here. Where did you think I went?"

Cassie looked up into the friendly, familiar face and said, "Oh, nowhere really... maybe into town. I am just really glad you're here." Cassie squeezed her tighter.

Feeling a little concerned over Cassie's behavior, Mrs. Vashon wanted to ask what all of this was about but did not want to make Cassie uncomfortable at showing her outburst of emotion.

"Well, Cassie, you would not believe me if I told you how happy I am you're here today. It has been a while since this garden and I have seen you. We have missed you very much."

Cassie still had not let go of Mrs. Vashon. Holding onto Mrs. Vashon made Cassie feel this was all real. Cassie was afraid to let go. If she did, would all this disappear? Would Mrs. Vashon disappear? Could this somehow be taken away from her?

"I've missed you too," Cassie admitted.

Mrs. Vashon did not care how long Cassie held on to her. She held onto Cassie back. She lightly wrapped her arms around Cassie and patted Cassie's back and held her head close to her. It did not matter how long this would take. Cassie needed to be held close in her garden, her sanctuary. They both stood there holding each other as time stood still in the garden. The sunshine lightly bounced around, sending its beautiful light to the tips of the flowers, the edges of the leaves. Bees buzzed from one flower to the next, looking for their sweet nectar. Cassie was held. Cassie was loved.

Saying nothing, Cassie finally pulled away from Mrs. Vashon. Turning, she ran and went to get her pail.

"I was pulling weeds before. Look at how many I found already! My pail is almost full."

Mrs. Vashon still concerned, decided to let it go, everything with Cassie seemed to be back to normal, "Cassie, you do a wonderful job taking care of this flower garden. You know those beautiful flowers would be choked out by those weeds, don't you? They take all the nutrients and leave nothing for the good plants."

"I don't want anything to hurt the flowers; they are too pretty," Cassie said, concerned.

"No, they are too pretty to be hurt," Mrs. Vashon agreed. Mrs. Vashon, looking at Cassie, was not just thinking of the flowers at that moment. Her heart went out to the flower standing in the garden with her. Was Cassie hurt? The question plagued Mrs. Vashon more then she would like to admit.

"You would like my grandma, Mrs. Vashon," Cassie stated in a very even voice.

The statement coming out of nowhere, and it took Mrs. Vashon a moment to catch up.

"I am sure I would like your grandmother, Cassie. Do I remind you of her at all?"

"You know, you do; you're very nice like her... I get along really well with my grandma. She loves me very much, you know."

"Oh, I am sure she loves you very much, Cassie. I would like to meet her. I am sure she is very nice too. Cassie..." Mrs. Vashon waited for Cassie to look at her. "Thank you for saying that I am nice like her. That is a lovely compliment."

Cassie looked very serious for a moment. She looked about to say something, but it took a few moments for anything to come out. "Mrs. Vashon?"

"Yes, Cassie."

"Well, I just want you to know... I love my grandma. I want you to meet her as soon as she visits the next time. And... I love you too, Mrs. Vashon." Looking down and then back up, Cassie said, "I just want you to know that."

Mrs. Vashon had never experienced anything so generous in her life. She felt as if she was given a most precious gift. Blinking back tears that threatened to fall, she smiled and told Cassie, "Cassie, honey, I love you too! You have been a gift given to me in my later years. *A gift,* honey, and I want you to know that also."

Suzanne Vashon knew later the tears would come when she could be alone and think on the precious gift handed to her that afternoon from Cassie.

Taking hold of each other's hands, they both started laughing. They laughed to cover up all the other overwhelming emotions they were feeling. They laughed because they both felt joy at having each other.

"Let's water the flowers... Mrs. Vashon, let's make rainbows together!" Cassie said, wanting this afternoon to go on forever.

Her heart swelling with love for this child, Suzanne felt so young she almost half skipped with Cassie as she began pulling the water hose out of its reel. "Yes, Cassie, they do look thirsty, and I love the rainbows!"

Later, sitting on a bench in the flower garden, Suzanne watched as Cassie made her rounds. She made sure every plant, and flower received their fill of water. Then all of the sudden Cassie took off in a run, having dropped the water hose. She was waving her arms all over the place. The water hose was throwing water up in the air, and Cassie was running this way and then that way.

Suzanne laughed. "What are you doing, Cassie?"

Cassie, looking all around and making sure the coast was clear, said, "It was a bee!"

They both got a chuckle out of that one.

"He sure made you dance a funny dance! I was thinking maybe you were doing an Indian dance for rain!" Mrs. Vashon continued to laugh.

Cassie laughed with her. She knew she had to have looked very funny running around like that.

"Nope, no Indian dances. I was trying to dodge the bee…" Cassie then wondered, "Do you think Indian dances *can* bring rain, Mrs. Vashon?"

"Maybe the faith of doing the dance for rain is what makes it work, I think."

"What do you mean?"

"Faith… faith is hoping in something that is not here yet. The Indians would dance, I do believe, with faith. Then the rains came. The dance was not what brought the rain but their faith that it would come." Mrs. Vashon hoped she explained that so Cassie could understand. "Did I explain that well?"

Cassie took it all in. "Yes, I think so. I think I know what you mean. It's like believing, believing in something until it happens." Cassie, deep in thought, picked up the hose and went about putting it away. The flowers were all watered.

Cassie went back over to the bench and sat down. Looking around the garden, she said, "You know, I don't want to leave, but I better get home and get some lunch. Then I should see what Larissa is up to. Maybe she will want to play today."

Patting Cassie on the head, Mrs. Vashon said, "Cassie, I don't want you to leave either. I like you here taking care of the garden. After lunch, you can always bring Larissa back. You girls could play here if you like.

This is your garden too. What are you having for lunch today, Cassie? Do you have something planned?"

Looking up with a smile, Cassie said, "Yep! I am having a peanut butter and jelly sandwich. That's the easiest, but I like it too!"

"Would you like to have lunch with me?"

"I better eat at home. But thank you for asking me, Mrs. Vashon," Cassie said politely. She was always thinking with her manners, but Mrs. Vashon did not miss the sudden change in Cassie.

Cassie jumped up and reached over and hugged her. "Thank you, Mrs. Vashon. I had another wonderful day in our garden."

Suzanne said, "Cassie, you are just full of wonderful surprises today!"

Cassie ended the hug and said, "I better go. See you later, Mrs. Vashon!" Then she walked backward quickly out of the garden, smiling the whole way and waving.

Suzanne laughed again. *Laughter is good for the soul*, she thought. Then she shouted out to Cassie, "Cassie, honey, please watch where you're going!"

Turning then, taking off at a run down the street, Cassie shouted back, still waving, "I will!"

Suzanne sat back down on the bench. She felt as if an angel had touched her. Suzanne felt so peaceful, so touched by the moment she wanted to stay in it. She had no idea how long she sat there, but it was late afternoon by the time she went back into the kitchen to make a lunch. She actually had missed lunchtime. Taking a small blue plate down from the kitchen cabinet, Suzanne decided she was not hungry after all. Knowing she should eat something, she decided she would have a small snack of cheese and crackers before dinner. She was thinking she would bake the chicken casserole she had prepared that morning for dinner an hour early.

After fixing herself a cup of coffee, Suzanne smiled as she stirred her coffee. Thinking out loud, she said, "My goodness, I have been truly blessed with that sweet child!" Hoping she could always be a part of Cassie's life, she prayed, "Lord, I thank you for Cassie. I thank you from the bottom of my heart for blessing me with her. Please protect her and keep her in the palm of your hand. Lord, she has truly been a gift to me! Bless her all the days of her life! Amen."

Shaking her head, Suzanne walked away from the kitchen sink thinking of what else she could do to fill her afternoon. Nothing was going to top her visit with Cassie, but she had to look for something to fill her time. It was hard that afternoon to say good-bye to Cassie. Suzanne would have liked it if she could take care of Cassie every day.

# CHAPTER 18

"Why isn't Cassie eating with us, Mary?" Paul asked as he scooped up some goulash from the pot on the stove and filled his plate. After filling his plate and grabbing a beer from the refrigerator, he sat down at the kitchen table.

"She said she didn't feel well and didn't want to eat," Mary finally said between spoonfuls of food. She had no manners when she was hungry.

"Is she okay?"

"Yeah, she's okay," Mary said, showing her frustration. *I just want to eat in peace. What is it with all these questions?*

"Well, don't get in a huff. I am just wondering, Mary; that's all," Paul said, annoyed.

"I told you she was," Mary said with finality.

Paul tried to look busy wiping up the tomato sauce on his plate with a couple of pieces of bread. He didn't want any trouble tonight from Mary. He was tired and wanted to just have a few beers while watching TV and get to bed early.

Nothing else was said. After finishing her dinner, Mary started cleaning up the kitchen. After piling up the kitchen sink with the dishes, Mary went out the back door. The screen door slammed into the silence of the night like a knife.

Paul was actually relieved she was gone. He'd do the dishes without one complaint. That's what she was saying to him, even though Mary didn't say a thing. Paul could hear her say as she swaggered out the back door, "I cooked dinner, Paul. You do the dishes." Her voice was loud and clear, even though she didn't open her mouth.

Looking around the kitchen, Paul resigned himself too. *This is as good as it gets. Does anyone have it any better, really?* Feeling even more tired than he did a few minutes ago, Paul rose from the table and set off to wash the dishes. Putting the kitchen back together seemed therapeutic somehow to Paul that evening. The quiet was welcoming.

Opening up his second can of beer, Paul stood at the kitchen counter looking out at the backyard that needed to be mowed. *Not tonight,* he thought as he sipped his beer. *It can wait until another day.* His truck needed some work on it too; it wasn't running right. *Hopefully nothing major,* he thought. He was too tired to even lift up the hood and take a look.

Paul peeked in on Cassie; she was sound asleep. Closing her bedroom door, he went into the bathroom for a shower. There was a purple flower in a glass vase on the counter. Paul smiled. The little touch was from Cassie. Mary would never think of such a thing, but Cassie would. Paul knew she'd probably found the flower in one of their flowerbeds and brought it in for all of them to enjoy.

Drying off with the towel in the steaming bathroom, Paul wiped off the mirror. The hot shower felt good, but it was too hot outside to enjoy the steam. Cassie's flower seemed to enjoy the moisture. The purple flower seemed to brighten in its vase. The color seemed deeper, like velvet.

Paul picked up the bathroom quickly and then fanned the bathroom door to help the steam escape. He went back to Cassie's room to check on her. Opening her bedroom door, she was still sleeping in the same spot. She looked so peaceful he didn't want to wake her. Reaching over, Paul touched her forehead just as his mom had done when he was little. His mother's rule was no fever you're fine; fever, then you're sick. Reaching, Paul laid his palm against Cassie's forehead. Taken by surprise at her temperature, Paul removed his hand and tried again.

Paul whispered, "Cassie, honey," and reached again to feel her. She was burning up. Paul was no doctor, but Cassie had one high temperature, too high.

Concern for his daughter made his heart pound. "Cassie, Cassie, honey, wake up."

Paul lightly shook Cassie by her shoulder. Cassie didn't stir. Fear bubbled up in his throat. *What in the world? This isn't right. What's the matter with her?* Paul ran out of Cassie's bedroom and grabbed a clean shirt from his bedroom, pulling it on as he ran to the back door.

"Mary! Mary! Something is the matter with Cassie!" Paul yelled on his way. "Mary, I just checked on Cassie. I can't get her to wake up!"

"What do you mean you can't get her to wake up?"

"Just that! Come on, we've got to get her to the doctor. She's got a high fever. She's out, Mary, I tell you, doesn't seem normal!" Paul said, motioning her to follow him.

Paul raced back to Cassie's room. He tried again, rolling her to her back. "Cassie, it's Daddy. Wake up, honey."

Cassie didn't stir.

"Oh my God, get me a cool cloth, Mary, and help me get her to my truck!" Paul yelled back at Mary. She was standing in the bedroom doorway.

"What's the matter with her, Paul? Shake her a little harder," Mary said as she went to the bathroom to get the washcloth.

Hoping that was what it was, that she just needed to be woken up better, Paul lifted her and gave her a good shake. "Cassie, Cassie, wake up, honey. Daddy wants you to wake up!"

Cassie heard something. She tried to answer the voice, but she was so tired. "Hmmm..."

"That's my girl. Come on, Cassie. Try really hard, honey; you need to wake up!"

Mary brought the cool cloth and said, "See, she is just really out; she's fighting a fever, Paul."

Paul looked up at Mary, thinking she was as cool as the cloth she just handed him. *How can she be this calm? This was not normal for Cassie.* "Let's get her to the truck. She needs to be seen. This fever is too high, Mary."

"Where are you going to take her now, Paul? The doctor's office closed at five."

Not believing what he was hearing, Paul snapped, "Mary, help me get her into the truck. I will take her to the hospital then! My god, Mary, she needs to get to a doctor! What is the matter with you?"

Lifting Cassie up from the bed into his arms, Paul carried her out to his truck. Talking to her the whole way, he told her she was going to be all right, that she was going to be taken care of.

As Paul laid her down in the passenger's seat, he buckled her in around her waist. Making sure his wallet was in the glove compartment, Paul then looked back one last time at the house. Mary was standing in the doorway leaning against the screen door.

"You're not coming with us," Paul accused, and it was not a question.

"No, you take her. You'll see, Paul, she just has a fever, and it is making her this tired. I used to get them all the time when I was little. She is just fighting something," Mary said evenly.

Running to the other side of the truck, Paul jumped in and didn't bother to waste any more time answering. Speeding off, sending gravel spitting up from the tires of the truck into the yard, Paul tried to think where the closest hospital would be to take Cassie.

Looking down at Cassie lying there on the front seat, Paul started patting her head with his right hand. She was almost too hot to touch.

"Cassie, baby, if you can wake up, I need you to. Daddy needs you to say something, honey."

Racing the truck as fast as it could go without endangering them, Paul sped down the road to the highway. He knew it would have been a waste of time driving by the doctor's office in town. They closed up every day at five in the afternoon and were closed on the weekends. If someone got sick between five p.m. and nine a.m., they were out of luck to be seen by a doctor in town.

Looking down at Cassie and really frightened now, Paul went off the road. Swerving back on the road, he sent rock and gravel everywhere. The tires spit up every size rock, the pings sounding off the metal bumpers on his truck. Paul wanted to curse Mary at that moment. She should be there holding her daughter while he drove.

Paul felt he was racing a clock. Cassie needed help now! The road seemed so long before him. It stretched out before him like an endless piece of ribbon weaving and blowing in the wind.

"Please, God, help me get her there," Paul whispered. "Cassie, Cassie, can you talk to Daddy? Let me know you can hear me, honey. Come on, Cassie. Daddy needs to know you can hear me." Paul felt her head move under his hand. "Cassie, can you hear me?" Hope filled him. There was another slight movement from Cassie. Paul looked down for a moment only. He needed to keep his eyes on the road. Cassie stirred again.

"Daddy? Daddy... so hot..." came the choked, whispered reply from Cassie.

"Cassie! Baby, Daddy is right here! I will get you a drink soon; then you can cool off. Stay with me, Cassie. You have a really high fever, honey. Stay with me!"

Cassie moved her hand and tried to touch him, but her arm was too limp. She could only move it an inch; then her arm lay still again. She had no strength. *What is the matter with me? Am I dreaming? Why can't I open my eyes?* She wondered. She wanted to ask but didn't have the strength to form the question. She knew she was with her dad though; he was taking her somewhere. There was movement. She was slightly rocking, and his voice faded in and out. It lulled her back into the deep sleep.

Paul drove for what seemed like hours. His hands were in a death grip on the steering wheel. Every few moments he pried his right hand loose and patted Cassie.

Paul didn't have much of an imagination, but the imagination he did have was going in directions he didn't want to think about. *What is wrong with my girl? How long was she like this and I didn't know?* The stress was pouring out of him, its evidence darkening his shirt.

Paul thought, *God, if you're out there, help us. Help me get Cassie to the hospital in time. For Cassie, God... Please listen to me for Cassie. I am sorry, God, so sorry. Something is very wrong here, and I don't know what it is. She needs your help. Oh my God...*

Paul hit the gas pedal harder. He felt like time was running out. There was an hourglass in his mind, and he could picture the sand running out; fear gripped his soul.

Pulling into the hospital parking lot at a high rate of speed, Paul swerved not to run up onto the curb. The tires squealed on the pavement, making his entrance known. Paul pulled the truck right up to the emergency door and threw the truck into park. Pulling at his seat belt, he couldn't undo the latch his hands were shaking so badly. Paul never wore a seat belt, but after swerving off the road, he had latched it just in case. Paul started shouting, "Help me! Please, somebody help us!"

An orderly came running from the inside of the hospital.

"Sir, can I help you?"

"Yes, my daughter! I can't get her to wake up. My God, I can't get out of this seat belt latch. I never use them, and tonight I put it on..." Paul was shaking so badly the orderly came to help him first. After unlatching the seat belt for him, the orderly ran back to the other side of the truck. Paul jumped out of the truck and ran to the passenger side while the orderly was already unfastening Cassie.

Paul ran behind the orderly, who carried Cassie into the hospital. "She's been unconscious. She spoke only once on the way here," Paul said, befuddled.

The orderly placed her onto a stretcher and started buckling her on so she could not fall off if she woke up. "Sir, please start giving them your information. We need to get her in to see a doctor as soon as possible." He nodded toward the nurse's station. A nurse was there ready and waiting.

Paul looked down at Cassie's face. She looked like she was sleeping and nothing was wrong. He fought to come out of the numb daze he was in. He couldn't catch his breath, and his arms were going numb. Rubbing his arms to get the blood to flow, he tried to focus. Where was he supposed to talk to someone about their information? Paul couldn't think.

"Sir, sir... right there," the orderly told him, pointing to the desk with the lady waving her hand trying to get his attention.

Getting a hold of himself and snapping out of the numbness, Paul panicked. "She's seven. I can't get her to wake up. She has to be seen now! Please get her to a doctor now!"

"Yes, sir, we will right this moment. Start telling this lady right there any information you can," the orderly said calmly.

At that moment, the two big doors that led to who knew where opened up with a man in a white coat and two nurses in green scrubs.

"Doctor! This is Cassie. She is only seven years old, and I can't wake her up. She didn't want dinner, her mother said. She said she wasn't feeling well. I checked on her after I ate dinner. I couldn't wake her up. She spoke once on the way here; she told me she was hot..." Paul spoke out the helpless words.

The doctor was already listening to Cassie's heartbeat. "Sir, we are going to take your daughter into this emergency room and start checking all her vitals. Please tell the nurse all you can; everything is important. Anything you remember. She has a list of questions for you." Then immediately they wheeled Cassie away.

Paul thought he would collapse on the floor. Cassie looked so small on the stretcher.

Turning, he approached the nurse waiting for him. "Okay, sorry," Paul apologized, taking a deep breath. "It's just that she is my baby girl, my only girl." Then he sat down and put his face into his hands and started to sob.

The nurse was feeling compassion for this poor father but, needing the information he might have, said kindly, "Sir, they are going to give her the best care. I need you to help her now by answering these questions."

That did it. Anything for Cassie now helped Paul focus.

Wiping his face on his shirt, Paul looked up, his face clear. "Yes, please ask away." He would get a hold of himself for Cassie if it killed him.

The nurse proceeded. Paul answered the questions to the best of his knowledge. He knew nothing really. Cassie had told her mother she wasn't feeling well and did not want dinner. Maybe she ate lunch, but he didn't know that either. She had a fever; he knew that well enough.

He felt useless. Swallowing down the sobs, Paul thought his chest would burst.

The nurse left him in the waiting room and went into the back rooms where the emergency rooms were, where Cassie was... Pulling both hands through his hair, Paul wanted to scream. He was thinking, *What is going on? Has Cassie woken up? Is she scared? Does she know what was going on?* As Paul paced the room, he thought he might be sick.

Looking for a restroom, Paul went back up to the front desk wanting someone to know where he was in case they were looking for him. There was another woman up there. The first nurse had not come back out front yet.

"Ma'am, I have to use the restroom. I am Paul Marvin, Cassie Marvin's dad. I just want someone to know where I am," Paul said, his voice slightly shaking.

"Yes, sir. The restroom is right there. I will let them know," the nurse told him with a kind smile, pointing down the hallway to Paul's left.

Once in the restroom, he leaned over the sink and washed his face with cold water. He kept his face in the sink and splashed it for what seemed like forever. The cool water helped him keep his stomach calm. Looking up in the mirror, Paul didn't like what he saw. He looked aged and worn out.

Using the paper towels, Paul dried off. Needing to get back out there, Paul turned off the bathroom light and let the door close behind him. The click echoed in the hallway, the sound reminding Paul how alone he was at the moment.

The waiting room was empty. Paul paced. *Is anyone going to come out here and tell me what is going on?* He needed to know something soon, or he'd go crazy.

Seconds ticked by into minutes. Finally the big steel doors swung open. A nurse with a mask on in green scrubs walked out. "Mr. Marvin?"

"Yes, I'm Paul Marvin."

"Mr. Marvin, the doctor would like to see you. Could you please follow me?"

The nurse in the green scrubs led the way. She took him to a room across the hall from the big room with all the beds lined up, some with pulled curtains around the bed. Cassie was probably behind one of those pulled curtains. The knowledge of that was not making Paul feel any better.

It took forever to walk the twenty to thirty feet to the room where the doctor was to see Paul.

"Can I see Cassie?"

Without turning back to him, the nurse said, "The doctor would like to talk to you first."

Opening the door, the nurse led Paul in. The room was empty except for chairs lining the four walls.

"The doctor will be right in, Mr. Marvin," the nurse assured him.

Fear slumped Paul's shoulders; he had to sit down. Paul had every ceiling tile counted and then counted by threes by the time the doctor came in. One ceiling tile had a chip in the corner, and it kept drawing Paul's attention. The ceiling would be perfect except for the one tile.

*Why did they leave the one tile there with the chip and not put in a good one?* The thought drove Paul crazy. Feeling sick to his stomach, Paul did not know if he was ready to hear what the doctor was going to say.

Looking away from the ceiling and facing the doctor, Paul swallowed and lifted his chin while straightening his shoulders.

"Mr. Marvin, may I call you, Paul?" Dr. Steven Hall asked as he sat down on a chair across from Paul.

Clearing his throat, Paul spoke quietly, "Yes, of course."

Smiling, Dr. Hall said, "Good. Paul, I am Dr. Steven Hall. Of course we spoke quickly in the hallway before admitting your daughter." Reaching his hand across to shake Paul's hand, Dr. Hall continued. "We are running tests on Cassandra, Cassie. She is very weak at this time, and her blood pressure was very low when she arrived here—extremely low; it was a very good thing you got her here, Paul."

Dr. Hall smiled and then got right back to the point of the conversation. "Paul, Cassie has some puncture wounds on the bottom of her right foot. Several of them, in fact, and they are infected. Do you happen to know what caused those punctures? The information may help us."

Paul was dumbfounded. He did not know anything about any puncture wounds. "No, I don't. I didn't even know she had any puncture

wounds..." Paul finished lamely, feeling stupid for not having information about them.

"No? That's not abnormal with children. They are getting cuts or
wounds all the time in their playing, Paul. I do believe she is fighting an
infection from this... blood poisoning. This is very serious. I am sorry,
but you should know. Does she have a family doctor we can get any
information from, her vaccination records?"

He felt even worse now. Why didn't Cassie have a physician over
the course of her life? Paul sadly admitted, "No, Mary, Cassie's mother,
never had a regular doctor for Cassie. Mary doesn't like doctors, and
Cassie's been really healthy..."

"We are going to do what we can. I would like you to see her now.
Her knowing you are here will help her."

"Has she woken up then?"

"No, Paul. Let's get you in there for a few minutes. Do you need to
call her mother perhaps?"

"Ah... no. Mary doesn't like hospitals. She just wanted to wait at
home. I'll call her later on with how Cassie is doing, but thank you."

Standing up on shaky legs, Paul followed Dr. Hall.

# CHAPTER 19

Not realizing things could get worse, Paul was hit hard when he pulled up a chair by the edge of Cassie's hospital bed. The vinyl chair made a crinkling sound when Paul sat down. Cassie was so small and looked so helpless lying there in the bed, which was big enough to swallow her up. Tubes were running out from her tiny arms, and monitors were connected to her, making her look even smaller than she was. Sitting on the edge of the chair, Paul reached for Cassie's hand. The seriousness of the situation crushed in on his chest. He could hardly breathe.

"Cassie, it's Daddy, honey," Paul tried, hoping she could hear him.

Dr. Hall nodded his head at Paul. "Yes, Paul, talk to her for a few minutes. It may help if she hears someone familiar. I will be right back. We are waiting for some results."

Paul looked back at Dr. Hall, having forgotten he was there, and replied, "Thank you, Doctor."

Rubbing his thumb over the back of Cassie's hand, Paul kept talking. "Cassie, Cassie, honey, you have to try and wake up. You need to wake up. I need you, Cassie, to wake up and show Daddy you're okay. You're going to be okay. I love you so much, Cassie, and I am so sorry."

The tears began to flow down his cheeks. He could not control them. "Oh honey, I am so sorry, so sorry. You must wake up, honey. You have to know I am sorry about so many things, Cassie. I should have known you were sick. I should have known you hurt your foot. Cassie, Daddy is here. Daddy loves you, honey. Daddy loves you so very much."

The tears dripped freely down his rough cheeks, splashing onto his shirt. Paul had no idea where they were coming from. He knew he had a reason to cry. The reason was lying on the hospital bed before him. But he didn't know he was capable of this kind of crying—crying that would not stop, crying that was silent, crying that was so quiet in its misery.

· · · · · · · · · ·

Cassie, deep in her fevered dream world, thought she heard her dad's voice. She tried to listen to make sure. She wanted to ask if it was him, but she was too weak to speak. She wanted him to know she was all right. If it was her dad speaking, he sounded worried to her, and she didn't want him to worry. It felt like he was holding her hand. Someone was holding her hand. If only she could wiggle her fingers, that would let him know she was okay and could hear him. No matter how hard she tried, Cassie could not wiggle anything. But it was nice to have someone holding her hand.

· · · · · · · · · ·

Nothing. No movement from Cassie. Just the beeps from the monitors and the drips from the medicine bags hanging from the IV pole were the only sounds in Cassie's hospital room.

Paul did not know what to do. He probably only had a few minutes left with Cassie until the doctor and nurses came back. There was a lot of movement and talking out in the hallway, so sensing his time might be up, Paul hurried to talk some more with Cassie.

"Cassie, Daddy may have to go out in the hallway soon, but I am here. I am close by. I will not leave you, Cassie. Honey, I love you. Please move your hand or blink your eyes, honey, if you can hear me."

Nothing.

"You are such a strong girl, honey; you can beat this. Try really hard and wake up for Daddy. We all love you, honey; everyone loves you. Oh, honey, please wake up for Daddy. Oh, Cassie, baby…"

Paul could not go on. He felt so alone, so helpless, he began choking on his tears. With no movement or sign from Cassie, Paul was feeling very hopeless. Looking around the room, Paul hoped someone would hurry up and get back here to help Cassie.

Only a few minutes had passed since the doctor and nurses left, but Paul felt he had been left alone in Cassie's room for an eternity. And during that eternity Paul felt even worse than the few moments before. He had not been able to do anything for Cassie. She lay still. The stillness of his daughter was torture to Paul. He placed Cassie's hand back down on the side of her bed. Then wiping his hands on his jeans because they were sweating, he got up and started pacing the area near Cassie's bed. He did not have much room to pace, but he couldn't sit any longer. Rubbing his hands over his whiskered face and then through his hair, Paul thought he would go crazy.

Two nurses entered the room. *Finally*, thought Paul. He could not stand to be alone another moment. One nurse began adjusting the drip on the IV, and the other nurse was checking Cassie's pulse.

"Any changes?" Paul dared to ask.

"No, Mr. Marvin. Her pulse is still really low. Some test results should be back soon. The doctor will let you know something soon," the nurse holding Cassie's wrist told him.

She had a kind smile, so the interaction helped Paul a little. He was so low, any dribble of human kindness that came his way was appreciated. He would not wish this situation on his worst enemy. This was bad, and he had never felt so bad.

Paul, not knowing what to say or do, continued to stand near the end of Cassie's hospital bed. The monitors started beeping some different kind of beep than what Paul was used to hearing.

"What is that? What's going on now?" Paul asked in alarm.

Both nurses seemed too busy to answer Paul. Maybe they didn't hear him. The fear crawled back up into Paul's chest. It was going to choke him. He backed up against the wall. He needed something to lean against; he needed to catch his breath. Dr. Hall was in the room now. Paul wondered, *When did he come in?* He hadn't noticed.

Another nurse was taking his arm, saying something to him, but he couldn't make it out. He couldn't hear anything. All the noise was muffled as if he were underwater. The nurse was still talking to him, lightly guiding him out of Cassie's hospital room. Paul let himself be pulled by the nurse. He did not have any strength to stop her. He followed her without a fight like a puppy dog.

The nurse led Paul to a chair and then pushed him into it so he was seated. Her face was kind, and she was still talking to him. He tried to focus on what she was saying. He wished he could surface. He felt a thousand feet under water. He couldn't hear. He couldn't catch a good breath. Opening his mouth, he tried to take in a bigger breath. Maybe that was all that was wrong with him. Maybe he was not getting enough oxygen.

The nurse was explaining, "Mr. Marvin, stay here. I am going to get you some orange juice. Please don't move. I don't think you will be able to stand on your own." Paul decided he needed to listen to her; she probably knew what was best.

When she returned, she was holding a plastic cup full of orange juice and what looked like a turkey sandwich on white bread. The sandwich was wrapped in clear plastic wrap.

"Here, Mr. Marvin, drink up; you need your strength. When was the last time you ate anything? I believe you have low blood sugar, and with the shock of everything, you need to counter all of this and keep your strength up."

Paul tried to remember when he last ate. "I had dinner. What time is it? I don't know the time. I don't know how long we have been here. Cassie didn't get to eat dinner." At the mention of Cassie, Paul's face crumbled. He could not hold it together.

"Mr. Marvin, I understand. Do you think you could take a few bites of this sandwich for me? It would greatly help you." The nurse named Beth, Paul knew from her name tag, stood before him opening up the turkey sandwich from its plastic wrapper. "If you take little bites, you will be able to keep it down. For your daughter's sake, we need you to be strong."

Paul, looking up into Beth's kind eyes, knew she was telling the truth. He replied with honesty, "I don't think I can eat, but thank you for the orange juice, really."

"Just a few bites. I need you to try. You could hardly stand in there," Beth said as she passed half of the turkey sandwich to Paul.

Paul reached for the sandwich and did as he was asked, hoping he could keep the food down. The sandwich actually tasted good, as if it was just what he needed. Did his body really need food right now for strength? Paul wondered how he could eat at all.

. . . . . . . . . . .

Dr. Hall was lightly shaking Paul's shoulder. "Paul, Paul, wake up…"

Paul did not remember falling asleep. He had finished the turkey sandwich the nurse had fed to him. He had ended up eating the whole sandwich. The nurse, Beth had stood there and talked to him while he ate. He remembered leaning his head back against the wall listening to Beth. He must have fallen asleep. Her voice must have relaxed him. Something she was probably hoping to do. Beth must have known he needed to relax. He was at the edge of pure craziness.

Waking up quickly startled Paul. He mumbled in disbelief, "I… I don't know how I fell asleep. I am sorry. Cassie… How is Cassie? Is she up? Does she need me?"

"Paul, Cassie… Cassie is gone, Paul. I am so sorry. She… she was too weak to fight the infection."

Dr. Hall waited. That was enough information to take in for anyone at the moment. He had learned that families, when suffering a loss, could only take in so much. Too much information overwhelmed them. Learning of their loss was enough. The questions would come later, after the shock. The whys would come, the questions of how could this happen would come. Dr. Steven Hall knew it well and hated it.

Paul paled. He could only stare at Dr. Hall. The emotions Paul was feeling were changing as every second ticked by. Shock, fear that what he'd just heard was true, and then panic that it was. When Dr. Hall reached out to hold Paul's hand, he did not say a word; he just waited. Paul held on to Dr. Hall's hand like it was a lifeline. He was slipping, drowning again. Bewilderment settled over Paul, and then grief slipped its cloudiness over his eyes.

Paul blinked. The contact broke. Paul crumbled as the helplessness hit him. The dam burst forth, and Paul wept like a baby. *Cassie is gone! Oh my God! Cassie is gone!* Paul's thoughts shouted again and again. He thought his head would burst. "My God, my God… I wasn't with her," came the whispered cry.

Dr. Hall stayed with Paul. Several nurses walked by in case the weeping man needed anything. Dr. Hall nodded his thanks and held unto Paul's hand.

Dr. Hall pushed a few tissues into Paul's hand. Paul's slight movement of his fingers showed he knew they were there. Dr. Hall waited. Paul was alone. And no man should be left alone after he just lost his daughter. No matter how long it took, Dr. Hall would wait with Paul while he grieved.

Paul finally lifted his head. The defeated look of acceptance was in his eyes. Taking swipes at his face with the sleeve of his shirt, he cleared the tears from his throat.

"Can I see her, Dr. Hall, before… before I leave?" Paul cleared his throat again, thinking the tears would choke him. He didn't want to say, "Before you take her."

Dr. Hall patted him on the arm and offered immediately, "Of course. Paul, she never woke back up. I don't believe she suffered. She was peaceful, like she was sleeping." Dr. Hall stopped and blinked back the tears threatening to spill. Clearing his throat, he went on. "Paul, I am sorry. I am so sorry for your loss."

Paul, wiping at his tears again, had to ask, "Was it an infection then? Just an infection could do this? Nothing could be done? There's no medicine that could have helped her?" There was no blame in Paul's voice. He just needed to know the answers to these questions.

Dr. Hall answered quietly, "Yes. Cassie was suffering from blood poisoning, an infection. There are medicines to help in these situations if caught in time but not always. And of course nothing is a guarantee. Cassie's body was fighting a fight too big for her. It weakened her. Her blood pressure was extremely low when she got here. Her fever was very high for a little one. She had a lot against her. There is no answer to why,

Paul. All I have is a few hows—how this could happen." Shrugging his shoulders in helplessness, Dr. Hall felt the weight of the world on his shoulders.

"I was out here sleeping..." Regret piled on Paul's shoulders, the regret in his voice.

"Paul, there was no time to wake you. All her vitals just dropped..." Not wanting to say more, Dr. Hall believed this poor father had heard enough. "One more thing, Paul... You could not have known this; no one is to blame here. There are so few signs until it can be too late. Unless Cassie had complained, you would not have known she injured her foot, which I do believe caused the infection. Children have high pain tolerances, and they sometimes don't complain about anything being wrong. Believe me, Paul. I have done many emergency surgeries on burst appendixes. The children of most of them never complained of pain, to their parents' grief."

Paul, knowing Dr. Hall was trying to help him, said, "Thank you. I hope what you just said will help me one day, Doc, but right now, well... right now I don't know..."

"Come, Paul, you can have a few minutes."

Paul, not knowing if he could handle this, had to see Cassie. He had to! He asked Dr. Hall, "Could you stay with me? I am sorry. I need to see her, but I don't really know if—"

Dr. Hall interrupted him, "I will be with you, Paul. This is all understandable. Don't worry. I'll stay with you."

Once they entered Cassie's room, Paul looked at his little girl and felt such loss that he thought his heart was being ripped right out of his chest. Cassie looked like she was sleeping. Her expression was peaceful. Paul turned quickly back to Dr. Hall. The question he wanted to ask was apparent on his face.

Dr. Hall replied instantly, "I know, Paul. I know. She looks fine. She seems so at peace. I do believe she is. I do believe she didn't suffer." Hoping to comfort with those words, Dr. Hall fell silent.

Looking down at Cassie, Paul could not believe she was gone. But she was, and he needed to say good-bye. He had so many regrets. He did not want to regret his last moments with her.

# CHAPTER 20

It was a lonely road home. In the early morning hours, there were very few vehicles on the road. Paul thought he'd never make it. His mind was spinning a million miles an hour. *What am I going to say to Mary? How do you tell someone news like this?* He was making a list of the people he had to call. They would have to make funeral plans. Funeral plans…

The tears started to flow. The shock would come and then wear off again as certain thoughts formed in his mind. *Funeral plans… oh my God! How do we go about making funeral plans?* Paul thoughts shouted at him.

*Elizabeth—we will have to call Elizabeth. Poor Elizabeth!* The thought made Paul's head hurt worse than it already did. He didn't want to go there. The sting felt real. He should have put his foot down and told Mary Elizabeth should have visited more. For that matter, he should have insisted they travel north more. Mary didn't want to see her family, Mary had won. Guilt washed over him again; it was too late to change anything now. He would never have a chance again to make a difference in Cassie's life.

Pulling up out front of the house, Paul thought he would have to drag one leg at a time to get into the house. The sun was coming up in a clear sky. It was going to be a beautiful day, but all was grim to Paul. He had the challenge of his life before him.

Paul went into the kitchen and started to make coffee. He needed something to do. He needed help, and black coffee seemed like the answer. Looking at the clock, Mary would be up soon. He would have woken her up, but he needed these few minutes. He also could not walk down the hallway right now and see Cassie's room. No, he needed a few minutes.

Sitting at the kitchen table, Paul waited for Mary to come out to the kitchen. He had heard the alarm clock go off a few minutes ago. She'd be up any time now.

Mary wondered what was going on when she saw Paul. She could tell he'd never come to bed. He was just sitting there at the kitchen table holding his coffee mug with both hands.

"What are you doing Paul? Did you sleep on the couch?"

Paul could not believe she did not ask about Cassie. *Did she forget Cassie was sick last night? Does she think Cassie was safe in bed sleeping?* "No, Mary, I did not sleep on the couch. I just got home from the hospital—"

Mary interrupted him. "Well, that took a long time. My God, it took all night for someone to look at Cassie?"

*She doesn't have a clue*, Paul thought. If Mary had taken a good look at Paul, she would have figured something was up. He looked awful, worn beyond worn.

"Mary, Cassie is gone." He waited for that to sink in.

Mary was adding sugar to her coffee. Not looking up, she asked, "Gone where, Paul?"

"Mary, look at me. I mean she is gone. She died, Mary." Paul didn't think he could go on. "She had blood poisoning from some punctures on her foot. They were infected. She didn't make it. The infection was throughout her body." Gripping his coffee mug tightly, Paul tried to relax his hands. He watched for some reaction.

Mary tried to work the news just told to her through her brain. She looked to be in shock, Paul waited. Was she going to blame him? What was she thinking? Paul could not tell. He needed a reaction. *Do something!* He thought. Mary was speechless.

"Died? She died?"

"Yeah, Mary, she never woke back up after we got to the hospital. It was awful, Mary. I still can't believe it. She looked so peaceful, like nothing was wrong. She just lay there like she was sleeping; then she was gone. Her blood pressure just dropped off..." Paul covered his face with his hands. "What are we going to do?" he whispered.

Mary had already left the kitchen and went back into their bedroom. She never heard the rest of what Paul said.

. . . . . . . . . .

Paul was not shocked by Mary's reaction. He didn't really know how she should have reacted. How does someone react when they find out they just lost their daughter or any other loved one for that matter. It looked to Paul like he was going to have to handle this all on his own. He needed to call Elizabeth. Elizabeth would know what to do.

*God, help Elizabeth,* Paul prayed absentmindedly. Grabbing the phonebook, Paul dialed Elizabeth's number.

When Elizabeth answered the phone, Paul felt relief for the first time in hours. Paul groaned out the news. Elizabeth was catching the first flight out. Paul would be picking her up at the airport later that afternoon. She would be there by dinnertime. Elizabeth comforted Paul even in the depths of her own loss. The cut through her heart was deep. It had taken her several tries to speak so he could understand her. But it didn't matter to Paul how long it took; he was crying too. Paul lay down on the couch when he got off the phone. Elizabeth was coming. He had someone to help, and he was on the verge of collapse.

Elizabeth mustered up the strength for Cassie. Cassie needed her now. Cassie needed to be put to rest in a proper way. Elizabeth did not know how she kept breathing. But she would take it one breath at a time. The squeezing around her heart was so painful; every breath was an effort.

After hanging up the phone with Paul, she fell to her knees, not able to hold herself up. Elizabeth covered her own mouth as to not let her scream escape. What came out was a muffled moan, a moan from the depths of her soul. Much later, a spent Elizabeth pushed herself back up from the floor.

She needed to pack. She needed to call her sons. Elizabeth would have liked to talk to Mary, but Paul said she was in the bedroom. Paul told Elizabeth she'd walked in there after being told and there was not another word from her. Better to leave Mary alone and just get there, Paul thought, and Elizabeth had to agree.

. . . . . . . . . .

Paul parked his truck in the airport parking lot. He was early, he decided to wait for a few minutes in his truck before walking in and meeting Elizabeth. Having something to do helped Paul. After his short nap on the couch from pure exhaustion, he made phone calls to work and a few friends, asking them to let others know of their loss. He then walked to the Stockards' home next door and told Barbara Stockard the news. The children were in their rooms, Paul had a private moment to talk to Barbara.

Barbara opened the door with, "Well, good morning, Paul. Is everything okay?"

"Barbara." Paul nodded at her greeting. "I have some really bad news, Barbara. Cassie... Cassie died early this morning at the hospital." Paul rambled on as Barbara's face crumbled, tears pouring down her face. "She had an infection, blood poisoning the doctor said. I took her early last night. We didn't know... We didn't know... she had some punctures on the bottom of her foot. I didn't even know about the punctures to her foot. She must have stepped on something. She was gone early this morning." Paul choked on tears. Clearing his voice, he tried to get control again. "You've been so kind to her. I know... she liked it over here. The kids were friends... I, I just wanted you to know." Paul wiped at his running nose.

Gripping the door jam for dear life, Barbara let the tears flow. "Dear God, I am so sorry, Paul, so sorry. We loved Cassie like she was one of our own, my sweet Jesus! How am I going to tell the children? This is breaking my heart... Paul, if you need anything, please let me help.

Could I help you by letting the neighbors and Cassie's school know?"
Barbara suggested.

Paul felt gratitude for the first time in a long time sweep over him.
"Yes, Barbara, that would help me... and Mary so much. I'm afraid I
don't know what all to do. Elizabeth, Mary's mother, is flying in this
afternoon. She is going tomorrow with me, us, to the funeral home.
There is so much to think of. Yes, anything you can think of I would
appreciate. Mary is taking this hard; she has hardly spoken since I told
her. Uh, she didn't know. She stayed home thinking this wasn't serious.
If she had known, I am sure she would have come with us to the hospital. Mary doesn't like hospitals. I can hardly blame her now."

Barbara Stockard closed the door and walked in shock to the kitchen
table. She sat there crying, staring straight ahead. She tried not to ask
why. She did not want to ask why.

That was where Larissa and Samuel found her. Her face was red
from crying; her beautiful eyes were swollen. They both knew something
was really wrong. When their mother told them the news, she tried to
be strong but choked out the words with tears. Both of the children
held on to each other and could not let go. Barbara lowered herself to
the floor so she could hold her children. They stayed there for most of
the morning just holding each other through each spasm of tears. Their
Cassie was gone. And she was *their Cassie*, their friend.

. . . . . . . . . .

What a day. Paul could only go over the day again and again. Everything
kept playing back like a bad dream. He hoped someone would wake him
up and tell him this was only a dream, that Cassie was fine and at home.

Elizabeth's plane was coming in on time. He'd called the airport a
few hours ago to double-check. He walked to her terminal; any moment
her plane would be landing. He came alone. Mary did not want to come
to the airport to pick up her mother. She knew Elizabeth was coming.
When Paul told Mary, she hadn't said a word; she'd just nodded. She
stayed in the bedroom most of the day. She had called work in the early
morning hours letting them know about Cassie.

Paul stood, looking out at the planes taking off and landing. He wished he was on one taking off. Where he would go, he did not know, but any place would be better than where he was. There were people walking everywhere around him, but he was alone... so alone.

Seeing Elizabeth made Paul smile. How he could smile at a time like this was amazing to him, but he smiled. "Elizabeth!" Paul almost shouted, relieved she was there.

Paul's parents had both died very young—his mother from cancer, and his father had a stroke when Paul was just a teenager. Elizabeth was really the only other family he had, and he was very glad he had her; he needed her. Cassie had needed her too. The guilt washed over him again. He should have done things differently by Cassie. He should have stood up to Mary.

Arriving in Tipton was terrible for Elizabeth. Seeing Paul reassured her she was here for a purpose, for Cassie and her parents.

"Paul, oh Paul, I wish I was here for so many other reasons. I still can't believe our Cassie is not with us anymore." Elizabeth hugged him tightly. Paul was so grateful. He had needed someone to hug him.

"I pray I can make it, Paul. My heart is torn in two. How are you and Mary holding up? You can't be any better off."

"I feel the same way. I don't know if we are going to make it. I don't think Mary and I are strong people, Elizabeth. But you're strong, Elizabeth, stronger than you think. I am ashamed to say it, but we need you here. I am... well, I don't really know what to do to be honest," Paul explained, hoping Elizabeth understood his weakness.

Elizabeth understood. Shaking her head and patting Paul on the arm, she told him, "Don't be ashamed, Paul. We will work this all out together, and we need each other, Paul. Now let's get going; there are plans to be made."

Maybe helping Mary and Paul with the funeral plans would help Elizabeth get through the next few days. Elizabeth could only hope. Mary's brothers were coming. They were driving their families down. They should be arriving late the next evening. Elizabeth felt sick to her stomach for all she had to face in the next few days.

# CHAPTER 21

Barbara had just left Suzanne's house. Suzanne Vashon was beyond grief from what she was just told. *How can Cassie be dead? How can she be gone? My God, my God!* Her thoughts did not want to believe the truth. Suzanne knew it to be true by the poor shape Barbara was in when she came to tell her. But... how? How? Her heart begged to understand. Sitting at her kitchen table, she let the tears flow. They shook her body to the core. Her heart was breaking and pouring itself out onto the kitchen table. It was more than Suzanne could bear. Her dear sweet Cassie gone. It just did not seem possible.

Suzanne thought back to her last visit with Cassie. It was probably one of their best times together. Cassie never said anything about her foot hurting her. Cassie did seem troubled the day she came to visit. Suzanne had thought something was bothering her. Cassie had seemed so relieved to get to the garden that day. Though her expressions had been so happy at times and Cassie showed so much love that day, Suzanne was feeling confused as she looked back over that day. Cassie was melancholy and that had troubled Suzanne. Suzanne wished now she had dug deeper, asked more questions. Maybe she would have found out something important.

Much later, Suzanne, weak from praying and crying, looked out to the garden. Her eyes seemed to be playing tricks on her. Like a vision before her, Cassie was dancing around the garden with the water hose. She was twirling and spinning, spraying the water over her and the flower garden. The smile on Cassie's face pierced her heart with love and peace. Suzanne did not want to blink for fear the vision would go away. The water fell in a transparent wall around Cassie. She danced and twirled inside the surrounding wall of water. Looking through the water, Suzanne could still see Cassie. She was a beautiful sight to see!

Opening the back door, Suzanne stepped out onto the back porch, hoping what she was seeing was true. Could Cassie be there? Could she be all right? The vision sparkled like diamonds; light reflected off each droplet of water. Cassie looked like an angel. As Suzanne slowly walked toward her vision, Cassie turned and looked at her. Both Cassie and Suzanne looked shocked they could see each other. Cassie's shocked look made Suzanne look shocked. Did Cassie see her? Suzanne asked, she could not stop herself, "Are... are you all right, Cassie?" Suzanne reached out to touch what she saw.

Cassie replied, surprised, "Yes, yes I am fine." The shocked look so apparent on her face said that she was surprised at being able to answer Mrs. Vashon and more surprised she had heard her question.

*Was this real? Could she really see Cassie? Did Cassie really just answer her question?* As they reached for each other, Suzanne's vision started to disappear. It was fading. Then Cassie was gone.

Suzanne looked around her, and she was standing in the flower garden all alone. She didn't feel alone though. An overwhelming peace engulfed her. Goosebumps were raised all over her body. She clutched at her chest and closed her eyes. She knew she'd just seen Cassie! Cassie was all right! Cassie was being taken care of. God must have given Suzanne the vision to help her. He gave her this gift in her time of grief. Maybe she could help the others. Overwhelmed, she knew what she had to do. The idea was excellent! She better get busy; she didn't have much time. She wanted to be able to share the idea with the neighbors and hopefully Cassie's family while they were still in town for the funeral. This would help! She believed this would help them all with their loss. Suzanne never wanted to forget the special moment that was just given her; it was for a reason. The energy surging through her for the task at hand helped her forget the pain that just a few minutes ago was twisting her insides. Suzanne did not doubt for one minute what had just transpired in the garden.

. . . . . . . . . .

Mary, Paul, and Elizabeth had just gotten back to the house after the grueling morning making the plans for Cassie's funeral. Her funeral was to be held in two days with visitation starting at eleven the next morning. They had stopped in town for a new dress for Cassie. Elizabeth had insisted. Elizabeth had picked out a white dress with flowers all over the print in the fabric. The flowers were yellow, blue, and pink with small green leaves. There was a pink satin sash at the waistband.

Mary picked up a new blouse and blue dress slacks. Paul bought a white dress shirt and brown slacks while they were shopping. Elizabeth insisted they look good for Cassie. Everything was for Cassie. No one argued with her, which was a miracle, and especially from Mary. For once, Mary kept her mouth shut. They had dropped off the items for Cassie at the funeral home before leaving town, which was one of the hardest things Elizabeth had ever done in her life. It was a quiet drive back to the house for all of them.

Mary stayed outside smoking a cigarette while Elizabeth and Paul made sandwiches. No one wanted to eat, but Elizabeth and Paul went through the motions of preparing the food anyway.

The evening before, Elizabeth stayed in Cassie's room for hours. She wasn't being nosy. She had just needed to touch Cassie somehow. Cassie's personality was everywhere, from her drawings to her stashes of precious things to her. Cassie had kept everything. All her things were tucked away neatly, some hidden in boxes or hidden under her clothes in her dresser drawers. Everything Elizabeth had ever remembered giving Cassie was in Cassie's bedroom. Cassie had stacks of finished pictures she had drawn and colored. Most were labeled to her grandmother, Elizabeth. After going through Cassie's things, Elizabeth sat on Cassie's bed to breathe her in and cried.

Mary came in from the yard and sat down at the kitchen table. Paul and Elizabeth were sitting there trying to eat their sandwiches.

"Could you do me a favor, Mom? Could you pack up Cassie's things before you leave?"

Shocked by the request, both Paul and Elizabeth looked up with surprise. Paul responded first, "What is the hurry, Mary?" He was disgusted. Couldn't they have some time to get used to this?

Mary ignored Paul. "Mom, will you do that for me?" Then looking at Paul, she added, "Not right now, Paul, but before she goes back home."

Looking back at her mother, she asked, "Will you? Will you do that for me?"

Mary looked very vulnerable. And she never looked vulnerable. Mary did not want the job of going through Cassie's room. For some reason that she could not put her finger on, she did not want to go in there. With Cassie dying, her room somehow scared Mary now. Mary would never admit it, but she felt nervous just thinking about going into the room.

"Of course, Mary. I don't know how long I am staying, but yes, I will take care of that for you before I go." Neither Elizabeth nor Paul had ever seen Mary like this. What did it mean?

"Thanks. I just know I'll never be able to do it," she admitted.

Wanting to stay on neutral ground, Paul wisely did not say another word. The last thing he wanted, was to have all Cassie's things removed as if she were never there. And already Mary was talking about it—Paul could not believe it!

Finishing their lunch was all they could tackle at the moment. Mary reached for her sandwich. Chewing and swallowing took a lot of effort for the three of them. The sandwiches were tasteless and went down like lead. But there they sat quiet, alone in their own thoughts.

Elizabeth went for a walk around the block. A connection to Cassie was what she needed and wanted. Elizabeth still had a hard time believing it was over two years since she had seen Cassie. The seven-year-old they had to bury in the next few days she was sure she would not recognize. Mary never sent pictures, it was always a guess to what Cassie may look like as she grew up. It saddened Elizabeth to the core that she was now in Tipton and Cassie was gone. Why did she ever let so much time go by? Why did she just not come visit? It was too late for those thoughts now, but they would haunt her forever. So many mistakes. *If only I'd known the future*, Elizabeth thought.

A few of the neighbors remembered Elizabeth from her last trip to Tipton. They spoke their condolences to her from their front yards. Elizabeth walked up the street to where she believed Mrs. Vashon's garden was. She knew when she found it. The yard was the greenest and most beautiful yard in the entire area. The summer heat had made most of the lawns look like golden wheat, but everything was green and very much alive in this particular garden.

The garden angel that Cassie had described was there. Cassie had done a wonderful job describing the garden. Elizabeth felt like she had been there many times.

The sun came through the mature trees, causing a stained-glass effect over the garden. It truly was a special place. No wonder Cassie had loved it there.

Elizabeth knocked on the back door hoping to introduce herself to Mrs. Vashon, but no one was home. Elizabeth wondered how Mrs. Vashon was doing. From everything Cassie had told her, she had had a friend in Mrs. Vashon. Elizabeth was sure everyone who knew Cassie was suffering from the loss of Cassie's death.

Elizabeth continued on her walk. When she was at the corner of Mary and Paul's street, Barbara Stockard came out to say hello.

"Hello, Elizabeth! It has been a long time. Could you come in for a cup of coffee?" Barbara wanted to spend some time with Elizabeth and did not know how long she'd be in town, so she jumped at a chance when she saw her walking down the street.

Elizabeth was so happy to see a familiar face. "I would love to, Barbara, and yes, it has been too long." Her eyes filling with tears, Elizabeth followed Barbara into the kitchen.

The coffee had been delicious, but being able to talk about Cassie was better. Barbara shared several stories with Elizabeth. They laughed; they cried. The experience was the start to a healing balm in Elizabeth's soul. Her granddaughter had been loved by so many people. Her granddaughter had been a wonderful person. The stories from Barbara's children told Elizabeth that Cassie had been a good friend, a true friend. Larissa had sat on her mother's lap and shared many funny stories about some of her times with Cassie. At one point, Larissa buried her head in her mother's neck and cried. She shook like a reed in the wind.

Lifting her head, Larissa told Elizabeth, looking right into her eyes with such conviction Elizabeth knew she meant it and knowing the statement would always be true to Larissa, "Mrs. Lauren, Cassie is and always will be my best friend. She was the best friend anyone could ever have had. I loved her, and she loved us. She really loved us." The tears began to flow again. Larissa sobbed into her mother's neck.

Barbara smiled at Elizabeth as she comforted Larissa. "We loved her. We all were really blessed to have her, weren't we?" Barbara asked as she patted Larissa's back, hoping to help her focus on a better thought. The question helped. It put a smile on each of their faces.

"Yes, Momma, I was," Larissa answered.

"Yes, Barbara, we were blessed," Elizabeth agreed. The tears were still there, but along with them was a smile. It was helpful to be reminded of the good in something.

. . . . . . . . . . .

The evening wore on for Paul. He thought he would go stir crazy. He drank a few beers and wandered around the house. A few of the neighbors stopped by in the evening with homemade casseroles and their condolences; stepping foot into the yard was the first for many of them. A death in a family changed things. The neighbors sent their kindness. Paul and Elizabeth received each of them and were so thankful for their kindness. They would have dinner for many days, which was such a help. Elizabeth had not thought of dinner, nor had anyone else. Some of the men who worked with Paul stopped by and talked with Paul on the front porch. The telephone rang all day. Elizabeth handled all the telephone calls. Cassie's teacher called. The florist called needing to know the details. The town was abuzz with the news of Cassie's death.

Who knew what was going on with Mary? She just stayed in the bedroom or sat on the back porch when she wanted a cigarette. She took a few phones calls from friends but for the most part stayed to herself. She wasn't saying much, and if she heard Paul and Elizabeth talking, she didn't add anything.

Mary walked through the kitchen, passed Elizabeth, and went out the back door without saying a word. Elizabeth knew Mary did not smoke outside to protect the house. Smoking outside was what Mary's father, Roy, had always done. Elizabeth wouldn't let him smoke in the house because of the children, and she didn't want the paint yellowed from the smoke. Roy Lauren had always enjoyed his cigarette smoking from the back porch. Watching Mary out there from the kitchen table made Elizabeth's heart break.

*So like her father… or is she? Is Mary like she is because she is like Roy, or is she like this due to him leaving her? Did she pick up his habits to have a little of her father around?*

Elizabeth had gotten over Roy a very long time ago, but she did not think Mary ever had. It was a shame how history repeated itself. If only Mary had realized what she was doing to Cassie. She might not have left Cassie like Roy had left her, but how she had treated Cassie was worse. Mary was there, and Cassie still never had her.

Cassie would never know the real reason why she was not treated properly by her mother. *It was never Cassie, never Cassie!* Elizabeth's thoughts screamed. Mary had been incapable of loving her. Mary was tangled in the web of her past. She was so blinded by her hurt, her anger. Mary did not see she was doing the very same thing to the people who loved her.

The telephone rang, and it was Mark calling from their hotel. The boys and their families had arrived. They were staying in Boonville at a hotel there. Not more than nineteen miles away, Mark told Elizabeth. They needed the rooms to accommodate their family. It was better that way. Mary had not seen her brothers in years. There was also no way they could put up all the children and the adults at Paul and Mary's home. Each of the boys had three children. Roy Jr. and his wife, Karen, had two boys and a girl. Mark and his wife, Amy, had twin girls and a boy.

Both of the brothers were very nervous about seeing Mary. They wanted to do whatever would be best for their mother and the situation. Mark's first questions had been about his mother's welfare. It was a relief to him his mother had had no problems with Mary. Losing her granddaughter had taken a toll on her. Trouble with Mary would just make a tragic situation worse.

The boys knew their mother loved their children, and she was a wonderful grandmother to them, but they also knew Elizabeth loved and missed Cassie dearly. The place in her heart for Cassie was a special place; no one could fill it. The knowledge of that never bothered the boys; they were always glad their niece had a great grandmother. Their wish had always been for the cousins to be close. That their children never had a chance to know Cassie was a hard pill to swallow.

"Let's meet at the funeral home tomorrow. It will be a long day, but at the afternoon dinner break, we can have dinner here together at Mary's. There is so much food here. I will have the house ready for us, and the children can play in the backyard for a while. I think it will be all right, Mark. Mary has been really quiet. We won't have much time before we have to be back for the evening visitation, a quick visit here should be fine. Oh... and the funeral is at ten the next morning." Elizabeth said the last words because she had too, but she hated saying them.

"Do you know how to get there?" Elizabeth wondered.

"Yes, Roy called and got directions; looks easy to find." Sighing into the phone, Mark added, sounding very tired, "Well, Mom, we will see you then. Love you."

"Love you too, honey. Please tell everyone hello from me, and I am glad you're here, Mark," Elizabeth replied.

"Night, Mom."

"Good night, Mark."

Hanging up the telephone, Elizabeth wanted a hot bath and then bed. She was beyond exhaustion. She had changed the sheets on Cassie's bed earlier and washed some of the clothes in the dirty basket. It had given her something to do. Cassie's bed had still been unmade from when Paul had carried her out. Elizabeth wanted to put Cassie's room back together. Cassie had always made her bed; Elizabeth wanted it made up clean and nice. Elizabeth knew Cassie would never sleep there again, but in her memory, Elizabeth wanted to keep things as they would have been had she still been there even for a little while.

Elizabeth would sleep in Cassie's room. At first she thought she would sleep on the couch and not disrupt Cassie's room, but Elizabeth knew Cassie would want her to sleep in her room.

# CHAPTER 22

The visitation at the funeral home was packed with the people of Tipton. It seemed like everyone who lived in the town of Tipton had come out to pay their respects to the Marvin family.

Cassie looked like she was sleeping in the casket, like a dressed-up doll in the pretty new dress. The funeral home had done a good job with her hair and dress. Cassie looked like nothing was wrong. *Maybe death did not steal her away*, was the thought of many who looked at her. They had folded her hands over one of her favorite dolls, which Elizabeth brought for them. She looked like a beautiful angel sleeping. It broke many hearts. Seeing her lying there was almost too hard to bear for many who knew her.

Paul, Mary, and Elizabeth stood to the left of the casket, which was surrounded by bouquets of flowers. Stuffed animals were set on the floor near her casket. The top of her casket had a blanket of every pink flower imaginable. The sash had *Our Daughter* written on it. The blanket of beautiful flowers and a big, pink teddy bear sitting on top was from Elizabeth. She wanted the best for her granddaughter. There were no pictures of her life, but her memory was living on in the hearts of the people who knew her. Paul, Mary, and Elizabeth shook every hand that was stretched out to them. Mary looked to the ground for the most part. Eye contact was not comfortable for her, but she greeted every person who came out for her daughter. Paul and Elizabeth thanked everyone. Roy Jr. and Mark introduced themselves and helped guide people through. The guest book was filling up. The florist in town was very busy with the continual runs over to the funeral home.

Mrs. Stockard brought the children, Samuel and Larissa. They both wanted to be at every visitation and the funeral tomorrow. Larissa told her mother that she needed to be with Cassie as much as she could. "Mom, I need to be there. I don't want Cassie to be alone."

Barbara asked her, "You know Cassie isn't really here anymore, don't you?"

"Yes, Mom, I know she's in heaven. But as long as I can still see her, I want to be around her. I guess I don't want to be alone or without her yet either."

Mrs. Vashon introduced herself to Elizabeth. Reaching for her hand, she spoke, "You must be Cassie's grandmother."

Elizabeth smiled knowingly. "And you must be Mrs. Vashon, the lady who owns the garden." They held each other's hand for a moment before either could talk.

"Yes, I am Suzanne. I am so sorry for your loss, Elizabeth, so sorry. Words could never say," Suzanne said, still holding Elizabeth's hand.

Elizabeth felt love for this woman, this wonderful woman who became a grandmother to her granddaughter. "Suzanne, thank you. And I am so sorry for your loss. I do believe you lost a granddaughter just as I did. Cassie talked of you often."

With those words spoken, Suzanne reached out and hugged Elizabeth with all her might. Elizabeth hugged back, sharing their love for Cassie. After a few moments, Suzanne opened her purse to take out a few tissues.

Passing one to Elizabeth, she said, "Thank you, Elizabeth, those were such comforting words. Not to take any more of your time, there are so many visitors, but I was hoping you could come to the garden this Saturday, say around one in the afternoon? I am inviting a few people who were close to Cassie for something special I want to show everyone. Could you and your family be there?"

"Yes, we would love to. I will let everyone know, and we will be there. Thank you. Thank you again," Elizabeth confirmed, wondering what it was Suzanne wanted to show them in the garden. *Something special, I am sure*, thought Elizabeth.

The crowds kept coming, mothers bringing children around Cassie's age. They must have been children who went to school with Cassie. The principal and several teachers paid their respects. Owners of the stores downtown took turns coming. A few of them were actually closing their stores during the funeral tomorrow so they could attend.

The kind words about Cassie continued to be said. Fun stories were told. Friends cried and then laughed when they remembered something together about Cassie.

Paul, watching the room and hearing some of the stories, realized there was so much more about his daughter he did not know. While he was at work or out drinking with his buddies, his little girl had a life. She was well liked, and she must have kept busy without Mary or him for all of these people to have known her, and she was only seven.

Mary was quiet and reserved.

The funeral home scheduled a three-hour break for dinner. The family left to rest back at Paul and Mary's home. Once at the house, Paul and Elizabeth started warming up some of the casserole meals that were sent over by the neighbors. It was nice for Elizabeth with Roy Jr. and Mark in the house. Their wives took the children outside to the backyard. They were running off some of their energy. Mary was out back by the porch having her first cigarette in quite a while. Everyone left Mary to herself. That was always the way she liked it, and by her quiet behavior, she seemed to be on a rocky boat, and no one wanted to tip it one way or the other.

Elizabeth had picked up paper plates at the grocery store, the good thick ones. *No sense in doing dishes*, she thought. She wanted everything easy. Easy was good. Paul was a help. He stayed by Elizabeth knowing she would show him what to do because he really did not know what to do. He was lost.

"This all looks good, Elizabeth. I wish I was hungry," Paul stated as he looked over the dishes that were prepared for them.

"I know, Paul, but let's gather everyone up. We have to eat."

Leaning out the back door, Elizabeth called to everyone who was outside. Roy, Mark, and Mary were standing in the driveway talking. The girls had the children playing a game in the backyard.

"All right, gang, come on in and eat; it's ready."

Then to her children, Elizabeth said, "It sure is nice to see the three of you together; it has been a long time." She laughed. "Sure makes me feel old; you all are so grown up!"

"Mom, you're not old, and you look really good for your age!" Roy laughed back at his mother. It was nice to hear her laugh.

"Yeah, Mom, you look good," Mary agreed, looking up at her mother.

Elizabeth loved hearing something nice from Mary; it had been so long. She laughed, wanting to keep it light, "Well, whatever it is you two may want with those compliments, forget it. Come on in now and eat; mother's orders."

"I love when she orders us around." Mark laughed. Standing at six two, he was way too big for his mother to order around.

Another rare moment for Mary, she admitted, "You know, I've kind of missed her ordering me around."

Both brothers laughed right out loud at that. "What? Mary, you never let anyone order you around and especially Mom!" Mark said.

Knowing what he said was the truth, Mary laughed at her own comment. "Yeah, poor Mom. I guess I never did let her. But I remember her trying; at least she tried."

Roy and Mark shared a look. That was probably the nicest honest moment they had with their sister in years. Reaching up and opening the back door, Roy smiled and said, "Well, let's get some dinner and at least let Mom think she can still order all of us around."

Mary followed them in and got in line for the food along with everyone else. Her behavior was so different it started worrying Elizabeth. This Mary was not normal. Was she going to crack right before them all?

. . . . . . . . . .

The evening visitation was like the earlier one: busy. Cassie's family was so impressed at how many people came out and paid their respects. Cassie's second grade teacher asked to say something at her funeral the next morning. Barbara Stockard asked to read a poem. The minister from the Stockards' church asked to say a word or two from the Bible. He felt he knew Cassie. Samuel and Larissa had shared many stories with him that included Cassie. The flowers kept coming; more stuffed animals were delivered. Looking at all the flowers surrounding Cassie, it would not be a surprise if the whole town of Tipton had run out of flowers.

Roy and Mark took their families back to their hotels. It had been a long day. Seeing the niece they missed growing up in her casket took its toll on all of them. What could anyone say? Time goes so fast? It's too bad we didn't visit more often? Their wives had a lot of questions. The kids wondered why they hadn't known their cousin Cassie. There were no answers to their questions. Who understood why families do what they do? Roy and Mark both came up empty when trying to answer their family's questions.

. . . . . . . . . . .

The next morning came quickly. The sun seemed to be in a hurry to rise in the morning. It was a beautiful day. For August, it was not too hot—around eighty degrees and no humidity. The funeral for Cassie was on this day. They all truly had to say good-bye to Cassie. It seemed like a dream, and someone would wake them all up and tell them it was a bad joke. Paul and Mary walked around like they were in a bad dream; they were disoriented. Elizabeth knew she was awake. Her granddaughter was going to be laid to rest. She prayed they made it through the day.

Mary walked in the kitchen. She had been the last to get ready that morning. Paul and Elizabeth were already sitting at the kitchen table having their coffee. It was still early, no one was hurrying. They still had plenty of time.

"It was a bag of rusty ole' nails," Mary said quietly. She poured some coffee and waited, staring at the kitchen counter.

Paul and Elizabeth looked at her.

"What?" asked Elizabeth.

As the moments ticked by, Paul thought maybe he knew what she was talking about. *Oh my God!* Paul thought as the fullness of what she had said hit him. *The punctures!*

"What was a bag of nails, Mary?" Paul asked, already knowing.

"I put a bag of dirty, rusty nails by the garbage pail in the kitchen awhile back. I went to get one out of the bag, and they were ruined. They must have gotten wet or something. I don't know. I just balled up the bag and threw it down on the floor, not in the pail. She must have stepped on them. I remember when I threw them out later a bunch of the nails were poking through the paper bag." It felt like a thousand pounds had lifted off her shoulders. It felt better to admit it.

Paul knew Mary had not been a good mother. He had not been a good father, but carrying the blame around for something like this had to be awful. He felt compassion swell for his wife as he watched her waiting for what they would say.

"Mary, you could not have known. Cassie never told us. She did not complain, did she?" Paul, hoping to help, also hoped there wasn't something else Mary had not told them.

Looking down at the floor, Mary said, "No, no, she never said a thing."

The nails caused the punctures. Now Elizabeth knew what had caused the change in her daughter. She was blaming herself for Cassie's death. She was many things, but she would not have wanted to cause her own daughter's death.

"Mary, Paul is right. You would not have known unless you knew of the injury. No one is to blame here, Mary."

Mary sipped her coffee and then looked at them—really looked at them. They waited. She looked like she was grasping at something. Mary looked out the window and then back at them.

She cried out, "That little girl died because of me. She got the puncture wounds because of me! And you know the worst part?

"The worst part is she couldn't have complained, Mom!" Mary admitted as she looked at her mother.

Mary then looked at Paul, and with the first tears in years streaming down her face, she cried, "She couldn't have complained about her foot hurting. Don't you understand? She wouldn't have told me! I would have just told her to stop complaining, to toughen up! My God, I didn't even go to the hospital, Paul! I didn't go... I was supposed to be her mother... and I didn't go. I didn't think it was important." Mary stood there shaking her head, trying to understand why she did what she had done.

Paul and Elizabeth were speechless. Their hearts went out to Mary.

Mary's shoulders slumped with a sigh. Taking a deep breath, she looked up. "It's too late now... but I am sorry, Mom. I'm sorry, Paul."

Elizabeth spoke up, "Mary, I don't want you blaming yourself for this. We... we can't control some things."

Mary smiled, the first real smile Elizabeth had seen in years. "Mom, you were always quick to forgive me, but please let me be sorry for this. Let me be sorry for Cassie, Mom. She deserved better."

Paul was shocked. He did not know this Mary. Her confession was like a healing balm over him. He had been no better than Mary; he had been lacking as a father. He had his own demons these last few days. But somehow he felt better listening to Mary. Maybe now they could grieve and remember Cassie together.

Elizabeth agreed with her daughter. Cassie did deserve better. Elizabeth wanted this day to be special for Cassie just in case she was looking down from heaven. "Well, let's go. This day will be hard for all of us, but let it be a very special day in Cassie's memory. Okay?"

"Yes... Stay with me, Mom. I want to make it through for Cassie."

· · · · · · · · · · ·

The funeral home was full. Every seat was taken. Tissues were being held in many hands. Sniffles were heard in the quiet. Everyone was in place waiting for Cassie's funeral to begin. Looking around the room, it would seem every family in Tipton was represented there. Mr. and Mrs. Chambers were both in attendance. Mr. Chambers, not having left his home in years, was there in his wheelchair. Mrs. Vashon, the Stockards, and the Colemans sat together behind Paul and Mary's family. Cassie's teachers and some of her classmates with their families were all there also. The town's business owners and coworkers of Paul and Mary were all there.

The minister started out with a prayer for Cassie and her family. He then went on to pray for all those who knew and loved Cassie. He spoke of the love of Jesus, the wonderful hope Cassie had. And though she was not with them any longer, her memory lived on, and they all had the hope of seeing her again.

Cassie's teacher, Mrs. Brooks, got up next. "I was honored to teach Cassie last year. She was a wonderful student. As a teacher, I will always feel blessed to have had Cassie in my classroom. She made us laugh. She always pointed out something good about others. She was a ray of sunshine in my classroom. She supplied me with beautiful drawings for my refrigerator every week. She asked me one day if I had children. I told her that I didn't, that my husband and I were not fortunate enough to have any yet. She brought me my first drawing the next day, and this is what she said: 'Mrs. Brooks, I drew this for you. Everyone should have a picture for their refrigerator. I will draw them for you until you and your husband have a baby.' That was the kindest, sweetest thing that has ever happened to me. My classroom was entertained and blessed from having Cassie in it, but my life was blessed even more. Thank you!" Mrs. Brooks finished up, barely containing her tears. She took her seat by her husband and some of her students.

Mrs. Barbara Stockard was next. The minister motioned for her to come up. Looking out at the people, Barbara began, "Thank you. I am Barbara Stockard. I was fortunate enough to live next door to Cassie, and she was very good friends with our children, Samuel and Larissa. We loved Cassie. Paul, Mary, she was a wonderful child. Words just aren't enough where Cassie is concerned. I am going to read a poem today, something I read recently that reminds me of Cassie.

> *I can see God when the sun comes up…*
> *He has given us another day.*
> *I can see God when a father reaches out to his son…*
> *He had taught us the same.*
> *I can see God when catastrophe strikes…*
> *He has brought us together.*

*I can see God in the rain...*
*He gives us the rainbow to remember his promises.*
*I can see God in a child's face...*
*Such wonder and grace.*
*I can see God in a rose...*
*Only he can make it bloom.*
*I can see God in the wheat field...*
*His breath blowing across it causes it to dance.*
*I can see God in the runner's face...*
*It says to never give up.*
*I can see God in the tears...*
*He washes my soul.*
*I can see God in the heartbreak...*
*He is the glue.*

Barbara looked up and said, "I would like to add to the poem because it is true and perfect for today. I could see God in Cassie. She was a gift to all who knew her. I can see God in the time we had together. He knew we needed her."

When Barbara took her seat, she put her arm around Larissa, hugging her close. Elizabeth held Mary's hand; she was staring straight ahead trying to compose herself. The minister said a closing prayer and then invited everyone to pay their respects by walking by Cassie's casket. There was a luncheon planned at his church for the family and visitors after the trip to the cemetery, thanks to Barbara and the ladies group.

Cassie's family surrounded her casket last to say their good-byes. Left alone in the room, each of them tried to muster up the strength to say good-bye.

Elizabeth tried to memorize her granddaughter. It was a moment Elizabeth wished on no other. Cassie had grown but still looked like the Cassie Elizabeth knew when she was five years old. Each of them was trying to handle the moment the best way they knew how. Elizabeth took charge. There was no easy way.

"Ready? Paul, Mary? They are ready to take care of Cassie now."

"Yes, I am ready. Mary?"

Mary nodded her head but did not speak. "Okay, let's get the cars."

It was time to lay Cassie to rest. It was time to let go.

. . . . . . . . . .

Later at the luncheon in the church hall, the atmosphere was lighter. People were visiting with each other while the church began to serve the luncheon. Children were running around releasing some of their energy. The food tables went on and on. Paul and Mary could not believe all of this was put together for them and their family… for Cassie. They actually had no idea this was all planned.

Elizabeth was so thankful for the people of Tipton. They had just taken over from the minister to the church luncheon. Their kindness saved them! Having this luncheon was a wonderful thing for them to do. The church had tables set up together in the front of the room for the family so all of them could sit together in one area.

The kindness continued with the people. One by one the neighbors came to Paul and Mary telling them something they remembered about Cassie. Children came up to them telling one story after another—how she was nice to them, how she helped them when they fell off the swings. On and on went the nice stories about Cassie.

Fellow coworkers were there for strength. Don and Julie Daniels were there. The funeral had been hard on Julie. She had felt a kindred heart with Cassie the morning at Paul and Mary's. Cassie had seemed to understand Julie's fear and hurt in the kitchen. Cassie's eyes had been so honest. Julie felt she had the perception of an old soul.

Mrs. Vashon invited the entire family to the garden the next day. She wanted to show them the beautiful flowers that Cassie kept watered and took care of.

Marty Coleman told Paul and Mary how she'd learned to swim the same day Cassie did. She tried it because of Cassie. She had been brave enough to try to swim because of Cassie. Paul and Mary were humbled by the stories of their daughter.

Mary was alarmed she was sitting in a church hall. But she was glad she had people being nice to her when she had never shown them kindness. She was glad for Cassie that these people were making the day the best it could be. She was glad her daughter had learned to garden, to swim. No thanks to her, but it helped Mary to know Cassie had not missed out on everything.

· · · · · · · · · ·

Sitting on the back porch, breathing the warm night air in deeply, Mary stretched her head to the side. Her neck had huge knots in it. She wanted some relief from the tension her body was suffering from. Reaching up, she massaged her neck, hoping that might help.

It was late. Her mother and Paul were sleeping. She knew they had been exhausted. The day they just shared would have taken its toll on anyone.

She should be sleeping but couldn't. Mary was wide awake. Too awake. She wanted to forget some of the things from the last few days but couldn't. Scenes replayed over and over again in her mind as if each scene was trying to tell her something. Mary felt afraid to listen. What could the message be? She had so much bottled up. How could she handle more?

*Those stupid nails! Those stupid nails! Why did I put the bag there on the floor? Why not in the garbage can? Why did I just ball up the bag and throw them down on the floor?* Mary's thoughts tormented her. And those were the good thoughts. There were others that tormented even more. *Will I ever get them to stop? Ever?* Mary wondered, overwhelmed.

In the cemetery earlier, Mary had felt like she was suffocating; panic had risen in her throat. *This is so final,* Mary had thought. *I don't have any chance to tell Cassie I am sorry.*

When the minister asked the family to shovel dirt on top of the casket in a show of putting Cassie to rest, Mary had thought with each drop of dirt she heard hit the top of the casket that she was being buried. Something was closing in on her. The pressure on her chest was heavy; she didn't think she could breathe. She had looked at Paul and her mother. Were they going through what she was?

This was her punishment; she just knew it. She would be punished the rest of her life, and she deserved to be. The memory of her actions over the past seven years slammed into her mind as each family member shoveled in dirt. Then it had been her turn. Staring into the hole, she felt the shovel passed to her. She didn't know if she could do it. Everyone was watching, waiting. Could she add more to what was burying her daughter? Hadn't she done enough?

Looking up at the sympathetic faces, Mary knew she would have to do this for Cassie. She couldn't make a scene now. Swallowing, she lifted the shovel full of dirt; then looking over the edge, she let the dirt go. She prayed Cassie could hear her.

Mary whispered, "I am so sorry, Cassie, so sorry. You really tried, didn't you? You really tried with me. I wish I could have been a better mother to you. Please forgive me."

As the last of the dirt fell from the shovel, an overwhelming sensation went through Mary. She felt lighter somehow... forgiven. Could that be possible? She wasn't sure what forgiven felt like, but something had made her feel a whole lot better than she had moments ago.

Going back over the day, Mary played the cemetery scene again and again in her head. It was very unbelievable for her. Dare she believe it? She still felt different. It was as if all the dirt in her had left as she poured the dirt over Cassie's casket. Did Cassie hear her and forgive her? Did God forgive her? Was this clean feeling that she was feeling inside what forgiveness was all about? Mary wasn't sure what had happened to her, but the one thing she was sure of was that she needed it.

# CHAPTER 23

Saturday morning woke bright and beautiful in Tipton, Missouri. Another nice day was in store for a usually warm August. Mrs. Vashon couldn't have been happier. It was going to be a glorious day for everyone to visit the garden. Suzanne had everything ready for her visitors: homemade cookies and fresh-squeezed lemonade in the refrigerator. She had a pitcher of sun tea on the porch. She was planning on making tea sandwiches made of tuna, cucumbers, and cream cheese and chicken salad. She would put those together at the last minute for freshness.

Looking out at the garden, Suzanne was pleased. The light filtered through the trees and danced all around the garden. The flowers were bright in color and blooming, their faces stretching toward the sun. She couldn't have asked for a more beautiful day. Stepping out on the back porch, she unfolded a yellow, gingham tablecloth and laid it over the table on the porch. Taking a pair of red-handled garden scissors, Suzanne went to the flower garden and clipped a few flowers for a centerpiece on the table. *Perfect*, she thought as she gathered the flowers into a bouquet.

Very early that morning, the gentleman, Mr. Davis, delivered and installed Suzanne's surprise for everyone. It was wonderfully done, a work of art, exactly what she ordered! He worked for two solid days to get it done for Suzanne and did not mind at all, he told her, due to the circumstances.

When Suzanne apologized for hurrying him, Mr. Davis wouldn't hear it.

"Now, Suzanne, this is for a very special reason. I wanted to get it done in time for you. With the family still here from out of town, this will be very nice for them," Mr. Davis declared politely.

Mr. Davis was a local wood worker, a cabinet designer actually. Some of his cabinetry was in some of the fanciest homes in the bigger cities of Missouri. In his spare time—the bit of time he set aside for himself—he carved more detailed, artistic woodwork. She could not wait to unveil it to Cassie's family and the neighbors. She had him wrap a green lawn bag around it to keep it a surprise. And if Suzanne was not mistaken with what she saw and felt yesterday, Cassie's mother, Mary, would be coming at one o'clock also.

Putting the last sandwich together and placing it on the platter, Suzanne cleaned the few dishes she had dirtied. Looking out the kitchen window, she thought, *Just in time!*

Larissa and Samuel had just run into the backyard with their parents coming up behind them. Suzanne started gathering the food out of the refrigerator.

The knock came on the back door. "Mrs. Vashon? It's Larissa! Do you need any help?"

"Come on in, Larissa, and yes, you can help me bring some of the food out."

Larissa came in ready to help. "It looks like you made a lot of nice things, Mrs. Vashon," Larissa stated the obvious when seeing the plates of cookies and sandwiches.

Mrs. Vashon laughed and then smiled, knowing Larissa would understand more than most people. "Well, Larissa, honey, I needed something to do. And I want this day to be a happy day to honor Cassie."

Larissa almost cringed at the mention of her best friend's name. It hurt so bad just hearing her name. But she wanted it to be a happy day.

"I need a happy day, Mrs. Vashon, I am going to try really hard to be happy... for Cassie, right?" Mrs. Vashon's heart went out to Larissa— to lose her friend at such a young age! "Larissa, this is a day to celebrate Cassie in a way. And she would want you happy. Remember that, Larissa. Cassie, more than anyone, would want you happy!"

Larissa smiled and sighed. "Thank you, Mrs. Vashon. Let's get all this yummy food out there."

A large group had gathered in the garden. Cassie's whole family was there! Suzanne peeked out the window. Elizabeth, Paul, Mary, and her brothers, Roy and Mark, with their families were among the group; everyone was on time.

"Please, everyone, come get some refreshments!" Mrs. Vashon called out as she placed a heavy platter down on the table. Plates, napkins, and paper cups were all arranged on the table. The plates of food looked delicious! Mrs. Vashon had outdone herself.

"Suzanne, this is wonderful. Thank you!" Elizabeth declared.

Everyone chimed in at the same time, "Wonderful. So nice! How lovely this is!"

Mrs. Vashon laughed at everyone talking at the same time, and then everyone laughed together. The laughter cut through the nerves, the sadness of the last few days, the loss.

"Well, enjoy the refreshments, and please eat it all. I don't need leftovers!" Mrs. Vashon laughed, patting her stomach.

Samuel, Larissa, and a few other children, with their plates full of food, sat in the shade near the bench, using the edge of the bench to hold their cups. Two of Cassie's cousins sat on the bench near the other children. The adults stood around talking about the good food they were enjoying and the flower garden. Most had not seen the garden up close.

Watching the guests, Suzanne felt the time was right. She wanted to share the reason why they were gathered. Walking over to the flowerbed near the surprise, Mrs. Vashon cleared her throat to get everyone's attention.

"Ahem… If you wouldn't mind coming over here, I want to tell you some of the reasons I invited you all here today," Mrs. Vashon started. "Please, bring your plates with you. I want you to enjoy this afternoon and thank you for coming."

Everyone gathered near her.

"Again, thank you for coming here today. I hope you stay for a while; please don't hurry off. Enjoy the refreshments and the garden! It really is a wonderful garden! Paul, Mary, Elizabeth, everyone, this is where I became friends with Cassie. She came to my garden on a regular basis. She'd walk in, take a look around, and then hurry out, not wanting anyone to catch her here. I knew she thought that she wasn't supposed to be in the garden, but I never minded her here. I was touched that she loved the garden enough to sneak in for a peek. And then I was lucky one day to catch up with Cassie before she could hurry away!" Suzanne laughed, remembering. "I wanted to tell her she was welcome any time and I would love to have her help. She helped me from that point on with the flowers, the watering, the weeding; everything here has Cassie's touch."

Mrs. Vashon had everyone's attention. "She was a blessing to me, to this garden. I loved her so very much. She was the granddaughter I never had." Suzanne looked at Elizabeth and smiled. "She showed me things, the beauty in things I never knew. I may have taught her gardening, the names of the flowers, but she taught me so much more."

Looking at Samuel and Larissa, Mrs. Vashon asked them both, "Samuel, Larissa, could you pull the hose over here and turn the water on for me?"

They took off on a run.

Suzanne continued, "I want to show you all something beautiful, something Cassie showed me. When she shared this with me, it gave me a peek into what a beautiful child she was, how she found beauty in such simple things that most of us miss."

Aiming the water hose over the flowerbed, Mrs. Vashon turned the valve on the water hose. With her back to the group now, she talked over her shoulder. "Cassie taught me 'looking through the water,' as she called it. She showed me the beauty of looking through to the other side. She showed me the rainbows, the colors, the transparency of water, how the colors from the other side will come through."

Suzanne opened the spray full blast. The sunshine was hitting the water perfectly. It was the perfect time of day to demonstrate Cassie's "looking through the water." Suzanne held the spray so it created a transparent wall, and all the colors from the flowers came through. The sunlight danced enough across the wall of water to create rainbows. Rainbows of every color danced everywhere. The droplets of water fell like diamonds sparkling to the ground.

Mary was transfixed and amazed at what see was seeing. Her mouth went slack. She reached for Elizabeth's arm. "Mom," Mary whispered.

"I know, honey. I know."

Suzanne moved the hose and made the water dance. The water created a cascade that twirled and swirled. Looking from above the garden that was shaded in spots and sunny in spots, the light danced around, creating its beauty. It lightly touched the edges of the garden fading into the shade. Elizabeth, holding onto her daughter, sensing her need, wished she could take a turn with the water hose. Elizabeth wanted to do what her granddaughter did. By looking through the water and seeing what Cassie had seen, Elizabeth knew she would keep a part of Cassie.

"This garden is as beautiful as it is because of Cassie!" Suzanne proclaimed as she lowered the water hose and turned off the valve.

Lifting off the lawn bag that hid her surprise, Suzanne turned toward her audience. "I invited you here today to dedicate this garden to Cassie! I had this made by a man who creates beauty from wood, and he did this in a huge hurry for all of us!"

Everyone became excited. They could not wait to see what Suzanne had made for the garden. A hush went through the garden. The quietness fell over them like a covering.

Lifting off the last edge of the cover, the hand-carved garden plaque mounted on a wooden pole, which was secured in the ground, the cement barely harden, was there displayed for them all. Cassie's dedication plaque.

It was enchanting. A small girl with flowing hair was carved into the left side of the wood plaque. She was holding a watering hose. The spray of water was carved into the wood and sprayed up and over the words on the plaque.

The plaque read:

## This garden is dedicated to Cassie Marvin
## Summer 1973

This is the place where Cassie showed us
the beauty of *looking through the water.*
May her rainbows always shine here.

. . . . . . . . . .

They will be like a well-watered garden,
And they will sorrow no more
Then maidens will dance and be glad…

*Jeremiah 31:12–13*

Elizabeth started clapping. Then everyone joined in. Suzanne turned to the plaque and started clapping. She turned back and looked at the group of people.

"For Cassie!" she said with a huge smile; there were tears in her eyes, but they were happy tears.

"For Cassie!" everyone said enthusiastically, a wonderful, warm feeling after the loss they all just suffered.

"If I could share with you one more thing... Paul, Mary, everyone... I would like to tell you what happened when I got the idea to do this." Looking at Barbara, Suzanne went on. "Barbara had just left my home after telling me the news of Cassie. I was brokenhearted. I sat at my kitchen table for... well, I don't know how long. When I got up, I looked out my kitchen window and thought my eyes were playing tricks on me. I saw Cassie in the garden with the water hose dancing in the mist of the water. She looked so happy, so peaceful. She was laughing and smiling! I came out on the back porch hoping the vision would not go away; it was so real. I walked toward her, and it was like she could see me. Then a surprised look crossed her face. I was just as surprised. Could she see me? Was I seeing her? I asked her if she was all right. I tell you, it was like I heard her tell me she was fine! Then she reached for me, and I reached for her; then the vision was gone. I was standing alone here in the garden. But a peace washed over me. I felt like I had seen the vision to reassure all of us that Cassie is fine; she is in a better place. The idea came to me in an urgency to get this done, especially for you, Elizabeth, and your family who have to travel home. To the rest of us, this garden will always be for you to enjoy visiting. I do believe this is a special place."

There was not a dry eye on anyone's faces. The tears came, but they came with relief, with joy, with peace. Mrs. Vashon received a thank you and hugs from everyone.

Elizabeth was so touched by the day. Her granddaughter had people who had loved her. The day comforted Paul. It had been an encouraging day. The garden dedication had been a great success.

Mary, being one of the last in line, came up to Mrs. Vashon to thank her for the dedication. She was nervous but offered immediately, "I don't know what to say, but thank you. I am so grateful to you for being so kind to Cassie, for being her friend. And then for you to share this with us…. well, it was so good to learn all of this. I am sorry to say I did not know any of this about Cassie. I… um…" Looking down at the ground, Mary was trying to come up with the words. "I… was not always there for Cassie." Looking up, searching Suzanne's face, Mary only saw acceptance in Suzanne's eyes and understanding. Mary gave half of a smile. "Would you mind if I visited the garden once in a while?"

Suzanne felt joy seep through her veins at Mary's request. Suzanne spoke sincerely, "Mary, you are always welcome here. Cassie would want you to visit. She would want you to enjoy and come to love the garden like she did."

"Thank you. Maybe it's not too late for me to get to know my daughter," Mary said, amazed she could admit it. What was happening to her? She felt thankful for the kindness shown her. When was the last time she was thankful?

"I think this garden will help us all keep her alive in our hearts. Her life was for a purpose, Mary. I do believe that purpose is still working in our hearts." Patting her chest, Suzanne felt the truth of what she just spoke to Mary. "We need to keep alive what Cassie has taught us; she saw beauty in things most of us ignore. She loved us, Mary, even when some of us were unlovable. She loved you, Mary, and probably understood you more than you knew. At my old age, I learned more from Cassie in just a few short months than I experienced in my lifetime."

Mary's heart was full and not full of bitterness for the first time in a long time. When did the bitterness leave and something gentler replace it?

"You know, it's funny, but I feel her love right here. I have felt her forgiveness. Maybe she knows how sorry I am for everything. Maybe God knows, and he's forgiven me." Mary was shocked by her words. Was this really her talking? She didn't care anymore. Needing to speak these words, this helped Mary express what she was feeling.

Suzanne grabbed Mary's hands and shook them excitedly. "See, Mary? Cassie's love is still working! And God? Oh, he never gives up on us! Never! His love is still working too! Mary, we are going to be all right! I do believe everything is going to be all right!"

For the first time in her life, Mary thought maybe, just maybe, everything was going to be all right!

. . . . . . . . . .

Paul, Mary, and Elizabeth waved to Roy Jr. and Mark's families as they pulled their cars away. They were on their way back home to Wisconsin. Both of the boys were so glad they had come. They both wished they had gotten to know their niece while she was alive. Life had some sad turns in it, but it was with a warm heart they had left their sister. They had Mary back, the very young Mary they remembered.

"They have nice families, Mom," Mary stated as they pulled away from the front of her home.

Elizabeth agreed, "Yes, they do."

Paul agreed also, "They are good guys, Elizabeth. I am glad they came down; it was good to see them again."

Elizabeth told Paul and Mary, "It will be nice having you both visit with me during Christmas. I am glad you're coming up!" Elizabeth laughed and added, "I am sure Wisconsin will give you a white Christmas!"

In one of the last conversations Mary had with her brothers, she told them they were planning on driving north to their homes for Christmas in December. She had whispered the night before to Paul, "Can we go home for Christmas this year? To my mom's house?"

Paul was almost asleep, before answering her, he questioned himself if he heard her right. He had. In these last few days, everything about Mary surprised him.

Paul whispered back, "Of course, Mary. We can go there if that is what you want."

Mary nodded in the dark and said, "Yes, that is what I want."

Paul reached over and held Mary's hand. Mary let him.

. . . . . . . . . .

Elizabeth stayed until Wednesday. This was also the same day Paul and Mary had to return back to work. Elizabeth's flight back to Wisconsin was leaving very early in the morning, Paul was going to take her to the airport before work.

Elizabeth and Mary had gone through Cassie's room together. Mary decided to keep it just like Cassie had left it. Mary wanted to make it into a spare bedroom but still leave it as Cassie's room. Cassie having so few things as Mary went through them she realized she wanted to keep almost everything. Mary found pictures and cards that Cassie had made her. They were saved! Mary knew she had probably thrown them out, but she thanked God Cassie had saved them. It cut through to Mary's heart picturing Cassie digging in the garbage, pulling these out. Mary would treasure them now and was so thankful she still had them.

"My goodness, Cassie, thank God you knew better than me, that you saved these! I didn't know then, but I know now. I will treasure these all the days of my life!"

Elizabeth and Mary cried, laughed, and smiled over the girl who tucked, hid, and kept all that was precious to her. Sitting on the floor looking at each other, they were both pleasantly surprised at how nice this had actually been. Mary had thought she would not have even entered this room let alone gone through Cassie's things.

On Wednesday morning Paul took Elizabeth to the airport. Mary thought getting back in a routine would be good. Work didn't look so bad that morning. Mary was heading back to work in an hour. With her mother going home, she realized how much she had come to depend on her these last few days. The house was lonely with Paul and Elizabeth gone. Mary wanted to visit Cassie. And if Cassie was anywhere, she was in the garden.

As Mary walked down the street, her heart pounded. She could hear her heartbeat in her ears. She felt excited and scared. Did she dare? Could she visit Cassie's garden? Should she? She didn't know if she deserved to.

Missouri had been blessed with beautiful weather lately. Another gift that Mary felt was given to her. The morning was gorgeous. Good weather for her mother to fly home and beautiful weather for her to visit the garden. Mary entered and took her time walking around. She also took her time to really look at the flowers. They were very beautiful she found if she looked. Mary has missed out on a lot of things, she realized. But thanks to Cassie, she would take the time now to look for the beauty. The beauty she was experiencing in her daughter was almost overwhelming. Cassie had truly been a wonderful girl. It was very sad to Mary she had been so blind before that she did not see this.

Walking over to the plaque, Mary started to read the words. Tears filled her eyes. She could still see the plaque through her tears. *Looking through the water*, she thought.

Out loud Mary said, "And they will sorrow no more... then maidens will dance and be glad..." Mary let the tears come. The wind blew softly, caressing. The leaves danced; the petals swayed. The sunlight grew bright over the trees, and the sun rose in the morning sky. Its rays beamed down upon the garden in streaks of light.

Her mind rejoiced. She welcomed the tears. She could still see what looked like Cassie holding the water hose beautifully carved in the wood through her tears. She would not blink. She now knew in part the beauty of looking through the water. God was on the other side. It was so transparent. He was there all along. Through Mary's tears, He reached for her.

In another realm in the garden, one Mary could not see, Cassie was there. She was where the beauty was. She had no more sorrow. She was dancing and was glad.

# READERS' GUIDE

1. When Cassie gets kicked out of the house by her mother, why does she blame herself? Do you think Cassie ever comes up with an answer to why her mother puts her out of the house?

2. Mary made Cassie nervous with her bad moods. Did Cassie take off and find something to do for herself or for her mother? Was it another way to please her angry mother?

3. What went through the minds of the people in Tipton that knew Cassie and knew Mary? What difference did it have on how they treated Cassie? Mary?

4. What did you think about Mrs. Vashon's thought-out approach to Cassie? How did helping Mrs. Vashon find a home for the statue help Cassie?

5. Was Cassie's imagination normal for a child her age? Why was it good that Cassie had such an imagination? Did her life benefit from having a good imagination?

6. Looking at Cassie's life, was she really alone? If she was alone in your opinion, how did she handle that situation in her life?

7. Without having ever visited a church or having any religious upbringing, do you think Cassie had a connection with God? How did she know He was there?

8. Mrs. Stockard had an unfriendly beginning with Mary. Why? Why do you think that never changed her feelings towards Cassie? What kind of person was Mrs. Stockard, who did not give up on Cassie and allowed her to play with her children even though she did not favor her parents?

9. What kind of father was Paul? Even though he knew it was wrong, how could he leave Cassie in the truck in a bar's parking lot? If he could leave her like that, why do you think he worried about leaving her with Mary at the same time? Was there a difference in how they treated their daughter?

10. What does Elizabeth Lauren feel about her daughter and granddaughter? Why does she feel there is nothing she can do? Could she have done something to help either of them over the years?

11. When Paul felt he had to whip Cassie instead of letting Mary, what do you think he went through, saving Cassie from a whipping from Mary but still having to whip her to satisfy Mary? Why didn't he stand up to Mary?

12. What do you think Paul was thinking when Cassie thanked him for telling her about his work? Why were those kinds of conversations so rare between father and daughter?

13. What does Cassie see looking through the water? Why does she share what she's found looking through the water? What does it mean to look through to the other side for Cassie?

14. When Mary is kind to Julie, what did that show Cassie that was so heartbreaking for her? Why did she need to run to the garden?

15. What was Mrs. Vashon to Cassie? Cassie was melancholy in the garden with Mrs. Vashon on her last visit there. What was she going through?

Was the reality of her life starting to challenge Cassie emotionally? If so, would that have started a change in Cassie?

16. Why did she not tell someone about the nails? When she became sick, why did she not say something to indicate how bad she must have felt?

17. What do you think of all the pictures Cassie made and were hidden or thrown away?

18. Mrs. Vashon was able to give them all something from Cassie's life. What do you think it meant for everyone involved? What did it mean to Mrs. Vashon? How could it help them all in their time of need?

19. How did you imagine Mary would react to Cassie's death? What did you think about Paul's compassionate attitude toward Mary?

20. Do you think forgiveness was given and received at the end of the book? Who received? Who gave?

CPSIA information can be obtained
at www.ICGtesting.com
Printed in the USA
BVHW041558240719
554236BV00016B/665/P